THE ZUCCHINI FAIRY MURDER

Also By Ann Philipp

Salty Sister Mysteries
Grand Theft Death - Book One

THE ZUCCHINI FAIRY MURDER

A Salty Sister Mystery

Ann Philipp

Salty
Sister
Publishing

ISBN: 978-0-9895654-1-7

Cover design by Tim Barber of Dissect Designs

First Edition 2024

Thanks to all my friends and family who are so supportive, even though I write slower than molasses. Cripes, that cliché's a bit overused. How about I write slower than a sloth taking a stroll on the moon. Wow, a sloth on the moon, what a fun kid's story, or even better Sci-Fi. I've never written Sci-Fi before...

Squirrel!

Chapter One

"Mom," I whispered into the darkness. "How many more cars?"

"Two," she whispered back.

"Where's the next one?"

"Across the street."

I squinted into the dim light. A wood-paneled station wagon stood helpless in a driveway, unaware of the bounty it was about to receive.

A flapping above our heads startled me. "What's that?" I sputtered.

"An owl," my mother responded. "Patricia, if I'd known you were going to be so edgy, I would have left you at home."

It took all my self-control not to let out an exasperated sigh. The last thing I wanted was my mother prancing around a suburban neighborhood at night by herself.

"Come on," she said, "we're almost done."

We sprinted to a large sycamore next to the sidewalk and then darted across the street. At the station wagon, I unzipped the huge pack on her back, took out five slender green vegetables and placed them on the front seat of the car.

"Did you get one with a face?" she asked.

Of course, my mother, Ms. Genevieve Schuster, artist and art teacher, couldn't garden the usual way. She forced her produce to grow in plastic molds, creating creepy gnome-like faces as the vegetables grew.

I checked. "Yes, Mom."

"Give 'em the big one too," she said. "With a car this size, they must have a lot of kids."

I reached back in and grasped the inedible three-foot-long squash that must have weighed ten pounds and placed it next to the others. A siren wailed in the distance, and I longed to be at home watching TV and scarfing ice cream.

"Okay. Next?"

My mother had plotted out every open car window —at least those without alarms—within a six-block radius. But that was at seven o'clock this evening; it was now almost ten. So far they'd all still been open. She consulted her map using a penlight.

"Five houses to the north."

We dashed to a low fence, stepped over it, and crunched across a gravel driveway onto a freshly mown lawn. A dense six-foot hedge blocked our path, so we veered for the sidewalk. A fluffy white dog on a leash appeared from around the barrier, pulling a man who was tying a knot at the end of a plastic bag.

We stood perfectly still, smack dab in the middle of the grass, as if being motionless would hide us.

"Genevieve?" the man called out. "I almost didn't

recognize you. How nice to see you!"

My mother had picked out my clothes for the night: a black turtleneck, black cargo pants, black running shoes, black leather gloves, and a black baseball cap, but I drew the line at black and green camouflage makeup. She wore the same—except with the camouflage makeup.

I stared at this man, baffled that he could identify her with all that goop on her face. He was tall, wore large black glasses, and had a clean-shaven face with a strong jaw line. A shapeless black and orange Giant's windbreaker hid his physique.

"Richard," my mother said. Her back stiffened, telling me that this was not a welcome encounter. A month ago my father had left my mother for a much younger woman. Since then, a load of single, middle-aged men had homed in on her; she was like a beacon of sexuality.

We slinked over to him and stood awkwardly, his nondescript terrier sniffing our feet.

"This is my daughter, Patricia," my mom said.

I would have reached out to shake his hand, but his bag of poop made me hesitate.

"Hello," I said.

"This is Cleopatra." He gestured to the panting mutt who'd plopped down on the lawn. "Beautiful night for a walk, isn't it?" he asked.

"It is," my mother said.

"Boy, those are some big packs you're hauling," Richard said.

We both carried camping backpacks, the kind you use for long hikes into the wilderness. Mine started out the night weighing close to 30 pounds.

"Hmm, yes," my mother said. I could tell she was searching for a lie.

"We're in training," I intervened.

"Yes. Training," my mother repeated. "For a marathon."

"Oh, which one?" he asked.

"Bay to Breakers." I blurted out the first long-distance race that popped into my head. My mom shot me a look, and I knew what she was thinking. Except for a few masochists, people thought of Bay to Breakers as more of a moving street party than a marathon.

"Oh." He sounded surprised.

"We're going dressed as campers," I said.

"Oh." More surprise. He studied my mother's face.

Before he could ask about the makeup, I gave her arm a tug. "Well, we better keep walking. Nice meeting you."

"Have a good evening," he responded, and called out after us. "Maybe I'll see you at Joey's Coffee tomorrow, Genevieve."

We headed up the sidewalk, and I spotted our last recipient: a small black sedan with an open rear window. Headlights turned the corner. I instinctively pushed my mother away from the street.

A shadowy area between two homes looked like a good place to hide, so we squatted there behind a low bush. Besides my heart pounding in my chest, I heard the sound of a TV. I imagined those inside lounging on a soft couch eating bowls of ice cream. Probably coffee flavored with homemade chocolate sauce.

A menacing growl behind us startled me. I turned to see two tall wooden gates, side by side. The closest one banged as a dog jumped against it, barking loudly.

"Dang," my mother swore. She stood up, reached over the far gate, and found the latch. It swung open and we stepped behind it. The canine continued to bark until the owner opened a side door and yelled, "Buster! Come!"

My mom peered between the gate slats. "Oh, crap," she said. "It's a cop, and he's stopped in the middle of the street."

With my luck it would be Officer Marc Romano—father of my almost boyfriend, Jake.

"We'll have to go over the back fence," I said.

I heard a snort and realized we were not alone. I held out my arms, positioning myself between my mother and whatever beast had us trapped. From behind a stack of firewood came an unenthusiastic "woof." A dog's head appeared, and he lumbered toward us. He was large, black, and even in the dark I could see a white spot just above his nose.

"Max?" I whispered.

He wagged his tail and softly woofed again.

"Mom, it's Max! I can't believe he's still alive. That means we're right behind your house." Between the ages of ten and twelve, I'd spent a lot of time climbing in the neighbor's magnolia tree by way of a large branch that hung over the fence. Back then Max was just a pup, and I'd lob pretzels or banana chunks into his yard for him to chase.

I gave Max a quick ear rub and peered around the corner into his backyard. On a large wood deck sat a barbecue grill and numerous types of mismatched outdoor furniture. The rest of the yard was lawn. In the corner, straight ahead of us, was our escape—the magnolia tree. We sprinted to it. I scrambled up the trunk. Reaching down, I grabbed my mother's arm and pulled her up. A branch stabbed me in the shoulder. I shifted sideways, ripping the arm of my turtleneck.

I found the limb that had provided my secret childhood passage, but at some point the branch had been cut off at the fence line. There was an eight foot drop into my mother's backyard, far enough to break an ankle.

Max looked up at us, a tennis ball in his mouth, still wagging his tail.

"Oh, look, he wants to play," my mom said. "Patricia, get down and throw the ball for him."

"Mom, this isn't a good time." I glanced back to the gate we'd come through, expecting a police officer to appear with gun drawn.

My mother dug around in her cargo pants pocket and threw something into the yard.

"What was that?" I asked.

"A liver-flavored doggie treat."

One thing I could say for my mom, she came prepared.

Max dropped the ball and chased after his quarry, which happened to land next to a trash can. As my mother tossed another treat in the opposite direction, I climbed down and ran to the can. It was made of indestructible plastic and full of weeds. I turned it upside down, dumping its contents, and ran back to the tree.

"Patricia, throw the ball," my mom said.

I tossed the tennis ball onto the deck, glad that my gloves protected me from the inevitable dog slobber. The back door opened and I crouched behind the can. A husky voice yelled, "Max!"

The old dog whined a goodbye, plodded up to the house, and disappeared inside. I returned, planning to heave the garbage can up the tree. After struggling with branches and backpacks, I had hauled the can high enough to drop it over the fence upside down. It landed on a shrub, a little cockeyed, but it would do. I put one foot on the two-by-four that supported the fence boards, held onto the cut branch, and reached out my other leg, touching the top of the can.

As I shifted my weight, the can sank into the bush and then caught. I stepped down with my other leg, and then jumped onto the ground. Turning around I took hold of my mother's outstretched arm and helped her to safety.

I leaned up against the fence, breathing hard. My mom brushed leaves off her arms, barely winded. A sea of thigh-high squash plants running from fence-line to fence-line surrounded us. I gestured to the lush greenery.

"Mom, why can't you just sell your zucchini at the Farmer's Market?"

"Farmer's Market," she scoffed. "Where's the sport in that?"

I really couldn't fault my mother for her odd behavior. Besides my father leaving her, she'd also recently lost her mother—my Nana. So what's a woman to do with all that anger and grief, if not take up an extreme hobby?

We slogged our way through the large, sticky leaves to the house. I was so tired I couldn't think about ice cream anymore; I just wanted to lie down on my mother's couch and sleep.

Dropping our packs on the back porch, we went in through the kitchen door. Flashing lights illuminated the hallway. Without saying a word we ran to the front door and peeked out the window.

"It's the police!" I said.

"They're on to us," my mother replied. "Oh, your father's going to have a field day with this."

My father worked as an estate attorney. A few weeks ago, I'd been arrested for grand theft auto. The charges were dropped, but that experience brought out some interesting facts about my not-so-pretty ancestry. I come from a long line of female criminals. My grandmother was an art counterfeiter, my great-grandmother robbed banks, and my great-great grandmother stole gold from a smelting company. My mother's indiscretion was stealing a $4,000 designer dress when she was in high school. Only my grandmother had done hard time. My father was embarrassed by my mother's family history, as if it somehow tarnished his profession.

I glanced out the window again. Officer Romano stood next to his police car.

"It's Jake's dad." I turned and looked at my mom. "Hurry, wash your face."

I followed her back to the kitchen, where she poured dish soap in her hand and rubbed at her camouflage makeup.

My overnight bag sat on the counter, and I pulled out a tissue to wipe sweat from my forehead. I took off my gloves, hat, and turtleneck and slipped on a t-shirt. I ran my fingers through my short, curly blond hair, which I knew would be sticking up in odd directions. I turned to my mom; her face was covered in lather.

"Rinse, Mom, rinse!"

She stuck her head under the faucet, spraying water everywhere. When she stood up, I handed her a wad of paper towels.

We hurried back to the living room window; Officer Romano was talking on the police radio.

"Looks like he's calling for backup," I said.

"Maybe he'll go easy on us. I hate being manhandled by cops." My mother plunked herself down onto an easy chair and dropped her head into her hands.

I sighed and looked again. Officer Romano was standing over something in the street.

"Oh, no. Mom, I don't think he's here for us."

At the officer's feet lay a body.

Chapter Two

A female sprawled on the dark asphalt. She wore a white sweater and jeans, her blond hair pulled back in a ponytail.

My mother joined me at the window.

"Do you want to go look?" she asked, sounding eager.

"No," I replied. Looking at a corpse was not my idea of a good time.

"Suit yourself." She sprinted down the front steps and out to the curb.

Officer Romano looked up as she approached. They shook hands and she pointed in my direction. He scowled at the house. They stood talking for a few minutes until sirens announced the arrival of the emergency crews. Two more police cars pulled up followed by an ambulance. Neighbors came out to take a look, standing around in clumps. I noticed Richard across the street; he appeared to be taking notes while Cleopatra sat at his feet.

The paramedics checked for vitals, shook their heads

and covered the body with a blanket. Two officers fanned out, examining the surrounding pavement and front yards. A third went from neighbor to neighbor, asking questions.

My mother finally returned with a report. "Okay, she's dead."

"How sad."

"Looks like a hit-and-run."

I scrunched up my nose, hoping she wasn't going to give me details.

"Officer Romano told me she was a postal worker. Maybe you knew her. She delivered to the downtown businesses."

"My mail lady?!"

I remembered a pleasant-faced 50ish blonde, who constantly talked on her cell phone. She communicated mostly with hand gestures and waves; in the few months that I'd owned Elsie's Antiques, she'd never spoken directly to me.

Footsteps thumped up the walk.

"Ms. Schuster?" Officer Romano said.

I opened the screen and poked my head out. "Hi."

"Are you having problems with your power?"

"No."

We still had the lights off. I flipped the switch and invited him in.

"Did you hear a car screech? Or maybe see someone speeding?" he asked.

In my peripheral vision I saw my mother shake her head ever so slightly. She must have already answered these questions.

"Not that I remember," I said.

"So, you were out back with your mom then?"

This time she nodded ever so slightly. Officer Romano looked back and forth between us and raised one eyebrow.

"Yeah," I replied.

"Someone called in about a prowler earlier. You two didn't notice anyone out on the street that shouldn't have been there?"

We both shook our heads.

He sighed and stepped back outside. "All right, be sure and lock up."

"We will," I said, closing the door and leaning against it.

"What did you tell him?" I asked her.

"I said that we were in the backyard making s'mores."

I rolled my eyes. "S'mores? What are we? A girl scout troop?"

"Well, I wasn't going to tell him we'd just climbed over the back fence."

"Ish. I'm going home."

"Don't you want to stay for a snack? I could make s'mores."

"Ha, ha, Mom. You're a riot."

I woke up to the smell of coffee and stared up at the cracked plaster ceiling of the California bungalow I'd inherited from my grandmother. Her death had coincided with my exit from the business world in San Francisco. I learned the hard way that artists don't fit well into corporations. I thought my graphic arts degree would let me live my creativity. How silly I'd been. Next to art, my other passion was surfing. Waking up early to get to the beach was easy; getting off the board and across town for an 8:00 meeting was close to impossible. Nana also left me her store—Elsie's Antiques—because I think she knew at some point I'd throw in the towel. Or in my case, have the towel thrown at me. I liked living in her house; it felt comfortable, like I was right where I was supposed to be.

The java aroma wafting from the kitchen was created by one of four women that had been friends of my Nana's. Sometimes it felt like I'd inherited them along with the house. The four gals belonged to a group I called "The Ladies." Three were ex-cons, and the fourth, Mrs. Sunny Russo, joked that she'd never been caught. For a variety of reasons the moral compasses of these four women had spun 180 degrees. At least that's what they said. Currently they performed undercover contract work for the FBI. Each woman had her own unique abilities, and I'd come to think of them as aging superheroes. After helping me out of a jam, The Ladies had asked me to join their crime fighting team. My ability to drive at night was my selling point. Cooking like goddesses was theirs.

They often showed up at my house to create a gastronomical masterpiece. But it could only mean one thing. They wanted something. My curiosity overrode my vanity and I entered the kitchen wearing my dancing sheep pajamas with my short blond hair sticking up like a pineapple top. Two of the four Ladies were cooking me breakfast.

Mrs. Sunny Russo stood at the stove. Even at this early hour she dripped with sophistication. She wore a white apron over a light pink cashmere sweater and black slacks. Diamond tear-drop earrings peeked out from her perfect silver pageboy as she stirred what looked like a hollandaise sauce in a double boiler. I considered Mrs. Russo fearless. Her last husband had ties to organized crime. With the help of my grandmother, she gave enough information to the district attorney to have her husband arrested for tax evasion. If it ever crossed her mind that she might have ended up in the San Francisco Bay wearing concrete shoes, she never let on.

Mrs. Betty Butterfield held a full pot of coffee in one hand. Her disposition was consistently as bright as her yellow apron. But behind her smile lay many talents; mostly coming under the headings of cars, languages and firearms. By her assessment she knew the two most important things about cars: how to fix them and how to steal them. Her knowledge of languages spanned at least five, but she was modest; it could be more. And as far as her shooting skills, I'd witnessed them first hand, and I'm glad we were on the same side.

"Good morning, sunshine," she sang out to me. "Let me pour you some coffee. And here's some of that organic cream you like so much."

I was served a plate of eggs Florentine with a side of crispy potato pancakes. Mrs. Russo and Mrs. Butterfield sat across from me and stared as I popped the first bite into my mouth. They watched patiently as I chewed.

"This is wonderful," I told them. "But I know you didn't come here just to cook for me. What's up, Mrs. R?" I liked to address The Ladies using the initials of their last names; their full names made me feel like a kid in grade school.

"We need help finding the murderer of a federal employee," she said.

I put down my fork. "You don't mean the postal worker, do you?" I asked.

Mrs. Russo nodded.

I glanced at my grandmother's wall clock, a china plate hand painted with purple and yellow violets. "The woman hasn't been gone for more than nine or ten hours. How can you be on this so fast?"

Mrs. Butterfield winked at me. "We take our work seriously, dear. Now, what do you know about her?"

I took a swig of coffee and thought for a moment. "She had a sweet tooth. She was always eating candy— and I mean always. The other day it was red licorice whips."

Mrs. Russo stared at me, I don't think she liked my answer.

"She talked on the phone a lot," I said.

Again with the staring.

"Did she have any enemies?" Mrs. Butterfield asked.

"How would I know? I only saw her ten seconds a day," I said. "She'd rush in, plop down the incoming mail, grab the outgoing, and run out the door. I wish I had more to tell you, but my interaction with her was minimal."

Mrs. Russo folded her arms, and squinted her eyes. She did not seem pleased. Mrs. Butterfield continued to look as chipper as a bright new day. I took another bite of breakfast, and savored the hollandaise sauce as if it was my last meal. I had an uneasy feeling I might regret sleuthing with these women, but being fed this way was powerful persuasion.

***

Something interrupted a perfectly good surfing dream. Nothing compared to the high of riding a wave. My surfing bud Chris called it "touching the divine." But instead of becoming one with the universe I felt an irritation that was equivalent to a mosquito buzzing in my ear. I opened one eye. Jimmy Chang stood over me, wearing a gray silk suit, a dark blue tie and sunglasses perched on top of his close-cropped black hair. A toothpick stuck out from between his front teeth.

"Hello, sleeping beauty," he purred.

"Ish," I said and sat up. I'd fallen asleep on a couch in Elsie's Antiques. Delivering zucchini by night and selling velvet covered settees by day was taking its toll. "What do you want, Jimmy?"

He was a snappy dresser, but his socks never matched. Which made me think he might be color blind. But if he was, then the rest of his outfit must be assembled by some type of adult Garanimal system. Jimmy's mother was a tall Swedish woman who taught every form of dance imaginable. His father, who taught martial arts, was Chinese. Jimmy inherited his mother's height and his father's looks. We'd met in grammar school, and he immediately began stealing items from me in a show of twisted affection. A few weeks ago Jimmy had been kidnapped, trapped in the trunk of Mrs. Russo's Cadillac, and hit in the face so hard one eye had swollen shut. During those stressful moments he confessed to having a lifelong crush on me. The feeling was not reciprocated.

"You know," he said. "I could report you to the head of the Downtown Lakeville Merchants Association for sleeping on the job."

"Jimmy, you are the head of the Downtown Lakeville Merchants Association."

He snickered at his joke and lowered his gangly frame down next to me. "Well," he continued, "as head of that fine organization I have come to inform you that you missed our meeting this morning."

"Oh?" I replied, wondering why he really was in my store.

"And since you did not attend, you do not know that next week's meeting will be on Friday instead of Wednesday." He straightened his tie. "I don't want you showing up at Tony's Pizzeria next Wednesday morning only to find the place empty except for the carpet cleaners."

His concern for me was a subterfuge; meeting times were communicated via emails. There was something he wanted to say, and I wished he'd get on with it. I glanced around the store, looking for my coffee cup. I needed more caffeine.

"Did you hear about our mail lady getting mowed down?" he asked.

Ah, there was the reason—Jimmy loved to gossip. The image of that poor woman lying on the street instantly shifted my mood from annoyed to sad.

"It happened in front of my mother's house," I said.

"Did you see anything?" He sounded hopeful.

"A lot of police and nosey neighbors."

"Too bad." His toothpick waved up and down, while the hairline-thin oval goatee that circled his mouth stayed impassive.

"Were you friends with her?" I asked.

He shrugged. "She liked to talk."

"I know. She was always on the phone."

"Huh, I never noticed," he said. "When she dropped off my mail, seemed like she could talk all day."

Jimmy's business—Chang's Used Autos—sat two doors down from Elsie's Antiques. How could Donna be on the phone every day when she delivered mail to me but ready to chat when she arrived at Jimmy's?

"Plus, she was my main source of sweets," he continued. "She always shared her candies with me: chocolates, licorice, Atomic Fireballs. Recently she had this amazing assortment of Life Savers; root-beer, peppermint, wintergreen, and all those fruit flavors, I'd forgotten what a simple pleasure those are. Wasn't a day that went by that she didn't have something for me." He sighed.

"She'd never offered me candy," I said. "Maybe she had a thing for you, Jimmy."

He shrugged and took the toothpick from his mouth. "I guess I'm going to have to buy my own sweets from now on. Yep, she'll be missed."

I raised an eyebrow at him. His depth was overwhelming.

He turned to me and said: "But you know who's really going to miss her is the Mastodon Association, the Guys & Gals Club and the Lakeville Senior Center." He used his toothpick to count off the list on his fingers.

"Why's that?"

"She was a bingo addict. Bingo is a big fundraiser. I think she attended games three or four times a week."

The Mastodon Association was a few blocks from my mother's house. Could she have been returning from a game last night?

"Bingo, huh? You play?"

He glared at me. "No, Patty Cakes. I don't play bingo."

I cringed at his nickname for me. "But, I thought you liked to gamble."

"Bingo pots are too low. If I'm going to gamble, I'm going to gamble real money. And win real money." He put his hands on his knees and hoisted himself up. "I can't help but notice that your store's looking a bit sparse." He made his way to the front door.

"I know." I looked around, there was enough empty floor space I could give dance lessons. I wished Nana were here so we could go antique hunting.

"I'm having the same problem; my lot's practically empty. Everyone is holding onto their cars; no one wants to trade up. Well, I got to go, and remember the meeting is on Friday, not Wednesday."

The second Jimmy was outside, Mrs. Rita Miller popped up from behind my counter.

I put my hand over my heart. "Oh, you startled me," I said.

All of The Ladies had a knack for appearing unexpectedly, and in one way or another they continued to surprise me. Recently I'd found out that Mrs. M was an electronics expert, who could RAM and ping talk any fifteen year old under the table. Her real name was Rita Martinez and she grew medical marijuana in Mrs. Taylor's garage. Her self-adornment of choice was a fresh flower tucked behind an ear. Today she wore a simple white daisy with a yellow center. The flower perfectly accented her shoulder length salt-and-pepper hair.

"Patricia, you need to be more welcoming to Jimmy. Be nice to the guy."

"What are you doing behind my counter?" I hoped I sounded calm and not startled. "And why would I want to be more welcoming to Jimmy? It just might encourage him to show up more often."

"In answer to your first question, I thought I'd look at your computer. I told your grandmother over and over that she needed to upgrade her system and install some security equipment in here. Do you know that you don't even have a surge protector?"

I knew she was right, I could hear the old machine grinding from where I sat. "That's so sweet of you," I said, "but I can't afford a new system."

"I have a used machine that I can give you. Stuff that is newer than what you have, and I won't charge you. Besides, I need a project."

I nodded and shrugged at the same time. "Thank you. That would be very helpful." I folded my arms in front of me. "Now, why do I need to be nice to Jimmy?"

"We need to stay on Jimmy's good side."

"Jimmy doesn't have a good side."

"Oh, Patricia, you are a hoot. But seriously, Jimmy has friends in low places. He can be a bit of a thug, you know. And unfortunately there are occasions that we need people like that."

"You give him too much credit. Jimmy only aspires to thugginess; he's never going to actually get there."

"Your grandmother worked hard on building a relationship with him, earning his trust, and for some reason he's transferred that trust onto you."

"Maybe it was our formative years together," I said,

referring to fact that Jimmy and I had gone through school together. If The Ladies ever found out Jimmy had a crush on me, they'd tease me six ways from Sunday—as my grandmother used to say.

"You need to make nice with him. Maybe find an activity the two of you could do together."

The Ladies had done a lot for me. Without their help, I'd probably be sitting in a tiny damp jail cell. Even now, the thought ignited my claustrophobia and made my stomach ache. Plus I didn't think prison would provide me with an adequate quantity of coffee I needed to survive. I really did owe The Ladies, and here Mrs. M was going to upgrade my computer out of the kindness of her heart. But chumming up to Jimmy Chang? Ish. I did my best imitation of a smile, but it hurt my face.

"Any idea on how to investigate Donna's hit-and-run?" I asked, wanting to get away from the subject of Jimmy.

"Now that we know she was a bingo fan, I'd say we start there," she said. "There's a game at the Lakeville Senior Center tonight, I'll call you later with the details."

"So soon?" I asked.

"Sure, the sooner, the better," she replied. "And one other thing—you need to change your locks. Your grandmother would give a key to anyone. If you pick some deadbolts up from the hardware store, I'll install them for you."

After we said our goodbyes, I called my mom. "I can't go on a zucchini run this evening."

"That's okay. I'll go on my own. Have plans with Jake?"

"No. I'm going to bingo with The Ladies."

"Bingo! I love bingo! Can I come?"

"Sure, I don't see why not."

That was a relief. Better to have my mother gambling than flitting around a dark neighborhood forcing vegetables on the fine folks of Lakeville.

While Mrs. Russo was at my house this morning making me breakfast, she also made me lunch: a roast beef sandwich on sourdough bread with horseradish sauce. My stomach growled, but before I ate, I wanted something to read. Directly across the street from Elsie's Antiques was the Lakeville Bookstore. Next door was the Yarn Barn, owned by the Yarn Barn lady who was the unofficial enforcer of Downtown Lakeville Merchants Association Rules and Regulations. To say the Yarn Barn lady hadn't warmed up to me was an understatement. She'd caught me closed for lunch and in her opinion, such indulgence screamed laziness and sullied the character of all the other downtown businesses. To be blunt about it, I was afraid of her, she wore knitting needles in a beehive hairdo that looked more like lethal weapons than hair adornments.

I poked my head out the door and looked up and down the street; it had been a quiet morning. But then again, I'd slept through most of it. I could see into The Yarn Barn shop, which looked empty. I put a sign in the window showing a clock with red hands to inform my nonexistent customers I'd be back at ten after twelve. I crossed the street, but instead of going directly to the bookstore, veered left toward Jake's.

Jake's Auto Body was housed in a red-brick building on the corner with a large roll-up door in front and an identical one in back. Behind the structure sat a dirt parking area, which was accessible from the side street. Jake and I weren't a couple, but we were leaning in that direction.

I jogged to the corner and looked into his shop. Every bay held a dented auto and three cars were parked in the center aisle. Since Jake had repaired Sunny Russo's Cadillac to its original pristine condition he'd been gaining a reputation with the vintage car enthusiasts in the area.

Jake stood in the back of the building, holding a clipboard and talking with a client. He wore his usual work clothes: a white cotton button down shirt and jeans. Another customer spoke with Reed, the shop assistant.

Jake shook hands with his client, then spotted me. He waved and strode my direction.

"Hi," he said, smiling.

"Do you have time for lunch?" I asked as he leaned over and kissed me on the cheek.

"Oh." His mouth turned down. "I'd better not; I'm swamped."

I looked into his cocoa brown eyes and felt disappointed.

"Maybe this weekend?" he said.

"Okay."

"Jake!" Reed called out from the back of the garage.

"I have to go." He kissed my cheek again and hurried away.

Feeling a bit deflated, I strolled back to the bookstore. Their window advertised a book club that met in a few days. The door chime announced my arrival, and the smell of fresh inked paper welcomed me. The store appeared empty. I slipped into the mystery aisle, looking for a story that might improve my detective skills. A book on the bottom shelf caught my eye. I squatted down to take a look.

A man and woman walked past heading to the front of the store. I glanced up, but they didn't notice me. My focus landed on a small dog the woman held in her arms. Dark gray with a hairless pink chest, it had the body of a Chihuahua and tufts of white hair on its head, tail and feet like a Clydesdale horse. The dog made eye contact with me and squirmed a hello.

I returned to my search and could hear the two talking.

"We're not going to weep, are we Kiki?" The woman said, making kissy noises.

"Now, Mitsy," the man replied, with a hint of reproach. His voice easily carried through the store.

"Well, after she threatened to write up a report on Kiki, then saying she wouldn't deliver our mail if we didn't restrain her, why should I be sad?"

"Still, you shouldn't speak ill of the dead," he retorted.

"We dodged a bullet and you know it. Could you imagine if that woman had filed a formal complaint? A citation against Kiki would have disqualified her from competitions for good. She could have ended Kiki's career!"

"Well, I for one, am going to miss Donna."

"Of course you are, a woman coming in here every day to flirt with you," her voice took on a hard edge. "Plus all the candy she gave you. Can you believe it,

Kiki?" The kissing noises resumed. "Giving a man sweets right in front of his wife. And, it's not like she ever offered me anything. Plus that package of taffy my sister sent me for my birthday mysteriously went missing."

"Now, dear," her husband said. "There's no way to know if she took it." The front door chimed as another customer entered the store. I could hear the man offering assistance and then Mitsy saying: "Go say hello, Kiki."

My focus returned to my book search, and I found one with a picture of a carving knife stuck into a chopping block. Its cover said it "offered an intriguing puzzle for the cozy mystery lover." When I emerged from the aisle the woman stood at a round table in front of a display of stationery. She had pulled a piece of taffy from her pocket and was removing the white waxy paper.

"Oh, I didn't see you there," she said, stuffing the taffy back in her pocket. Kiki's mom was a small woman, barely up to my shoulder.

"I'm Patricia Schuster," I said, holding out my hand. "I'm the new owner of Elsie's Antiques."

"What's that?" she asked, cupping a hand behind her ear. She wore a bright pink jacket, black Capri pants and platform sandals. Her fake eyelashes scrapped against her eyebrows, and her short cropped hair was dark maroon.

She took my hand and I repeated my introduction, speaking louder.

"Oh, you're Elsie's granddaughter. I'm Mitsy. I'm so sorry for your loss. I miss her so."

"Thank you. Me, too."

"Hubby!" she yelled. "Come meet Elsie's granddaughter."

Kiki trotted over, sitting at my feet. I reached down

to pet her. What hair she had was soft. She looked at me adoringly as I stroked her head.

A tall man with a thick waist walked to the counter. Balding on top with some silver hair on the sides, he wore a yellow, orange and brown plaid shirt, covered by a yellow windbreaker. His ensemble clashed with his pink complexion. He bent over and picked up Kiki, placing her gently on a blue velvet pillow which sat near the cash register.

"Hubby," Mitsy said, "this is Patricia. She's running Elsie's Antiques."

"Hello," he said with a fleeting smile. "Did you hear about Donna, the mail lady?"

I nodded. Since he didn't tell me his name I wondered if I should address him as Mr. Hubby.

He leaned toward me, and his glasses slipped down his nose. "Do you have a dog?" he asked, sounding accusatory.

"No," I said. This must be the dog-lover's equivalence to the 'Do you have a husband?' question.

"If Donna had a dog, this never would have happened. A woman shouldn't live alone without a dog." He looked at me as if I'd committed a crime.

"Hubby, go help that customer," Mitsy said.

"He didn't want help."

"Well, help him anyway," she said, giving hubby a little shove. Then she grabbed a paperback from a pile and handed it to me. "Would you like to join our book club? This is what we're reading now." She tapped on the front cover; it showed a woman in a flapper dress under an umbrella next to a man in an overcoat and hat. "It's all about a scandal of a very wealthy couple in the 1920's.

Fiction, of course."

"Sure, sounds interesting."

She tucked a flyer about the club inside the cover and moved behind the counter to ring up my purchases. Lowering her voice and nodding in the direction of Hubby, she said: "Sorry about that. He had a little crush on the mail lady. She brought him candy and talked his ear off."

Well, wasn't that interesting. Donna had treated Hubby the same way she'd treated Jimmy. It appeared that Donna had enjoyed flirting.

I put my mystery book on the counter. Next to Kiki sat a small trophy that bore the inscription: "World's Ugliest Dog. Sonoma-Marin Fair. Honorable Mention." A silver-framed picture showed a dog similar to Kiki but with a tongue that hung out the side of its mouth and eyes that popped out of its head.

"That's Bartholomew," Mitsy said, gesturing to the photograph. "He was my first Chinese Crested dog. His winning Honorable Mention at the Ugliest Dog competition was one of the highlights of my life. He was Kiki's grandfather, and one day Kiki will follow in Bartholomew's paw-steps."

As if on cue, Kiki opened her mouth and her tongue fell out sideways, just like grandpa's.

Chapter Three

Some consider the 1959 Cadillac Biarritz convertible kitschy; others consider it classy. Twin bullet tail lights sat below massive fins trimmed with chrome. Sunny Russo's model sported a white exterior and a maroon interior. Its length ran almost 19 feet and was large enough to carry the four Ladies, my mother, and me. When I rode in it, I felt like a mayor in a parade. Driving with the top down, I wanted to sit up on the back seat and wave to the pedestrians.

The passenger seat was filled by the fourth member of my grandmother's friends who made up The Ladies group: Mrs. Audrey Taylor. She typically wore button-up paisley dresses and ludicrously large hats to convey an old-fashioned lady persona. Perched on the brim of this evening's head attire sat a bird's nest with three small, blue, speckled eggs. I had come to believe that Mrs. T's head gear was inspired by the musical revue *Beach Blanket Babylon*, and if she could balance a replica of the San Francisco skyline on her head, she probably would. What few knew was that beneath her distracting head gear was a wicked-smart brain and a ton of initials behind her name, mostly having to do with psychology.

We arrived at the Lakeville Senior Center early enough to find a group of seats next to each other in the third row. The large auditorium was filled with long tables and metal folding chairs facing a stage. Reproductions of famous oil paintings decorated the paneled walls: The Mona Lisa, Boy in Blue, Girl with the Pearl Earring, a self-portrait of Leonardo De Vince, and, a little surprising, The Scream.

An elaborate flower arrangement sat on the front table with a small sign that read: "In Loving Memory of Donna." A teddy bear held a red heart between its arms and behind the heart someone had tucked a purple dabber. A woman stood at the table. She smiled and sang softly under her breath while adding flowers to the bouquet. She had curly bangs and wavy brown hair that hung below her shoulders where the ends of her tresses also curled. Her outfit consisted of a green skirt and a peach vest over a simple beige blouse with full sleeves. An eclectic collection of bracelets covered both wrists.

As we sat down, I noticed two women at the table directly in front of us, one had mini muffins arranged in a semicircle around her bingo cards. I recognized the two from a funeral I'd attended some weeks before. Their names were Mary Belle and Janie, and both looked to be in their early seventies. Mary Belle didn't wear makeup and had very short gray hair. Janie's gray hair was also short but tousled on top, as if she couldn't control it if she tried.

"Oh, Janie, those look good. What kind are they?" Mary Belle asked.

"Zucchini with mini chocolate chips," Janie replied. "I made them myself this morning."

"Can I have one?" Mary Belle asked.

"No. I brought one mini muffin to eat before each game. They're going to bring me luck."

"How are muffins going to bring you luck?"

"They're special," replied Janie.

"What do you mean, special?"

Janie put one of the muffins on the palm of her hand and held up her prized possession for Mary Belle to admire. "This little baked good contains magic zucchini."

My mother and I exchanged a glance.

"What are you talking about, magic zucchini?"

"Three zucchinis were in my car this morning. One even had a face. The face of a wise man."

My mother covered her mouth, stifling a laugh.

"That doesn't make sense, Janie. Who'd put zucchini in your car?" Mary Belle demanded.

"I don't know." Janie put down the muffin and repositioned the other muffins to make a perfect semicircle. "The Zucchini Fairy, I guess."

"The Zucchini Fairy?" Mary Belle asked. "There's no such thing."

"Well, there must be, if zucchini magically appeared in my car."

"Helena," Mary Belle said loudly, and the woman with the bracelets looked up from Donna's memorial bouquet. "You ever heard of The Zucchini Fairy?"

The woman snickered and shook her head. "No, but Sam Roberts found zucchini in his car this morning. He lives around the corner from you, Janie."

"See Mary Belle, there is a Zucchini Fairy."

Helena stopped adjusting the flowers and leaned over and said: "Maybe it was her." She pointed to the memorial in front of her. "You know they found her a few blocks from your house."

"It couldn't have been her," Janie said. "She might give Sam Roberts zucchini, but she sure wouldn't give me anything. You know how she was about women."

"Maybe she thought she was at your neighbor's house," Helena continued. "Who lives next door to you?"

"Well, Juan and his uncle live on the south side." Janie wiggled in her chair, and her head tilted back like she was thinking hard. Her voice dropped to almost a whisper. "And a new guy just moved in on the other side."

"Maybe she mistook your house for one of theirs," Helena said.

"Oh, blast it," Janie said. She picked up a mini-muffin and slammed it down in front of Mary Belle.

Mary Belle quickly peeled back the wrapper of the little baked good and took a bite.

The lights flicked on and off and a man wearing a beige cardigan walked onto the stage. He took the microphone, repositioned his glasses on his nose, cleared his throat and addressed the audience: "Good evening. I'm Harvey, and I'll be calling the numbers tonight. Would everyone take their seats, please?"

A woman walked in behind him, her short dark hair cut close to her thin face. She sat down at a table and put on a pair of reading glasses, peering at the audience over the top of them.

"This is Judy. She'll be manning the bingo board

tonight," Harvey said. Judy waved. "After a number is called, Judy will light up the corresponding number."

In front of Judy sat a control box and behind her a large board. The word bingo ran down the left side in large bold letters. The numbers one through seventy-five were divided into five rows.

"Before we get started," Harvey continued, "I'd like to have a moment of silence to remember our dear friend Donna, who passed yesterday." He bowed his head.

Chairs screeched on the floor; people coughed and sneezed. A child prattled nonstop, ignoring a chorus of shushing. I glanced up. Judy had removed her reading glasses and was giving them a good cleaning with the edge of her T-shirt.

Harvey's head popped up. "All right, is everyone ready?" He looked over the crowd. "We'll start off easy with your basic two-bingo game. You must get two regular bingos on one sheet in any direction to win. We'll start with the red sheet." He held up a sheet of six squares, each outlined in red. I had the same type of sheet in front of me.

He turned a round brass cage full of white ping-pong balls until one rolled out into a small metal holder.

"N-33," he spoke into the microphone. "N-33, dirty knees."

He passed the ball over to Judy and the number 33 lit up on the board in the N row.

I looked over my four cards, and not seeing N-33, I looked to my mother's, she had N-33 twice. Then I glanced at Mrs. B's four cards, each one contained the picked number.

After about five or six minutes of numbers being called, I heard Janie in front of me say: "Come on, B-10. I need B-10."

"O-74," Harvey called. "O-74, the candy store."

An unusually long moment passed, and I looked up. Harvey removed his glasses and wiped his eyes.

"Harvey?" Judy said.

Harvey didn't bother to put his hand over the microphone. "The Candy Store," he sniffled. "It reminds me of Donna."

Judy sighed.

Harvey took a deep breath and pulled out another ball. "G-56," he said. "G-56, pick-up sticks."

Someone shouted from the back of the room. "Bingo!"

"Shit!" Janie said, slamming her hand down on the table, and like an echo, Janie's exclamation was repeated throughout the hall.

After three more games, no one in our group had won a thing, and Harvey called for a break. I stood in the snack food line with a list of orders: Two chocolate chip cookies, two oatmeal cookies, three coffees, and a hot chocolate.

A woman tall enough to meet my eyes, with very short dark hair, turned and appraised me. Her nails, lips, and jacket were a trio of intense red. The jacket covered a white silk blouse and blue jeans.

"Hello, I'm Cecelia. Cecelia Bronson, no relation to Charles. You can call me Cece." I placed her in her mid-forties. She had pretty blue eyes and a big smile that showed a lot of teeth.

"Patricia," I responded.

"Have you won anything?" she asked.

"No."

"Me neither, but I came close. Twice." She kept her eyes locked onto mine. "What do you do, Patricia?"

"I own Elsie's Antiques."

"The antique business, huh?" She reached into her jacket pocket and produced a business card. "I work at Green's Used Cars."

Green's was at the opposite end of the main boulevard from Chang's Used Autos. This gal worked for Jimmy's competition.

"What kind of car do you drive?" she asked, still staring. "No, wait, let me guess. A Lexis?"

I shook my head.

"A Nissan Sentra?"

"No," I said, wishing the line would move a little quicker.

She looked down at my clothes. "Honda Accord?"

"An '05 Civic," I said.

Furious blinking tried to hide her disappointment in my less-than-optimal vehicle status. "Well, when you want a replacement, I'm your gal. We've got gads of hybrids in; always want to be thinking about the environment!"

"Next!" the cantina woman yelled out.

As Cece placed her order, I listened in on voices behind me.

"You know, I heard Donna delivered zucchini to needy citizens, they're calling her the Zucchini Fairy," said one man.

"Sounds just like her," the other replied, sighing. "Such a generous soul."

I couldn't wait to tell my mother. The rumor that Donna was the Zucchini Fairy was moving faster than an incoming tide.

Holding the four cups in a cardboard carrier I squeezed through the crowd to where Mrs. Taylor stood in a small group.

"This is Elsie's granddaughter, Patricia," Mrs. T said. "She's taken over Elsie's Antiques." She motioned toward the used car dealer. "This is Cece."

"Hello, again," Cece said.

"And Earl and his grandson, Andrew," Mrs. T said. "They recently came back from Alaska."

"That sounds adventurous," I said.

"Oh, that reminds me," Cece said, digging into her purse. "I need to give you your house key back."

"Cece was kind enough to house sit for me while Andrew and I were away," said Earl.

Earl looked to be in his fifties and wore a black bowling shirt with two white pinstripes running vertically down one side. A closely trimmed salt and pepper beard covered his face, and his dark hair was pulled back into a pony tail. He wore thick black glasses and had a diamond stud earring in one ear. Both he and his grandson, Andrew, shared a tall frame and a thin nose.

Andrew wore jeans and a long-sleeved plaid shirt with the sleeves rolled up over a white T-shirt. His attention was on his phone. I judged him to be in his late teens. He gave me a head nod when he looked up, and I noticed he had a scratch on his check that looked like an exclamation point.

"My daughter and her husband work as fishing guides in Homer," Earl said. "Andrew usually spends winters with me while he's in school and summers in Alaska with his parents, but this summer he decided to come back early. Luckily, I had some vacation time coming, so I went up and stayed with them for a few weeks and got some fishing in before the two of us came back."

"Gramps, can I get the keys?" Andrew asked.

"Going to see Maggie?" Earl asked.

"Yeah."

"Are you coming to the restaurant for pie? I'll need a ride home."

"I can give you a lift, Earl," Cece said, sounding flirtatious.

"Thanks," Earl and Andrew replied in unison.

Andrew smiled at his grandfather. "You can keep my winnings."

"Your winnings? I paid for those cards." Earl grinned as he dug into his pocket and dropped keys into Andrew's open hand. "Be home by eleven-thirty," he said. "Just because you're not working is no reason for you to stay out all night."

My ears perked up at Andrew's employment status. "I may know of something," I said, thinking about Jake's auto body shop.

"Oh, yeah?" Andrew replied.

"Jake—the owner of Jake's Auto Body—is looking for some help. Why don't you give him a call?"

"Okay, thanks," Andrew said, as he headed out the door.

"Did you know Donna?" Earl directed the question to me.

"She was my mail carrier," I replied.

"Andrew dates her step-daughter, Maggie. She's having a hard time with Donna's death. Understandably so." He nodded his head for emphasis. "Maggie was the real reason Andrew wanted to be here this summer, instead of in Alaska."

Earl took out a business card and scribbled on the back. "This is Andrew's number; maybe you could pass it on to Jake. When it comes to work, Andrew has a tendency to be forgetful." He grinned handing the card to me. The front read: Earl Gray, Guitarist.

"And before you ask: Yes, I like tea, and yes my parents are English with an odd sense of humor." He said this with a tilt of his head and a bit of a smile. At his age, he must have handled that question a thousand times. His smile faded and he said, "Donna was lead singer in our band."

"You know, I'm always available to fill in, Earl," Cece said.

Earl frowned. "I'm not ready to make any decisions."

Cece's focus moved beyond Earl. "Fred! Hey, Fred!" she yelled.

An older gentleman leaning on a smooth oak cane stopped and turned, his eyes narrowing in irritation.

"That glass bottle doesn't go in the trash, you know," Cece said. "It goes in the recycle bin." Fred hobbled back to the large plastic garbage can, fitted with a black plastic liner. He reached down, pulled out a clear glass bottle and dropped it into the blue recycle bin. He walked on, but one hand came up flipping Cece the bird.

"Old fart," Cece muttered. "Doesn't give a second thought about polluting the planet."

The lights flickered. I started to turn, but a graceful

hand moving high in the air caught my eye. I leaned sideways and looked down a long corridor that led to offices and an emergency exit. Helena, the woman wearing multiple bracelets, had both arms above her head and her hands crossed and uncrossed while her thumb and fingers tapped against each other as if playing invisible castanets. She swayed sideways, hip first, her skirt following with her movements. Her flat shoes were decorated in gold sequins. Two women stood on each side of her and a little behind. They were dressed casually in jeans and T-shirts. They watched closely, mimicking her movements.

"Helena teaches belly dancing," Mrs. T whispered in my ear. "She's also in Earl's band."

Others around us turned to watch as Helena leaned backwards, her long hair almost touching the floor, while her arms undulated above her like ripples on a lazy river. The dancers came upright, then bent forward at the waist, every part of their bodies exuding a rhythmic sensuality. Suddenly Helena straightened up, raised one knee to her chest, pulled off a slipper, dropped to the floor and—WHAM—smacked her shoe on the vinyl.

"Die! Die! Die!" she yelled, continuing her assault.

The violent movement made the crowd, as well as her fellow dancers, jump back in surprise, quickly realizing this wasn't part of the dance. Helena's head came up. Her upper lip curled into a snarl. Her eyes flashed over the silent crowd.

"There was an ant." She pointed to a spot on the floor.

I leaned over to Mrs. T and whispered, "Do you think Helena could have run down Donna?"

Mrs. T grabbed my arm. "Let's go back to our seats."

We returned to our table, and I passed out the drinks and cookies I'd gotten from the cantina. Harvey spoke into the microphone to explain the next game.

Our luck finally turned and Mrs. B won $125 when she hit a solo bingo. Mrs. T won a few bucks on some pull tabs. I won the last game, called a picture frame. It was Donna's favorite and played in her honor. It netted me $50 after splitting it with two other winners.

In the parking lot Mrs. R opened the door to the Cadillac, then passed me the keys. "Do you mind? You know how I hate to drive in the dark."

A white Prius sedan silently backed out of its spot. The driver's window rolled down, and Cece's head emerged, her eyes landing on me.

"I thought you drove a Civic," she said accusatorily.

My first thought was to explain, but I kept quiet. I didn't care for her bullying tone.

Cece's interior light flipped on, and I could see Earl fiddling with the radio. She grabbed his arm and pulled it away from the knobs. "Driver picks the music," she said, then turned back and surveyed our little group. "You know cars like that shouldn't even be on the road, filling the skies with carbon monoxide." She wagged a finger. "You need to replace that with something more fuel efficient, maybe even a hybrid."

"Hey, what's this?" Earl asked holding up a lacey purple bra and swung it in front of Cece's face.

She pulled back a bit as if trying to focus.

"Where did that come from?" Cece asked.

"The floor." Earl laughed.

Cece grabbed the bra, dropped it behind the seat and

rolled up the window. As she drove away, Mrs. B raised her arm and pointed at the car. "What a hypocrite. Do you see that?"

"See what?" Mrs. T asked.

"Her car? It's spotless. You can see the sparkle of the street lights off the roof."

I glanced around the parking lot, she was right; the other car roofs were dull with dirt and dust.

"And?" Mrs. R said, trying to get an explanation, since none of us seemed to understand Mrs. B's outrage.

"That means she's washing her car!" Mrs. Butterfield said. "We're in the middle of a drought, people. Remember, the drought? You're not supposed to be wasting water by washing your car. And just a minute ago she was being snippy about the Cadillac's gas mileage."

The Ladies, along with my mom, mumbled a litany of replies: "Hmm, okay. Right. Oh, yes, of course. Awful, isn't it?"

Chapter Four

The next morning I woke to the smell of coffee. The Ladies were back. I sat up and inhaled deeply, attempting to decipher what scrumptious breakfast they had created. It smelled sweet and doughy.

Amid the laughter and talking coming from the kitchen was a voice I didn't recognize. I decided to shower and dress first; since meeting a visitor in my sheep pajamas might not make for a good first impression. But when I entered the kitchen it wasn't a stranger, it was Beatrice Johnson, the FBI agent who served as liaison between The Ladies and the Bureau.

"Good morning, Patricia," she said, rising to greet me as she held out her hand.

Ms. Johnson was the quintessential professional. She wore a navy blue suit and tiny gold hoop earrings. Her dark hair was pulled back into a bun, with minimal makeup. I guessed her to be in her mid-forty's, but her smooth ebony skin hid her true age. She didn't look a day over thirty.

"Ms. Johnson, what a nice surprise," I said.

The veneer of Ms. Johnson's professionalism cracked. One eyebrow pointed upward. "Sunny," she said, "didn't you tell Patricia we were having a breakfast meeting at her house?"

Mrs. R opened the waffle iron and poured in some batter. As per usual, her silver pageboy didn't have a hair out of place. Without looking up, she said: "Hmm, I must have forgot. Patricia, we're having a breakfast meeting this morning to go over our strategy for catching Donna's killer, and our FBI liaison will be attending." Mrs. R gestured to Ms. Johnson. "From here on out, we'll be using your house as Command Central."

I looked around Nana's small kitchen with its restaurant style booth beside the large picture window. Two easels crowded the space between the table and the built-in wall hutch. One held a flip chart and the other photos attached to a whiteboard. I admit I felt a pang of disappointment that Ms. Johnson hadn't brought along a floating hologram like they have on the CSI TV shows.

"I'm sorry," Ms. Johnson said. "Now I feel like we're intruding."

"It's all right," I said, pouring myself a cup of coffee.

Ms. Johnson's eyebrow lowered to its usual place, and her professionalism returned.

I grinned at the other Ladies sitting around the kitchen table. Mrs. M wore a purple Gerber daisy behind her ear, which matched her form-fitting plum-colored dress. Mrs. T had one of her classic blue-and-purple paisley dresses. I glanced at Mrs. B's yellow shift, which was so bright it made me blink against its intensity.

I took a seat and poured organic cream into my

coffee, then helped myself to some scrambled eggs and a waffle.

Ms. Johnson stood next to the whiteboard and easels. "Okay, here's what we know about Donna Olsen." Ms. Johnson pointed to a photo that looked like it came from her employee badge. "She was fifty-two years old, lived on the west side of Lakeville, and was married to Steve Olsen, no children."

"Married? Really?" I said. "The bookstore owner implied she was a bit of a flirt."

"Well, Donna and Steve were married for three years, they separated about a year ago and she filed for divorce a little over six months ago. But the final papers weren't filed."

"What's Steve going to get?" Mrs. M asked the agent.

"An insurance policy and some savings. He'll end up with close to $145,000 and a small portion of her pension. She recently bought a house, but we don't have any details about what she put down."

"In some circles $145,000 is enough of a reason to knock someone off," Mrs. B said.

Ms. Johnson pointed to a second photo that was clearly a mug shot. A middle aged man stared into the camera with untamed dark hair graying at the temples and eyebrows in need of restraining. She tapped on the picture.

"Donna's husband, Steve Olsen, fifty-four, occupation—artist and musician."

"What was he arrested for?" Mrs. R asked.

"Assault. He's dabbled in graffiti art, and about a year ago he got into an altercation with another artist who had painted over some of his work. It was his first offense. He got off with some community service. Interestingly enough, it was around the time that he and Donna split."

Ms. Johnson then gestured to a picture of a young woman. She had a smiling round face, with short brown hair, and her eyes registered a hint of embarrassment. "Steve Olsen has a seventeen-year-old daughter, Magnolia, also known as Maggie, from a previous marriage."

The last picture on the whiteboard was a music group on stage.

"Donna was in a band called The Stokers," Ms. Johnson said. "Mrs. T, you know Earl, don't you? Why don't you fill us in on what you know about the group?"

I had a feeling that Ms. Johnson knew all about The Stokers and their history. After all, she did work for the FBI.

"I met Earl some years back when his band played at a friend's wedding. He and Steve are the core members, and have been playing together for years. They're mostly a cover band. Earl plays guitar; Steve plays the drums."

"What about other members?" Ms. Johnson asked.

"Different people have cycled in and out over the years. Their most recent incarnation has been Earl, Steve, Helena and Donna. Helena had been lead female singer until Donna came on board and took her place," explained Mrs. T.

"You mean belly dancing, ant hating Helena from last night?" I asked.

Mrs. T nodded.

"So there could be bad blood between Helena and Donna," said Mrs. Russo.

"It's possible," Mrs. T said, "but Donna joined the band three or four years ago, seems like a long time to hold a grudge."

"This is an old photo," Mrs. T said, tapping on the picture. "The fifth member shown here is Cece Bronson. Patricia, you met her last night at bingo. She's had a tumultuous relationship with Earl, and she has connections with a traveling band. So when she and Earl would have a drag out fight, she'd run off and join up with the other band. This last time she came back Earl wouldn't let her back in the band. He said she caused too many problems."

"Looks like there's a bit of an age difference between those two," said Mrs. R.

"Yes," said Mrs. T, "Earl's close to twenty years older. People that far apart can have very different outlooks on life."

Ms. Johnson cleared her throat to get our attention. "Now, before we go too far down a rabbit hole, let's keep the big picture in mind." She paused and looked around the group. "We're here because there is a chance that Donna's death is related to her job as a federal employee. So let's brainstorm some ideas that revolve around her job at the Post Office."

"What about Donna having access to the FBI's most wanted list?" Mrs. M said. "It hung inside the post office, something she would see on a daily basis. What if she'd spotted a fugitive on her route?"

"Good," Ms. Johnson said.

"Or she could have uncovered someone doing a mail scam." Mrs. R said. "Even a coworker."

Ms. Johnson nodded. "Okay, let's start some lists."

She wrote FBI Related as a heading on the flip chart. Under that she wrote Fugitive and Mail Scammer. Then the next headings: People, Activities, Personality.

"Let's start with the obvious," said Ms. Johnson, as she wrote Mail Carrier and Singer under Activities. She then listed all the people we'd talked about: Donna's husband, Steve; Earl, Cece and Helena from the band; and Maggie, Donna's step-daughter.

"Other friends?" Ms. Johnson asked.

"Men," I said.

"Can you be more specific?"

"She flirted with the owner of the Lakeville Bookstore and Jimmy Chang, too. Maybe she's ticked off other women besides Helena."

Ms. Johnson wrote the word "flirtatious" under Personality. "What about other activities besides singer?"

"Bingo," we all said in unison.

Our stoic FBI agent's lips twitched, it was almost a smile. "Anything else come to mind?"

"Statistics always point to the husband," said Mrs. T.

Ms. Johnson put an asterisk next to Steve's name.

"Mitsy, the bookstore owner, wasn't sad to see her go," I told them. "Donna threatened to end the career of her dog." I explained about the ugly dog contest.

"Killing someone over a dog show seems a bit of a stretch," said Mrs. R.

Ms. Johnson nodded, but added Mitsy to the chart.

"What about means and opportunity?" Mrs. B asked.

"If they wanted to hide a car, they could be in Mexico or Canada by now," said Mrs. R. "Besides, so many crimes are done with stolen vehicles, I'm sure the police will be looking for that."

Mrs. T jumped in. "We can't rule out it was an accident."

"Right," said Ms. Johnson, "and speaking of that, let's not step on any of the local law enforcement's toes." Her face took on a stern look, as if it had happened before. "Okay, let's talk strategy."

Mrs. R jumped up to pour another batch of waffles. Mrs. M pursed her lips and adjusted the daisy behind her ear. Mrs. T stared intensely out the window. And Mrs. B decided we all needed more coffee.

"All right ladies, I can take a hint. I know you don't want to discuss your plans with me." Ms. Johnson gathered up her things. "You'll find all the details in the file folders, plus a list of the FBI's Most Wanted. I've highlighted the ones that have ties on the West Coast. It's a long shot, but I want to cover all our bases."

Underneath all our plates were dark green folders. I opened mine, the top sheet showed the picture of Donna, her address, phone number, and work schedule. Another page had her mail route. The other pages contained similar facts on Steve; his daughter, Magnolia; and the band. The last pages were the FBI's most wanted.

I walked Ms. Johnson to the front door. She turned and held out her business card. The FBI's blue and gold logo decorated one corner. The center held the name Beatrice Johnson in gold embossed letters, her title was Liaison. Nice and vague. Below that was an 800 number plus an extension.

"Watch your step, Patricia. These ladies don't have a lot of inhibitions, and sometimes they can get off course. I'm hoping you'll be an even keel for the group."

Mrs. M's voice carried to the living room, "Ay carumba, stakeouts are boring! I say we do a little breaking and entering!"

"See what I mean?" Ms. Johnson said. She tapped on the card. "I can help with information, but a run in with local police, and you're on your own. Leave a message if you need me, but just to give you a heads up, depending on what other cases I'm working on, it may take some time, and I can't always communicate by traditional means." Her eyebrows went up and she smiled.

When I returned to the group, Mrs. Miller, Mrs. Butterfield and Mrs. Russo were all talking at the same time.

"Break into her house."

"Hack into her computer."

"Let's do a stakeout and watch the husband."

"We have to find the car that ran her down."

"The police have better resources to locate a car than we do."

"We need to talk to her co-workers."

"Let's cross check arrest records with her postal route."

While the other three women continued to brainstorm, Mrs. T leaned over and softly asked. "How's your mom doing, Patricia?"

"I'm worried about her," I said. "Her teaching job doesn't start until September, and she has been keeping busy with gardening and Tae Kwan Do." I sighed wondering how much I should reveal. "But, you know mom; she has a tendency to be a bit extreme in her activities."

Mrs. T's eyebrows creased with concerned. She'd

been my mother's guardian for two years when my grandmother was in prison for art counterfeiting. She loved my mother like a daughter.

"Such as?" she asked.

"Mom is the Zucchini Fairy."

At that pronouncement the remainder of the group stopped talking.

"Your mother is the Zucchini Fairy?" The Ladies asked in unison.

I nodded.

"Oh, dear," Mrs. B said. "She's been smelling too much bat guano."

Later that morning, when all my customers were of the "just looking" variety, I decided it must be a window shopping day and not a buy something day. I called Jake's Auto Body, and his assistant, Reed, answered the phone.

"Hi, Patricia. Jake's with a customer, do you want to leave a message?"

"I ran into someone looking for work, and I thought I'd pass the information along."

"Shoot," he said.

I rattled off Andrew's name and phone number from the back of Earl's business card.

"Thanks, I'll let him know."

I hung up the phone feeling disappointed. Even though it was technically a business call, it still would have been nice to hear Jake's voice. I sighed and returned to my internet search for cheap antiques. Even with furniture from Steve on the horizon, in the antique business, "the hunt never ends," as Nana used to say.

My front door jangled, and I looked up to see

Mrs. M and Jimmy.

"Patricia," Mrs. M said. "I'd like to get started on installing your security system." She looked up at one corner of the room. "Let's start over here."

Jimmy followed behind her, carrying a large cardboard box which he gingerly placed on the floor.

"Do you have a ladder?" Mrs. M asked.

"It's in the storeroom."

Mrs. M looked at Jimmy, and he trotted off.

"This is your chance to be nice to Jimmy," Mrs. M said.

"Okay," I said.

It was hard to argue with someone who was working for free. I went over to her as she opened the box. Inside were security cameras and lots of wire.

"I know, using wires is old school," Mrs. M said, "but you get a much better picture."

"I don't mind," I said, then lowered my voice. "You told me you wanted a project, Mrs. M. But what is Jimmy expecting in return?"

"We're bartering," she said. "I'm going to install a security system for him, too."

Jimmy used a rickety old office trailer to conduct business at Chang's Used Auto.

"You mean he doesn't have a system in place already?"

"He has a pretend system, cameras that aren't hooked up to anything. It's very risky."

Jimmy returned and opened up the ladder.

"How are you today, Jimmy?" I asked, trying to sound pleasant.

"Fine." He pulled out a small black tube from his

pocket, took off the lid and slid out a toothpick. "Want one?"

"Sure," I said, hoping accepting something from him would be enough niceties and I could get back to work. I popped the pick in my mouth. It was sweet and hot. After a few moments it started to burn. I smiled, pulling my lip away from the sting, but it was spreading to the side of my tongue. I removed the pick, but not before my eyes began to water.

Jimmy grinned. "They're atomic cinnamon. Do you like it?"

"Yeah. Great," I said, and began to cough.

I retreated behind the safety of the counter. Mrs. M shot me a dirty look; obviously she didn't think my small exchange with Jimmy was sufficient. Too bad, as far as I was concerned. Catching my mouth on fire was enough of a sacrifice for the team.

After work I parked across the street from a steel-blue Victorian home with white trim. I walked up the driveway to a small unit in the back where Steve, Donna's almost-ex-husband, lived. The front and back houses were painted alike with pink tea roses edging the front of both dwellings. On Steve's front porch, a lounge chair upholstered with green and peach tropical fabric sat next to a wicker end table. A small piece of tape covered the doorbell so I knocked. No one answered. I peered through the window and checked out Steve's living room. Books and newspapers lay scattered about. A large screen TV took up one corner and beer bottles were lined up in a row on the coffee table. Apparently cleaning wasn't on the top of Steve's to-do list.

This seemed like a perfect time to snoop. The front house had a six foot hedge that created privacy from the street. Fences delineated the properties on both sides. I snuck around to the back of Steve's unit and peeked into his backyard. An old convertible sat with its hood up. I walked around the car; the body was in good shape. After listening to Jake talk shop, I knew that these older models could require any amount of tinkering.

My backup plan to find Steve included checking out the one area in town that welcomed graffiti artists, a fence that ran between the old train tracks and the road to the Lakeville Animal Shelter. In high school, I'd visited the incarcerated cats, giving them love and a moment's escape from their temporary confinement. I'd walked dogs on occasion, too, letting them stretch their legs along the dirt road. But a lot had changed since then. The shelter had been remodeled. The entrance was on the south side now, on a paved road lined with new businesses. On the sidewalk, a man walked two dogs: a black lab pup and an adult sized German Shepard. The big dog sat calmly while the man bent down to rub the pup's ears.

The wood fence that I had remembered covered with colorful graffiti had been painted over with whitewash. The only place left for the graffiti artists was an abandoned three-car train. It stood on the old railroad tracks, covered in a base coat of rust. One lone teenager worked on a wild design that looked like the word "Stop," with a grotesque hand growing out of the top of the S. His jeans rode low on his hips, showing off blue and white striped boxers. A cigarette dangled from his lips. I wanted to point out the dangers of smoking while standing in dead weeds, but a safety lecture wasn't a great way to start a conversation.

"Excuse me," I said.

He stopped to shake his can of paint.

"I like your hand."

He turned to me unsmiling.

"I'm an artist too," I said. "Hands are tough."

He grunted. I took that as an invitation for further discussion.

"I'm looking for a guy named Steve."

"Old guy?" he asked.

"Yeah."

"I haven't seen him, I heard he got a job downtown."

"What kind of job?"

He gave me the adults-are-so-stupid look. I probably only had seven or eight years on him, but at his age enough to make me ancient. "Guess," he snapped.

I got back in my car and made a U-turn. The dog walker was facing me. I recognized the man as Hubby, the bookstore owner. He wore the same light yellow windbreaker as the day I met him. He looked right at me, so I waved, but he put his head down, acting like he didn't see me.

I drove back to the center of town and cruised slowly down the main drag. With Fourth of July on the horizon I hoped to spot Steve painting a flag or a fireworks display on one of the storefront windows. But instead I spotted a man standing on a single story flat-top roof that abutted the three-story Phoenix Building. Once a theater, the Phoenix had been transformed in the '80s into a small concert hall and hangout for local teens. I'd spent many nights there, listening to music and meeting up with friends.

He stood on scaffolding and stretched to his full height to paint a brilliant yellow-orange sun in the top left corner. The man's whole body was involved, as though he were dancing. I was overcome with a sudden desire to take up mural painting. I'd never painted without the limitation of a canvas. It appeared daunting, yet freeing at the same time. I drove to the back of the building and parked in the alley.

An aluminum extension ladder leaned up against the brick wall. I took hold of the dirty round cross bars and climbed. It rattled as I ascended, and about half way up I could feel it flexing under my weight.

"Hi," I said, when my feet touched the solid roof.

Steve looked better than he had in his mug shot. He was freshly shaved. His salt-and-pepper hair had been trimmed but still appeared tussled as if he'd just risen from bed. Like the kid painting the railroad car, he didn't acknowledge me.

"Your mural's beautiful," I said.

"Thanks."

"My name's Patricia."

"Steve."

"Mind if I ask you some questions?"

His mouth turned into a thin line. He looked down and loaded up his brush with more paint. "I'm getting paid through a private donation," he said. "No precious taxpayer money is going to support this project."

"That's nice," I said. "But I wanted to ask you about Donna."

His head snapped up. "Who are you?"

"Patricia Schuster. I'm moonlighting for a private

investigator," I lied. "I'm investigating Donna's death."

"Well, Moonlight. What's there to investigate?"

"I'm trying to find out who hit her."

"What difference does it make? It was an accident."

"Maybe."

"Who's your client?" he asked.

"I'm not at liberty to say."

He shook his head. "I can't talk now. I'm working."

"How's this?" I said. "Let me buy you dinner. McNear's in a half-an-hour?"

"All right, Moonlight. You've got a deal."

I heard the ladder clattering. A petite young woman, with shoulder length brown hair and long dangly earrings, hopped onto the roof. She wore cargo shorts, chunky sandals, and a T-shirt with lightning bolts across the front partially covered by a tailored jacket. I recognized her from the photo Ms. Johnson had provided. She was Steve's daughter, Magnolia.

"Dad," she said.

"Hi, Maggie," he replied. "What are you doing here?"

She ignored his question while appraising me with intelligent eyes.

"I'm Patricia," I said.

"Magnolia."

"Why aren't you at work?" Steve asked.

She raised her hand up and flicked at her hair. Two bandages wrapped the edge of her palm. "Dad, it's a volunteer position. I can take a break any time; no one's going to get mad."

"When you make a commitment, people come to rely on you."

"Dad, there's not going to be any docent-related

emergencies at the Lakeville History Museum in the twenty minutes I'm gone."

"How's your knee?" he asked, then glanced at me. "She took a spill last night, hurt herself and totaled her bike."

"Fine," Magnolia replied, looking away and pulling at one of her earrings. "I took an aspirin before bed."

I got the odd sense that she was lying. I'd fallen off my bike many times, but the only way to total a bike was to run into something.

Steve turned his attention back to his paint can. "Moonlight just offered to buy me dinner," he said.

"Moonlight?" Maggie asked.

"Patricia moonlights for a private investigator. She's looking into Donna's death."

"What's there to look into?" she asked, her eyes darting back and forth between Steve and me.

"Nothing," Steve said. "But Moonlight is still willing to feed me."

Maggie's mouth turned into a straight line, reminding me of Steve's just moments earlier.

I backed up a step. "I'll see you later then, Steve." I looked at Maggie. "Nice meeting you."

Her expression stayed ridged as she folded her arms in front of her.

Halfway down the ladder, I heard her voice: "Does she think you had something to do with Donna getting hit?"

"Honey, people with money like to throw it around. It's nothing; forget it."

McNear's Saloon and Dining House had been around

since the late 1800s. A stuffed mackerel hung on the wall above the bar mirrors; suspended from the ceiling was a plastic, inflatable, bright-green alligator. The opposite brick wall held a collection of mismatched items: A Pabst Blue Ribbon Cold Beer sign; an antique wood sleigh, doubtful that it was used locally; and a picture of an oversized chicken sitting on an oversized basket in downtown Lakeville during its egg production heyday.

Steve wandered in a few minutes later, blue paint smeared on the thigh of his ripped jeans. He went to the bar, ordered a beer then joined me at the table. He looked tired after a day of painting, but underneath the fatigue he seemed content.

We both ordered fish and chips and made small talk about how he got the mural gig, and I told him about my art background. After the meal arrived and we'd had a few bites of fish, the topic changed to his daughter.

"She jumped a grade, so she just graduated. Got a scholarship. I just hope she doesn't screw it up."

I raised an eyebrow as a question.

"She's involved with this guy." He shook his head as if that was enough of an explanation.

"Andrew? Earl's grandson?"

He nodded.

"I met him at bingo last night," I said.

"She's a good kid though, especially under the circumstances. Maggie was six when her mom divorced me, moved to Arizona, and started another family. There've been some rough times over the years. When Donna and I got together we seemed like a happy family, at least for a little while. But the stepmom role is tricky. Donna tried to be Maggie's friend, and that left me to be law enforcer. Once Maggie started dating, my knee-jerk response was to lock her in her room until she was eighteen."

I smiled. "You sound like my dad."

"I just felt that Donna was way too lenient with her. After Donna and I separated, they got even closer. She started staying the night at Donna's for part of the week. I think Maggie felt comfortable talking to Donna about boys."

"How is she taking Donna's death?"

"Hard. In a way, she's lost two mothers."

I felt bad for him. He was back to being a single dad. A difficult place when Maggie was six, probably even more difficult with Maggie in her teen years. I popped a fry in my mouth, and while I thought about how to word some personal questions about Donna, a woman's yelling broke my concentration.

"Hey! Hey!"

I looked up and Mitsy, the bookstore owner, was coming our way. She teetered on her huge platform sandals. A bulge on the side of her tote bag moved; poor Kiki was in hiding. Mitsy slammed a half-empty beer stein down on our table.

"So how's your business doing, Patricia?" She asked, but before I could answer she turned to Steve. "Don't I know you?"

"I'm painting a mural on the Phoenix Building," he replied.

"Oh, right. You're the artist fellow," she said, nodding. "You paint our windows at Christmas." She looked back to me. "He's too old for you."

I grimaced, feeling embarrassed for Steve. His

eyebrows went up at the accusation of being the creepy old guy.

"This is a business meeting," Steve said. Stating what he thought would have been obvious had Mitsy known of my imaginary private eye profession.

Mitsy looked at me, her eyes studying my face or trying to focus; it was hard to tell. I could see the wheels spinning behind her blood-shot orbs. She leaned on the table, stabilizing her wobbly legs and turned to Steve.

"Well, if you've got something to sell, she's your gal."

Steve tried to explain, "She's investigating Donna's death." He evidently thought that Mitsy was the one confused.

"You investigate people?" she asked me.

Out of the corner of my eye, I could see Steve's eyebrows come together.

"I moonlight."

She nodded her head in approval. "Huh, I'll keep that in mind. So how's your store doing? The book business is in the crapper." She looked back to the bar and abruptly walked off.

Steve got up and followed her to the bar. He gestured to the bartender, then spoke to him. The bartender pointed to a group of women that Mitsy had joined. Since it was so early in the evening, I couldn't help but wonder if drinking heavily was a common occurrence for Mitsy.

Steve returned to the table. "She's got a ride home." Then he pushed his beer away and took a gulp of water.

"I own Elsie's Antiques," I stated, hoping that would explain the misunderstanding. "Elsie was my grandmother. She left me the store."

"I'm sorry," he said. "I mean about her passing. I liked her." He dunked a piece of breaded fish into a small plastic cup of tartar sauce. "Donna had some furniture that will need a new home, also some odds and ends. Do you do consignment?"

"I prefer to buy outright; it's less paperwork. But I'd have to see the items before I commit." Wow, having inventory just drop into my lap. This meant, at least temporarily, that I wouldn't have to drive around to garage sales, searching for those elusive unique pieces to fill up my store. But an uncomfortable prickly feeling was starting at the base of my neck. I was mixing my business life with a suspect.

"I'd like to ask you something about Donna," I said.

"Shoot."

"Why were you two getting a divorce?"

He reached into his pants pocket and pulled out a mashed up wad of cash and change and slapped it on the table. Nickels, dimes, and quarters rolled every which way. He put his hand out, gesturing to the mess.

I raised my eyebrows; he could tell I didn't get it.

He passed his hand over the money. "I'm unorganized. My daughter says I shouldn't even carry cash, just a debit card. Now, Donna was organized, ridiculously organized. She kept track of everything, had a diary for this, and a diary for that." He looked down at the money. "I lost my wallet a few weeks ago. But my rent's all paid up, so is the electric bill, and I have enough money for coffee and a bagel tomorrow morning. That's the important thing, right?"

I indulged him with a smile.

"You know, Donna kept track of all the dogs on her

route—which ones were mean and which ones she could bribe with a dog bone, after checking with the owners of course." He finished off the rest of his beer, and swept the cash and change into a pile. "I know what some people thought: that it was because of her flirting. But she wasn't always like that." He stared intensely at his beer while peeling a piece of label from the long-necked brown bottle.

"Had Donna been married before?"

"Twice. I was number three." His eyebrows pulled together. I didn't know him well enough to read his face, but embarrassment was a possibility.

"How'd you meet?"

"I'm in a band. We were playing at a wedding." He shrugged one shoulder. "She came up on stage and started singing with us; she was good, so we signed her up."

"Whose idea was that?"

"Well, Earl's and mine. Earl started the band. We'd been without a fourth member for a while. But Helena wasn't so crazy about it. She was our lead singer at the time." Steve stopped making eye contact with me, and I wondered if he felt guilty hiring Donna. "I can't blame Helena. If I was her, I'd be mad too."

"Can you think of any reason why someone would want to hurt Donna?"

He shrugged. "She'd had a run-in with a gal on her route, something about a dog. I guess Donna could have seen something illegal, but if she had, she'd have gone to the police. But there was an odd thing with some packages."

"What do you mean?"

"Maggie mentioned that Donna had lost some packages." He used air quotes around the word lost. "I can see someone stealing packages from her truck, but losing them? I was completely baffled by that. With her organizational skills, she'd never just lose a package."

We both ate in silence for a few minutes. I felt the evening coming to a close, so I hurried to make a point.

"Since you and Donna are still married, are you going to make money off her death?" I asked.

"I didn't run her down, if that's what you're thinking." He sighed, side stepping my question. "Look, you're wasting your time investigating this. The cops think it was an accident, some drunk probably. This has nothing to do with me."

I nodded, grabbed the check and stood up.

"Here's Maggie," Steve said, his eyebrows coming together.

I turned to see Maggie. She looked distraught.

"Dad, someone went through my bag while I was working at the museum," she said, sounding a bit out of breath as she plunked her backpack on the table.

"Aren't you going to say hello?" Steve asked, gesturing to me.

"Hi," she said, forcing a smile.

"So how do you know someone went through your bag?"

"I left it behind the counter on a shelf below the cash register," Maggie said, "and at the end of my shift, the zipper was open. I never leave it open."

"Was anything taken?"

"No, but it's just creepy."

Steve's face visibly relaxed. "You don't leave anything

valuable in it do you?"

"Yes," she said emphatically, "my laptop."

Steve stood up, and put his hand on Maggie's arm. "Why don't we ride home together, sweetie." He turned to me. "Thanks for dinner, Patricia. Anything else you want to know?"

"What kind of car do you drive?" I asked.

"A '67 Schwinn. It's parked at the bike rack out front. Would you like to see it?"

I wanted to challenge him, since I just saw a car in his backyard, but revealing that I'd been poking around his house wouldn't win me any points. After all, the car I saw had its hood up. Maybe it ran; maybe it didn't. Maybe it wasn't even Steve's car; maybe he made extra money being a mechanic. I was making excuses for him, and the prickly feeling in my neck returned.

Chapter Five

The barista at Joey's Coffee handed me two large cups, which I doctored with cream and plenty of sugar. My mother had grabbed a prime table next to the window. I slid into the chair across from her. She wore a big grin and seemed usually perky for so early in the morning. I feared the worst.

She leaned over and whispered, "I'm going on a zucchini run tonight. You in?"

I took a gulp of coffee before replying. "Mom, this whole sneaking around—"

"Hi, Genny," a voice called from across the room.

I looked over to see a tall dark man with tight black curls in a white dress shirt and blue tie waving. His large grin made me suspect this was another man after my mom's heart.

"See you in class," he said.

My mom waved back. "He's in my Tae Kwan Do class. Such a sweetheart."

"He ask you out?" I asked.

"No, but if he doesn't soon, I'm thinking of asking

him." She wiggled her eyebrows up and down at me.

I wanted to be supportive, but I didn't think my mother was ready for dating. Not only was it too soon after the breakup with my father, but any talk of my mother being the Zucchini Fairy could put the kibosh on any budding relationship.

She watched him drive off, and for a moment I thought she'd forgotten all about zucchini. When she looked back at me her eyes had touch of wildness in them.

"So, ya in?" she asked.

I sighed. "Mom, this whole sneaking around at night thing isn't a good idea. Really, we're going to get caught for trespassing." I thought about Max, the neighbor's dog. "Or bit."

She grabbed a piece of her brunette hair and twirled it around her finger, her green eyes turning turquoise with excitement. This made me nervous; I was afraid she'd become addicted to zucchini drops.

"I have a new idea," she said. "We'll hit the bowling alley, the theater parking lot, and maybe a bar or two. You know—public places—so no trespassing and no dogs."

Oh, boy. The new school year, and my mom going back to teaching couldn't get here soon enough.

"But there'll still be people coming and going," I said.

"Exactly! We'll blend in."

"Mom, it's just too risky."

"You know what else we could do for the folks out drinking?" She said. "Come up with a hangover recipe that includes zucchini, like a zucchini smoothie." She tapped her index finger on her chin. "I wonder what vitamins are in zucchini."

As I racked my brain for more objections, Richard approached our table.

"Hello, Richard," my mom said. "Patricia, you remember Richard. We met him on our last walk."

In the light of day Richard was mid-fifties, with gray hair and high cheek bones. His black glasses looked even larger in daylight. This morning he wore a navy blue sweater vest over a red, white and blue plaid shirt. His overall look reminded me of Clark Kent. I wondered if underneath his shirt he had an S splayed across his chest.

"Hello," I said.

"So how's the training coming?" Richard asked.

My mother and I locked eyes. What the heck was he talking about?

"It's admirable of you to start so early," he continued.

Then I remembered, we'd lied about training for Bay to Breakers, the marathon that takes place in the spring. This was July.

Richard looked from me to my mom and back again. He had something on his mind.

"Would you like to join us?" Mom asked rather unenthusiastically.

"Sure." He sat and looked at my mother. "So do you know that I was the last one to talk to Donna before her untimely demise?"

"Oh?" my mother replied.

"I was walking up Fourth Street, when she came up behind me. She walked very fast and seemed very excited. Had to show me her winning bingo sheet. All those purple dots, looked like something you'd see under a microscope."

He smiled, looking at my mother, then at me. He seemed to like having our attention.

"She also gave me a Tootsie Roll," he continued, reaching his hand into his pants' pocket and dropping said Tootsie Roll on the table. We all stared at the brown-and-white bite-sized morsel, its waxy paper ends still twisted closed. "You know, I was the last person she talked to and the last person she gave candy to." He sighed deeply. "So what did you tell the police about the accident?" he asked.

"Nothing," Mom answered a little too quickly. "We didn't see anything, did we dear?"

I shook my head. "You know how it is when you're in training. You have to focus. No distractions. Keep those blinders on, just like horses." I put my hands up on each side of my face.

"Really? Nothing? Gee, I saw two small trucks in the neighborhood, a couple of sedans, at least six big SUVs. Heard a siren. The police questioned me that night of course. But when I got home I realized that I had left out a few details. I called Sergeant Romano and left him a message." He reached through the neck of his vest to his shirt pocket and pulled a small spiral bound blue notebook. "I take this with me everywhere; you never know when you're going to need to jot down a reminder."

"What details did you leave out?" I asked.

"Well, for one, that I'd seen you two," he said.

I started to panic and had a sudden urge to reach out and snatch his little blue notebook and make a run for the door.

"I'm sure Sergeant Romano doesn't want to be bothered with details about us," I said.

"Well, I think he would want to be bothered with information about an old truck in the area," Richard said. He opened his notebook and started flipping pages. "Here it is. Like from the '40s, with the big fenders. You don't see trucks like that anymore. And I do want to be thorough. Good thing I have my little book." He tapped his finger on it, looking pleased.

Even as I wanted to rip Richard's notebook into pieces, I realized maybe it could be helpful.

"Say, Richard, you didn't happen to see Maggie Olsen on her bike the other day, did you? I heard she took a spill."

His eyes lit up and I knew I'd hit the jackpot. He started flipping pages again.

"Here it is. It was the night after Donna got hit. Young woman sitting on curb, her knee and hand were bloody. Young man with her was favoring one leg. I asked if I could be of assistance, and she shook her head." He looked up from his notebook. "I did not recognize either one of them, nor did I ask their names."

"Young man?" I asked, thinking that Steve didn't mention that Maggie was with someone. But why would he? "Was he tall, thin nose?"

"Could be," Richard replied.

"Did you notice her bike?" I asked.

"The front tire was twisted in a way she wouldn't be able to ride it. She said she hit a rock and ran into a parked car."

This confirmed my theory that Maggie was lying to her father about the accident. She didn't just fall off her bike, she actually ran into something.

"You know what they're calling Donna, don't you?" Richard asked as he snapped closed his notebook. "The Zucchini Fairy. I prefer the term *Cucurbita Pepo* Fairy." The corners of his mouth twitched upward as he attempted to suppress a grin. "That's the botanical name for squash."

My mother's fake smile had turned to a grimace, and I realized she was not happy that Donna's title of Zucchini Fairy had stuck.

He glanced at his watch. "Oh, look at the time. I've got to run."

"When you bumped into Donna, was she carrying zucchini?" My mother sounded casual, but I could tell, she was getting wound up over this rumor.

"Well, no. But it was late. Maybe she'd delivered the zucchini early that evening," he explained.

"Before bingo? When it was still light out?" my mom snapped.

He shrugged, unmoved by this observation. "If she was wearing her postal uniform, no one would think twice about seeing her walk up to a house." He snatched up his little blue notebook. I winced as it disappeared back under his vest. "I've got to go. Nice seeing you two."

After he left I leaned over the table and hissed: "Mom, do you realize what this means?"

"What, what means, dear? That people can't put two and two together and realize that Donna can't be the Zucchini Fairy?"

"Not about that. We lied to Sergeant Romano, a lie that you started. You told him that when Donna got hit we were in the backyard making s'mores."

"So?"

"So, Richard's little notebook says otherwise. Richard's little notebook is going to say he saw us, and talked to us. It probably even mentions that you had camouflage makeup on. What if he tells Sergeant Romano?"

She gave me a dismissive wave, then leaned over and asked: "So the zucchini run, you in or out?"

"Aren't you the least bit worried?" I couldn't let this go. "We lied about where we were when a crime took place. It looks like we're covering up something."

"Zucchini run," she repeated, "in or out?"

Oh man, she was jonesing bad.

I sat back in my chair. I didn't like this one bit. "In," I said.

When I arrived at Elsie's Antiques I found a crowd gathered. Mrs. Miller and Mrs. Butterfield were sitting on a loveseat in my display window sipping from tea cups. Mrs. B wore a blindingly bright yellow pantsuit. Mrs. M had donned a white shift embroidered with orange flowers around the neck and hemline. A peach rose was tucked behind her ear. On the floor between them sat a thermos. When they saw me they raised their cups, as if toasting to my good health.

As I unlocked the door and propped it open, Mrs. B called out, "Morning, Sunshine!" She held up the thermos and wiggled it back and forth. "We brought you coffeeee!" She sang out. "With organic cream!"

"No, thanks. I'm full up." Actually I wasn't, but I

didn't have enough to do to warrant that type of caffeine high.

"We're here for a stakeout," Mrs. M said. "I hope you don't mind. We let ourselves in."

"What stakeout?" I asked, stepping up into the display window with them, hoping that none of the onlookers could read lips.

"The stake out of Donna's business postal route. From this spot we can see up and down the street. But we're going to focus on that Mitsy woman, the one who owns the bookstore across the street," Mrs. B said. "I think her beef with Donna over the dog was too quickly dismissed."

"How is that going to work? I thought the point of doing a stakeout was watching someone who didn't know they were being watched."

"It's the hiding in plain sight idea," Mrs. M explained. "We're pretending to be your new decorators. Your displays are a bit lacking." She took a sip from her cup, which I now recognized as a piece of fine bone china that had been sitting in my teacup display at the rear of the store. Mrs. B's china cup, decorated with tiny yellow roses, also looked familiar.

But Mrs. M was right; my window did look empty. The day before the display had held two end tables, a floor lamp, and a crystal Mikasa vase, but I'd sold the lot. When I'd closed up last night the only thing left was a vintage poster of a cruise ship. The other window held a player piano with a mismatched bench that had been sitting there since I was in grammar school. Now, with The Ladies moving a pink satin upholstered loveseat from the back of the store, and a small rosewood coffee table, the window looked better already.

"We thought we'd bring up those nice marble-topped end tables you have," Mrs. M continued. "And maybe that lamp with the mission-style shade."

"Look at all the people outside," Mrs. B said, waving at a little girl, whose nose was pressed against the glass.

"Oh, I see someone over in the bookstore," Mrs. M said, pulling out a pair of binoculars from her large tote and taking a look.

I gently took her spy paraphernalia from her hands and placed it back in her purse. "Mrs. M, could you at least wait until the audience is gone?"

"But I can't see what books people are buying with my bare eyes. I'm low on reading material; maybe I can pick up a recommendation or two."

Across the street the Yarn Barn Lady stood with her arms crossed, glaring my direction. She wore a gray suit with two lethal knitting needles sticking out from the back of her head creating an X shape. She couldn't look any more disapproving of the folks gathered outside my store if she held up a sign that said, "I object."

Next door to her, a young brunette woman with loose long hair and wearing a light-blue summer dress propped open the bookstore's front door. She went back inside and returned with a stack of newspapers and placed them in a stand. She disappeared for a moment, and returned with a broom, and began sweeping the sidewalk.

I was just about to turn away when a red-and-black Mini Cooper drove up and parked directly in front of the bookstore. Mitsy exited the passenger side carrying Kiki. Hubby opened the driver's side door.

"Just look at that car," Mrs. B said. "Paper license plates. That's brand new." She turned to Mrs. M and nudged her. "I wonder if they had to replace their old car because of a big dent in the hood and a broken windshield."

"Hmm," I said. "I think we'll need more evidence than a new car."

"Well, it's a place to start," Mrs. B said.

"Oh, here comes the new meter maid." Mrs. M stood up and pointed down the street. "Oh wait, that's a meter dude."

As the glorified golf cart came closer, the crowd in front of the store turned to stare. I wondered where our previous meter maid was now—after avoiding capture by the authorities—probably in Mexico, relaxing on a sunny beach.

As the new parking enforcement officer came closer I realized the man was handsome enough to pass as a model, with short straight black hair and olive skin. He leaned his broad shoulders out of the cart and waved, flashing a radiant smile at the shoppers.

"Buenos Dias!" he called out and stopped his cart. "How is everyone on this fine morning?"

The crowd approached him to chat.

"Mmm, mmm," Mrs. M purred. "You could write me a ticket any time."

After a few minutes, the attractive meter dude continued on his route. I could hear one of my cuckoo clocks ticking the time away. Unfortunately, the crowds in front of my store did not translate into crowds inside my store.

"Okay," I said, looking at the empty room. "I've got

dusting to do. Give me a holler if Mitsy or Hubby run into the street and yell out a confession."

I left the display window to boot up my grandmother's computer behind the front counter. Except her clunky monitor was gone. In its place was what looked like a small flat screen TV. I glanced on the floor and there sat a thin black box—my new CPU. I touched the space bar on my new ergonomic keyboard, and the screen lit up. I gasped with delight. I clicked on the browser icon and was logged onto the internet in a matter of seconds and without the horrible grinding noise the old computer made. Mrs. M had even installed bookkeeping software.

I went back to the window display. "Mrs. Miller, I don't know what to say. The computer—it's great. Thank you." I held out my arms and hugged her, and heard applause from outside. "I guess your audience isn't gone yet," I whispered into her ear.

"They probably think we're performance art." She giggled and pulled away. "The security system should be hooked up soon. It will all be run through your computer, and it also will be linked to your phone. Someone breaks in at two o'clock in the morning, your phone will let you know. But you'll have to sign up for a service if you want the police alerted. I'll let you take care of that."

That afternoon my mother called, asking me to drop by her house after work. She said she had a surprise for me. I arrived around six o'clock and let myself into the front room. Michael Jackson's *Thriller* video played on my mom's big screen TV. I called out her name while

Michael sprouted hair on his face and claws grew out of his fingertips. MTV brought back fond memories. When I was a kid, my mom used music for painting inspiration and also as my babysitter. She'd turn it on, plop me down on the couch and dance down the hall to her studio. While most kids my age were learning their ABCs on *Sesame Street*, I was learning how to moon walk.

My mom came in the room. "What do you think?" she asked.

I stood transfixed. My mouth flopped open. I thought she'd worked through the various stages of grief over the loss of her mother and her marriage, and I had hoped that the extreme gardening would be the worst of it. But I was wrong. She appeared to be starting back at the beginning again, like a grief loop.

She wore a neon-pink jumpsuit, tight at the ankles, but with extra material at the hips. The sleeves were rolled up to three-quarter length, and a four-inch-wide black elastic belt synched in her waist. The outfit buttoned down the front, and the collar was turned up, like she was about to put on a tie. On her feet were high-heeled black sandals. Her jewelry consisted of oversized triangular purple metal earrings and a gold cuff bracelet three inches wide. Her hair reminded me of a poodle: curly on top, but close to her head by her ears.

This needed to be dealt with quickly, like pulling off a Band-Aid. I put my hands on her big, puffy shoulder pads and stared into eyes that sported too much makeup.

"Mom," I spoke slowly, enunciating my words. "Do you know what year it is? You're having a 1980s flashback."

She grunted, pulled away from me, and started

dancing the zombie shuffle, her eyes wide and the rest of her face impassive.

Behind my mother another pink jumpsuit appeared, assaulting my eyes.

"Mrs. M, what are you doing here?" I asked.

"We had an idea of how to get into Donna's house. So we asked your mother to help us by sewing these outfits." She turned around. On the back of the pink jumpsuit in purple letters were embroidered the words "Flock of Maids." She turned back. "We're going to walk right in Donna's front door."

"Ah, Mrs. M, can I talk to you in the kitchen?"

When we were alone I turned to her.

"Why did you get my mom involved in this?" I hissed.

"You implied that she needed something to do," Mrs. M said.

"But not something illegal!"

She then quoted me a line I'd heard before: "It's not illegal if you don't get caught."

"Yes, I'm familiar with your mantra, Mrs. M, but that woman is on the edge." I pointed down the hallway. My mom had her arms high in the air, her hands curved into claws. She tipped back her head and howled.

Mrs. M shrugged. "Patricia, divorce hits some women harder than others. When my tía went through a divorce, she wore a tortilla on her head for three months."

"You know it's not just the divorce; it's losing Nana too. The woman needs structure and our support. Not lessons on breaking and entering."

I went back into the living room and paused the

video. The best way to get her out of the house was to put her to work. Honest work. The kind of work that won't get you arrested.

"I have a favor to ask," I said. "Could you come down to the store and help me out?"

"Sure, dear," she replied, lowering her arms at the same time her face returned to normal. "I'm surprised you haven't asked me before. You know I helped out when your grandmother was alive."

"Good," I continued. "Because every time I close for lunch I'm afraid I'm going to get a lecture from the Yarn Barn Lady."

"That Yarn Barn Lady." She huffed and crossed her arms. "I think she's dropped a stitch."

Chapter Six

That evening, all four of The Ladies descended upon my kitchen. The table was decorated with a bouquet of fresh roses—yellow with pink edges. Next to the flowers sat two scrumptious looking shepherd pies topped with grated cheddar cheese. The whole house smelled heavenly. These women could cook me dinner any time.

After eating the main course, Mrs. T placed a bowl of strawberries on the table and a bowl of whipped cream. Mrs. B got up and made a fresh pot of coffee while Mrs. R handed out a meeting agenda. The highlights were as follows:

1. Update information on Donna.
2. Plan Operation Search Donna's House.
3. Check on stolen vehicles.
4. Assign person to attend Donna's funeral.

"Okay, does anyone have new information that can shed light on Donna's accident?" Mrs. R asked. She looked classy in a peach sweater set, a pearl necklace and matching earrings, very à la 1950s.

"I had dinner with Steve," I said. "He told me he gets

around on a bike, but when I went by his house earlier I found a car in his backyard. It was an old sports car. The hood was up, so maybe it's not working."

"His car's not working? Oh, maybe I can help," Mrs. B said. "I hate to see a man without a car."

"Did it look like it had been sitting for a while?" Mrs. M asked.

"What do you mean?" I asked.

"Well, was it dusty? Were there tire marks leading to it, or had it been sitting so long that the tire marks had disappeared?"

"What difference does that make?" I asked, feeling irritated with myself for not paying attention to such details.

"Well, it would help to know if he was lying to you."

"Ah," I nodded my head. "Unless he's working on the car for someone else. But, anyways, there weren't any dents, so it wasn't the car that hit Donna."

"What else did you find out, Patricia?" Mrs. R asked.

"It was Donna's idea to get a divorce," I said. "He's disorganized, and apparently she wasn't."

"That's a nice way of saying he's a slob and she was a neat freak," Mrs. T said, shaking her head. "Oh, that's a tough match."

"I also met his daughter, Magnolia—she goes by Maggie."

"What's she like?" Mrs. R asked.

"Smart, graduated early. Wary of me. Protective of her father."

"So, does Steve have an alibi?" Mrs. R asked.

"Alibi?" I said, my voice squeaking.

Mrs. Russo continued: "Just because he rides a bike

doesn't mean that he didn't steal a car, then dump it on someone's property out in the country. We need to know what he was doing that night."

"I, ah, um," I stammered. "I forgot to ask." Besides being embarrassed, that prickly feeling in my neck returned, just like I had when I spoke to Steve about selling Donna's furniture. Now I knew what that feeling meant. It was a warning not to mix business with a suspect. Details like alibis get overlooked.

The Ladies suddenly didn't want to make eye contact. I slumped in my chair. "Sorry." I mumbled. "I'll talk to him again."

Mrs. R cleared her throat. "Moving on. Who wants be in charge of Operation Search Donna's House?"

Mrs. M stood up and smoothed down the front of her bright pink shift. Her hair ornament this evening—a pink peony—tumbled onto the plate of strawberries in front of her. She picked it up and replaced it behind her ear.

"I'm in charge," Mrs. M said. "We're planning on breaking in early in the day, and we'll be dressed as house cleaners."

"Who will be participating?" Mrs. Russo asked.

"Patricia will be—"

"When is this supposed to happen?" I interrupted and fumbled with my phone, trying to find my calendar.

"Monday," Mrs. M replied. "And also Genny, Patricia's mom."

Mrs. T frowned. She didn't like my mother's involvement in illegal activities any more than I did. But my mother owned a big, generic SUV that could hold all of us plus cleaning equipment.

"Okay, on to stolen vehicles that might have been used in the incident," Mrs. R said. "Betty, any news?"

"There were two that occurred the week before Donna was hit," Mrs. B replied. "One vehicle turned up on a road outside of town after it had been stripped of its catalytic converter, the other turned out to be a grandkid borrowing a car without telling his grandma. Neither had been in any kind of accident."

"And last on our agenda," Mrs. R said, "one of us needs to attend Donna's funeral." Her eyes landed on me.

"I don't have any reason to be there," I said quickly. "Steve thinks I'm moonlighting for a private eye. It would look like I'm spying on him." I started to feel hot, like I did when I felt claustrophobic. I wasn't a fan of funerals. They were so sad, and I had a tendency to cry when I saw others cry, like how some people react to a yawn.

"You don't need a reason to attend a funeral; you just go," Mrs. T said.

"But you have to have some connection to the deceased," I continued. "What about one of you pretending to be one of her teachers?"

Mrs. R replied: "Donna grew up in Washington, D.C. Do you really think someone of our age is going to fly across the country to go to a student's funeral?"

"Well, what about an aunt?" I asked.

"She didn't have much family, and her husband would know that," said Mrs. T.

Mrs. M leaned over and whispered, "Patricia, you could go with Jimmy Chang. He knew Donna."

A funeral and Jimmy? The shepherd's pie I'd eaten

summersaulted in my stomach.

"That would be a good excuse to spend some time with him," she continued, her voice still low. "Then you can make up for being rude."

"You were rude to Jimmy?" Mrs. R asked.

Mrs. R had hearing like an insectivorous bat. I looked down and pushed a piece of strawberry around on my plate.

"Well, it was only two or three offensive things," Mrs. M said.

"He didn't even notice," I said. "Besides, I was nice to him when you installed my security system."

"We can't lose our connection to Jimmy Chang," Mrs. R said. Her voice took on an authoritarian tone. "We need every advantage we can get. Your grandmother worked hard for that relationship. You wouldn't want all that effort to go to waste would you?"

Oh man, playing the guilt card, now that was low.

She continued, "Ask him to take you to the funeral."

"Like a date?" Good thing I didn't have food in my mouth. A statement like that is choking fodder. "No one goes on a date to a funeral."

"Sometimes we have to make sacrifices for the greater good," Mrs. R said, rather decisively.

I folded my arms in front of me like a defiant child.

"Have some more coffee dear," Mrs. B said, pouring me a cup and sliding the organic cream across the table.

Unfortunately, Mrs. R had a point. My grandmother had done a lot to cultivate a relationship with Jimmy Chang. She must have had good reason. I reluctantly nodded my acquiescence. "Okay, I'll ask Jimmy if I can go with him to Donna's funeral."

Ish, I needed ice cream.

I paced in front of the trailer that Jimmy used for his office at Chang's Used Autos. The morning sun felt good on my face, but even the two cups of coffee I'd drunk couldn't get rid of this irritating sensation that felt like a rock in my shoe. I needed a favor from Jimmy, and until I spoke with him, it would annoy me to no end. I started up the metal steps. The door swung open, and there stood Jimmy, gallantly holding it for me.

"Patricia Schuster," he said, a toothpick bobbing between clenched teeth. "To what do I owe this unexpected visit?" Jimmy's penchant for toothpicks developed at an early age, and over the years, he'd learned to talk around the tiny wooden sticks.

"I need a favor," I responded with equally clenched teeth.

"Please, have a seat." He moved aside, gestured to a metal folding chair, and took his place behind the desk.

The trailer's interior felt dreary, with gray carpet, and taupe-colored paneling. A bright-red tablecloth covered a corner table. In the past, I'd seen it decorated with fruit, but today it sat empty. A small camera aimed at the chair I sat in was fixed on the wall above Jimmy's head.

"I see Mrs. Miller got your security system installed."

I waited for a lurid comment, but he just sighed deeply. Resting his fingertips on the edge of the desk, he tapped out a quick rhythm. Something was bothering him.

"Please tell me that you're ready to upgrade your Civic," he said, "I need inventory in a bad way." He looked down at his desk. "You wouldn't believe the people that come in here and jerk my chain. This gal here." He picked up a folder and shook it in the air. "She came in with a ten-year-old Nissan, got a price from me, said she 'had to think about it,' and when I called her a few days later, she'd gone to Green's Auto and traded in her car there."

He slapped the folder down and picked up another. "This guy wanted to sell his dead aunt's little sedan, and the same thing happened. I give him a price and he turns around and takes it to Green's."

When he picked up the third folder I tried to interrupt him, but he was on a roll.

"Now, this guy, Nick Something-or-other actually works for Green's Auto, so he starts telling me that he's having a midlife crisis, and he's going to quit his job, dump his crazy girlfriend, go back to playing music, and start living right." Jimmy rolled his eyes. "You know, I deal with a lot of guys going through a midlife crisis, but that's way too much personal information for a car salesman to know about their customers."

I nodded, he was right, this was way too much information.

"So we fill out the paperwork, but he doesn't want to leave the car with me, because he hasn't told his girlfriend yet or his boss. So he gives me an extra set of keys and tells me his car will be at the bus stop the next day at a certain time. So I walk down to the bus stop, and there's no car. I tried calling him, but he didn't answer." He slammed the folder down. "At least I hadn't given him any money."

I jumped in before I had to hear more woes of the used auto business.

"No, it's nothing about my car," I said. "I want to go to Donna's funeral." My throat started to close up, and my words came out as a wheeze. "I need a, a…" I couldn't bring myself to say it.

His demeanor changed in an instant. "A date?" he asked, with the eagerness of a shark smelling blood in the water.

I swallowed hard and snapped at him: "No one needs a date to attend a funeral."

The grin inside his pencil thin oval goatee turned evil.

"Then what shall we call it?" he asked. "You need me to pretend to be your boyfriend."

"Maybe you could pretend I'm your adopted sister," I said.

"Why would my parents adopt a twenty-five-year-old?"

My hands uncontrollably closed into fists, and I realized I was developing a craving for firearms.

"What's the cop's kid going to say when he finds out you're dating another guy?" he continued.

"Jimmy, it won't be a date, and I'll tell him ahead of time."

"Ah, the honest type." He leaned back in his chair, folding his hands behind his head. "But still, you don't need me to go to this event. You can just go." His lips pursed together and his toothpick stuck out like the stem of a cherry. He jerked forward and leaned across the desk. "Wait a minute, are you hoping the heirs may have an antique or two you can sell?"

I hesitated. Letting Jimmy think money was my objective would keep him out of the realm that I might actually want to spend time with him. "A person's got to make a living," I said.

"So ghoulish," he replied. "I like it. So we're back to the boyfriend plan."

I could feel myself losing my nerve. "Okay, this was a bad idea." I stood up. "Let's just forget I asked. I'll figure something else out."

"So what are you going to do? Make up a story of being a long-lost cousin from Minnesota and don a northern accent?" he said. "Or maybe if you mumbled no one would ask too many questions." He pulled the toothpick from his mouth and pointed it at me. "Besides, it's too late for that. You try and lie your way in; I'll point it out. The widower might not take kindly to you crashing a funeral for monetary gain."

Jimmy was slime, and that was insulting slime. But, lucky for me, he'd taken the bait.

"Fine. We'll pretend to be friends. But you try any funny stuff, and I'll make a scene that will upstage the deceased."

"I'll pick you up at eleven-thirty."

"No, I'll meet you in the parking lot."

Ish. I was definitely going to need three cups of coffee to get through that day.

Jake and I sat under a rusty red-and-white umbrella at a round, concrete picnic table in the dirt lot behind his auto body business. The side street ran in front of us, with noonday traffic just starting to pick up. Fine dry soil settled around my flip-flops, covering my recent home pedicure with dust. Surrounding us were a variety of dented and dinged vehicles, all waiting for Jake's magic touch to bring them back to life.

I'd picked up burgers and fries for lunch, and then stopped by the pastry store to buy two coffees. I'd added plenty of sugar and organic cream to both cups.

"Andrew starts work today," Jake said. He opened one of the bags and handed me a burger. "It's going to take him a while to get up to speed. But he took an auto body class at the junior college, so that should help."

I opened the ketchup packet and squeezed the contents onto a corner of the fry container. This was a good time to mention that I'd be going to Donna's funeral with Jimmy, but what made me hesitate wasn't telling Jake about me spending time with Jimmy, it had more to do with me going to a funeral for someone I barely knew. Unless I told Jake about The Ladies extracurricular activities, I'd have to lie about something, which I really didn't want to do.

"I'm going to Donna's funeral tomorrow with Jimmy."

Jake pulled the bun off his burger and sprinkled salt over the meat. "I bet there'll be a big turnout; she was awfully friendly." He tried the burger. "These are really good."

I also took a bite. He was right. The burgers were good. And I'd worried for nothing; he clearly trusted me. I liked that. I really didn't want to be involved with someone that had an opinion about every little thing I did. Especially since his father was a cop who might label some things I did inappropriate. Okay, I was being easy on myself. Inappropriate wasn't the right word; illegal landed closer to home.

"My dad said she was found in front of your mom's house."

I nodded.

"He knew her."

"How?" I asked.

"Have you heard about the real estate scam going on?"

"Yes, but I don't understand how it works."

"Well, a person breaks into a house when the owners are out of town and pretend like they own it. They put up a rental ad online, and meet with potential renters. They write up a fake lease, give them a fake key, and take a cash deposit. In a hot market, it can happen in one afternoon."

"So, how could a postal worker help?"

"Since Donna would know when folks are gone, she might see activity at a house that should be empty. He'd talked to her a couple of times, but she hadn't seen anything. He knew it was a bit of a longshot."

"Huh," I said. I thought all this was interesting, but I couldn't see how that would get Donna killed. The person doing the scamming wouldn't know Donna's bingo schedule or even that she lived here in town, unless the person knew her from someplace else besides her mail route.

I wanted to ask more questions, but a yellow tow truck pulling a black pickup stopped on the street. The tow truck reversed and began maneuvering the vehicle into the lot. It came in at a perfect angle, avoiding the building, and avoiding the other banged-up cars.

Jake put down his burger and stood up. "Uh, oh."

"What's wrong?"

"That's Andrew's first project. I should have driven out to his place and looked at it before I had it towed."

The truck's tail end was up in the air. The windshield was shattered and the hood dented.

The tow driver stopped and jumped out of the cab. I recognized the driver as Mel, who worked at Marino's Tow and Impound.

The passenger door opened and Andrew slid out carrying a backpack. He reached into the truck bed and hoisted out a bike. He wore flip-flops and came toward us walking with a limp.

"You do something to your leg?" Jake asked.

He shook his head. "I fell off my bike, and sprained my ankle. My foot's too swollen to get my shoes on."

Mel finished disconnecting the pickup, climbed into the tow truck, and waved as he drove off.

For a moment, I wondered if Jake was going to make an issue of opened-toed shoes inside his shop. But he rubbed the back of his neck, and asked: "How did the window get smashed?"

"Granddad hit a deer," Andrew said, looking down.

"When was this?" Jake asked.

"I don't remember, a few weeks ago." He looked back up, his eyes wide. "But this is going to be a big surprise for him. He's been keeping this in a barn that we rarely use, so I'm hoping he won't notice it's gone."

Jake stared at the truck, and his lack of response grew uncomfortable.

"How's your grandfather, Andrew?" I asked.

"Fine," he replied.

"I'd like to hear him play. Is he doing any gigs this weekend?"

"Nope." Andrew's focus moved inside the garage. "Oh, man, is that a '66 Camaro?" He asked, disappearing into the building.

Jake took out his cell phone.

"Dad? You have time to come by before work? I have a truck here you may want to look at." He hung up and turned to me. "I don't feel good about this."

"Why'd you call your dad?"

"The police look for certain things when there's been a hit-and-run, and unfortunately, this is exactly the type of damage." Jake pointed to the truck. His eyebrows came together and he looked deep in thought.

We returned to our burgers and ate in silence. I could see Andrew inside talking to Jake's assistant, Reed, while they went from car to car inspecting every inch.

Officer Romano arrived in his street clothes: jeans and a polo shirt. Years ago, he'd been a homicide detective in San Francisco but was let go due to an alcohol problem. He lost his job and his marriage. After he got sober, he ended up in Lakeville. He was tall and handsome like his son, graying at the temples with a swagger in his step that came from a natural self-confidence. He greeted us, made a beeline for the truck, and inspected the windshield.

"I'll send forensics over," he said. "They'll need to take a look."

Andrew emerged from the garage.

"What should I get started on first?" he asked Jake.

"We're going to need to hold off on your project for a while," Jake replied.

"Do you have something else for me to do?" Andrew asked, looking confused.

Sergeant Romano stepped forward, introduced himself to Andrew, and suggested they go inside to talk.

I dug into my purse to find Beatrice Johnson's phone number. When her voice machine answered, I left a message asking for information on Earl and Andrew, giving her the truck's license plate number. Since I'd dropped the ball on getting an alibi from Steve, maybe I could redeem myself by coming up with some information on Earl.

A few minutes later, Andrew hobbled out with his backpack and grabbed his bike. "My grandfather didn't kill anyone," he yelled over his shoulder before riding off. Sergeant Romano nodded in my direction as he strode off the lot.

"That didn't go well," said Jake. He sat down next to me, his eyebrows furrowed. He picked up the last bite of his burger, then put it back down. "I hate accusing someone."

I thought back to when I met Earl at bingo. He seemed to really care about Andrew. I had a hard time believing that he'd hit Donna, on purpose or on accident, and just drive away. Plus, Earl had referred to Andrew as his driver. Even though he hadn't said why, it was clear that Andrew had driven the two of them to bingo, and Earl had planned on Andrew driving them home.

Something else crossed my mind, but I didn't want to add to Jake's angst by saying it out loud. Andrew could have been the driver, not Earl, and I had a feeling that Jake's dad would think the same thing.

Chapter Seven

The book club met in the children's section of the Lakeville bookstore. Rolling shelves had been moved to make room for a circle of chairs. A pile of pillows sat in a corner next to a kid-sized plastic table and chair set. Mitsy held Kiki in her arms and chatted with Mrs. M who wore a white gardenia tucked behind her ear. The smell of chocolate and sugar steered me to the refreshment table where I vacillated between a chocolate chip cookie and a piece of carrot cake with cream cheese frosting. Hubby approached me, smiling awkwardly.

"Ah, Patricia, isn't it?" he asked.

I nodded, "But I've forgotten—"

"I have a favor to ask," he said quickly, deflecting my attempt to learn his real name. "I'd appreciate it if you wouldn't mention seeing me at the animal shelter the other day." He stood just a little too close, locking his eyes with mine.

"All right," I said, taking half a step back. I hoped he was going to offer an explanation, since it seemed an odd request.

He glanced away, and I followed his gaze to Mitsy, who snuggled Kiki close to her face while the dog licked her chin. "Mitsy's been hinting she wants another dog, so I'm thinking of surprising her on her birthday."

"That Lab puppy you were walking with was cute," I said. Even though I had a hard time imagining Kiki frolicking with a Lab; Kiki was a take-me-shopping kind of dog, while Labs were more of a take-me-to-the-park kind of dog.

"She's cute, but I'm thinking of the German Shepard."

"Oh," I said.

"She's a sniffer dog. Got kicked out of K9 School for getting pregnant. You know institutions don't take kindly to that." He sighed. "But, taking on another dog is a big decision." He reached out and shook my hand. "Thank you, I appreciate your discretion." He gave me a nod and ambled over to another club member.

Movement at the front of the store caught my eye. Above the racks of books I saw what looked like the rings of Saturn: blue, orange and green bands bobbing around a yellow globe. Then a hand came up, and I realized I was looking at one of Mrs. T's hats. She was waving, trying to get my attention.

"You're not going to believe this," she said when I reached her.

"What?" I said, taking a moment to digest her wild bonnet. I was disappointed to discover that there were no moons.

She nudged me toward the window and pointed outside. "See that truck?"

It was a monster of a thing, with big rounded

fenders over tires three feet high. The sides of the bed were made of wood slats. The whole thing was covered in dust; in fact, the dirt was so thick it was hard to see through the windows. The front windshield wipers had scraped two half-moon sections clean. I had to admire the driver for taking the no-washing-cars-during-the-drought rule seriously, but even that seemed a bit much.

"Inside the cab," Mrs. T continued, "is our widower, Steve Olsen, and another Stoker band member, Helena, locking lips."

A dim interior light came on in the truck. Steve slipped out of the passenger seat and crossed the street. Helena got out and looked around. Was she nervous about being seen? We stepped back from the window and pretended to look at greeting cards as Helena sashayed into the bookstore.

"Hi," Helena said, grinning at us as she ran her fingers through her mass of wavy hair. She wore a colorful quilted vest with a long peach blouse that hung over a blue and green skirt.

After she passed us, Mrs. T raised an eyebrow: "Well, that puts Steve back in the hot seat, and her too."

I felt disappointed and let down, I was getting to know Steve, and I didn't want an accusing finger pointed at him.

"You don't look happy about that. Why?" she asked.

"Because I like Steve."

She eyed me as she removed her celestial headgear.

"Well, he's an artist and I'm an artist," I continued.

"Sounds like you're becoming sympathetic with a suspect," she said.

Of, course, she was right. Darn Mrs. T and her

insight. She must have sensed my discomfort because she slipped her arm through mine as we walked to the back of the store. "How did you like the book?" she asked.

"I only read three chapters," I replied. "Does the philandering husband leave his wife and run off with his mistress?"

"He's run down by a horse and carriage. Then the mistress moves in with the wife and they live happily ever after. The author leaves it up to our imagination as to which of the women did him in."

As we returned to the children's area, Helena was in the process of repositioning the chairs. She made a space big enough to place a large pillow on the floor and sat down on it. Mary Belle and Janie had also arrived.

"Do you know Janie?" I asked Mrs. T. "The woman in the light-blue shirt and white skirt? She was at bingo the other night."

"Our paths have crossed. My only impression of her is that she likes to gossip," Mrs. T said.

"Mine too. I wonder if she has any information about Donna that might be helpful."

Mary Belle and Janie stood in a group with three other people. Janie stood next to a rack of journaling books. The kind that have pretty covers meant to inspire. I loved to buy them and hated to use them; I found all that beautiful blank paper intimidating.

Mrs. T took my arm. "Maybe we can get her alone to talk. I have an idea, but I'm going to need some bait." She pulled me to the refreshment table and grabbed a large chocolate chip cookie. "This should flush her out. Wait here."

Mrs. T walked up behind Janie and held her cookie

up in the air. "Oh, isn't that pretty," she said loudly. Janie turned; her face was just inches from the sweet-smelling chocolate. "I like this one." Mrs. T pointed to a book with a pretty ocean scene, but Janie couldn't take her eyes off the cookie.

Mrs. T took a small bite and turned to Janie. "Umm. Have you tried these?" she asked.

Janie shook her head.

"They're to die for," Mrs. Taylor crooned, then returned her focus back to the decorative notebooks.

For a few seconds Janie's eyes stayed firmly planted on Mrs. T's treat; then her focus hopped to the refreshment table. A few moments later Janie stood next to me munching away.

"Chocolate chip and macadamia nuts. Yum!" she said.

I grabbed one too, handed her a napkin and we both chewed for a few moments.

"Sure has been a lot of excitement downtown," I said.

Janie locked her eyes on mine, sensing a fellow gossip. "Oh, yeah?" she said around a full mouth. "Like what?"

"Donna, the mail lady, getting run down and no one knowing who did it."

Janie's eyes darted back and forth and her voice lowered. "You think someone hit her on purpose?"

"Do you?" I asked.

Janie nodded vigorously. "She wasn't exactly loved by the female population, but to the men in town she could do no wrong." She looked to the circle of chairs where we'd all soon be sitting. Helena adjusted the folds of her skirt to make a circle around her, while her lips moved as if she was singing to herself.

"Take Helena. She's suspicious."

"Why?"

She looked back at Helena. "I saw Donna and Helena arguing that night."

"Really? Where?"

"Just in front of the Mastodon building. I'd gone out to get a breath of fresh air, and I heard voices. They were standing in the shadows of the trees."

"Arguing over what?"

"A man. Helena said something about 'leading him on.' Then Donna said something like 'he can think for himself.' When they noticed me they lowered their voices. Who knows what people are capable of?" She paused to chew for a moment before adding, "But I doubt that Helena sideswiped Donna's daughter, Maggie."

"What?" I asked, trying to hide my shock. "When did this happen?

"The day after Donna was killed. Mary Belle was driving home from the store and saw a car swerve then speed off. Unfortunately, she was too far away to see the car, but when she got closer she saw poor Maggie sitting on the curb, along with a young man. She stopped and asked if she could help, but Maggie said she was fine." Janie grabbed another cookie. "Odd coincidence, don't ya think? Her mom, then her."

I took another bite of my cookie, and chewed slowly. I didn't like the idea of someone purposely trying to hurt Maggie, and I certainly didn't like coincidences.

Janie picked up another cookie. "I bet Mary Belle would like one of these. See you later." She merged back into the crowd.

The club members began taking their seats, so I sat down next to Mitsy in the circle. I reached into my tote to pull out the book that we'd be discussing that evening, and my winning bingo card came out at the same time. It fluttered to the floor and landed next to Kiki, who gave it a whiff with her tiny pink nose. She was not interested.

"Do you go to bingo?" Mitsy asked.

"Just recently; it was my first time." I picked up the card.

"My husband goes all the time. He just loves it. Me —not so much. I have a hard time hearing the numbers when they're called, so I have to look for them on the board. I could never keep up. So I let Hubby go alone. He needs a night out by himself once in a while anyway. He fills me in on the details when he gets home. You know, what games were played, who won what."

I pointed at my card. "This was fun. I won the memorial game for Donna."

Her eyebrows came together over her nose. She looked confused. "What?"

"This was Donna's favorite game, getting all the numbers on the outside. So in memory of Donna, it was the last game of the night. See, it makes a square, but it also makes a D, for Donna."

She had the oddest look on her face, so I thought I'd try to explain it again, but speak a little louder. "You have to get all the numbers in the B column and then—"

"I understand the game," she said curtly. "But what I didn't know was that Donna went to bingo."

Oh, boy. I just dropped Hubby in it. I could see Mitsy's mental wheels turning. Hubby told her all about his time at bingo. That meant Hubby was purposefully leaving Donna out of his play-by-play recap of the evenings. Maybe I could distract her before she thought Hubby went to bingo just to see his candy-loving friend. I tapped on the book we'd be discussing that evening. "How did you like the book?"

"What night was this?" she asked.

Ah, oh. Too late. "Just the other day."

"Was it at the senior center?"

I nodded.

She stared up at the ceiling. "Tuesday? Was it Tuesday?" she asked.

"Yes," I squeaked.

Her eyes narrowed, and she jumped up from her chair. Stomping over to Hubby, she grabbed the sleeve of his sweater and pulled him away from a small group that Mrs. T happened to be a part of. Even though I couldn't hear what Mitsy was saying, I got the gist.

She poked at hubby's chest over and over. His pink complexion turned even pinker, and he looked like he was trying to explain, but I saw no forgiveness or understanding on her face.

She stomped back to her seat, held up the book we were to discuss, and addressed the crowd, "Let's get started everyone. So was the husband a lying jerk face, or what?"

A gigantic neon-purple bowling ball reflected light onto the hood of my mother's SUV. It was late, and I wished I was at home eating ice cream rather than sitting in my mother's car in front of the Lakeville Bowl about to distribute zucchini to the fine bowlers of Lakeville.

My mother and I wore casual clothes this time—just jeans and T-shirts and no camouflage makeup. But I did have my hair tucked up under a baseball cap. Before my mother picked me up she'd cased the bowling alley's parking lot. It was a tournament night, so we'd have plenty of cars to choose from. At the moment, the parking lot was void of people. I glanced into the back seat, and saw two large boxes of lunch-sized paper bags and two brown grocery bags full of loose zucchini.

"I've improved my marketing," my mother said, holding up one of the paper bags. Its top was folded over and held closed by a smiley face sticker. She opened the bag and pulled out an index card. "This is my hangover recipe. I've added one to every bag, along with a zucchini, and sealed it with this sticker." She put the package back together. "Isn't that cute? Just like party favors." She waved it in front of me, pleased with her creation.

I forced a smile, wondering how long her strange behavior was going to last and how long I'd be able to tolerate it. After all, large quantities of caffeine can only take you so far.

My mother handed me half a dozen zucchini-laden bags.

She pointed. "Okay, I'll head down this row, you take that one. You know the drill. Look for older cars without alarms. Keep hunched over, and watch for people coming or going."

I moved out, searching for the elusive older vehicle. Miraculously I found one with a back window that was down just enough for me to pop in a bag. I hoped they'd notice it before Halloween. As I approached the next open car, I could hear laughing and noticed the windows were fogged up. Then I realized the car was rocking.

"Oops, occupied," I mumbled to myself.

Still half bent over, I tried the next row, inspecting five cars, all with windows safely secure. At that point my thighs started to burn. I looked around for a car to lean against, but I was surrounded by newer vehicles that were probably equipped with alarms. The pain in my legs snapped me back to sanity. I felt ridiculous.

I stood up straight, walked back to my mom's car, and got comfortable in the front seat. Just because she needed to get rid of extra vegetables in a silly way didn't mean I had to participate.

I heard a siren in the distance that progressively got louder. My mother emerged running at full speed from the cars. She pulled open the door.

"Oh man, busted!" she yelled. She threw her backpack at me, jumped in, started up the car, and zipped out of the parking spot. As she screeched to a stop at the driveway, we looked up the street.

"Those aren't police," I said, as two fire trucks sped by.

"I've got an idea," she said, not at all embarrassed by her overreaction.

She turned onto the main drag and, putting her foot on the gas, began chasing the emergency vehicles.

I put on my seatbelt, grabbed onto the door handle, and thought about looking up meditating techniques when I got home. Learning to find my happy place might be a necessity to get through the summer with my sanity intact.

After driving through downtown Lakeville, the fire

engines stopped in front of a small business complex. We saw smoke and flames through the windows of an office and parked half a block away while firefighters rushed out of their trucks.

My mother grabbed two grocery-sized bags of zucchini, bolted out of the car and down the dark sidewalk. She headed straight to the fire truck's open passenger side door and scrambled up the steps. After depositing both bags of zucchini on the front seat, she returned looking pleased with herself.

"You know," I said, "that's not a bad idea. Cooking for all those firefighters could burn through a lot of zucchini."

"Well, don't sound so surprised. I have lots of good ideas."

On the drive home we approached McNear's Restaurant. My mother pulled into an open parking space, grabbed three sealed bags from her backpack, and got out of the car. She crept toward a group of cars that were deeply shadowed by a pair of large redwoods.

The restaurant had large removable front windows, so on warm summer evenings, like tonight, the lively atmosphere tumbled out to the sidewalk. I spotted Earl and Cece standing inside at the ornate wood bar. Earl swayed slightly from side to side. Cece grabbed his arm, helping to steady him.

My mom got back in the car, minus her bags.

"There's Earl and Cece," I said, explaining who they were and how they were related to Donna's death. "His truck has been impounded because it might have run down Donna."

"I went to a yard sale at his place the other day."

"Did you buy anything?"

"No, all he had were tools," she said. "He had a beautiful backhoe in an old barn. Boy, what a garden I could create if I had one of those." She sighed. "He told me the original house burnt down in the '30s. He lives in a mobile home now. You know, he looks like a guy that might need a hangover tonic. Let's drop off a bag of zucchini on his front porch."

Before I could object, my mom backed out and turned right onto D Street. Earl lived on the edge of town. On the way we passed several houses that were listed with the National Registry of Historical Places. If we'd kept going, we'd reach Bodega Bay and the Pacific Ocean. We drove past Earl's house, found a place to turn around and pulled to the side of the road. My mom rolled down her window.

The buildings on his property sat in an L shape. Closest to us, on the left was a large red barn. The sliding doors on the building sat perpendicular to the road. Next to that was a mobile home that had two lights on; one inside, plus the porch light. Two more garages faced us, behind them the land rose in a gentle slope as far as I could see in the dark.

"Okay, I'm going in," my mom said. She grabbed a bag of zucchini.

"But what if Earl's grandson's there?"

She shrugged. "What's he going to do? Shoot me?"

"Yes." I fervently nodded. "It's a possibility."

"Patricia, stop being such a worrywart. But, why don't you slide over here to the driver's side, just in case we need to make a quick get-a-way."

I wanted to sigh and roll my eyes, but what would be the point?

My mother crossed the road and made it to the first barn. She disappeared into the shadows, then reappeared on the porch. A dog barked from inside the house. I hoped she'd brought her stash of dog treats.

Headlights blinded me. I ducked down. All I needed was for Sergeant Romano to drive up and find me sitting alone in the car. I peeked over the steering wheel and watched a car turn into Earl's driveway. It was Cece's Prius. I couldn't see my mother. Hopefully, neither could Cece.

As Cece helped Earl to the front door, the barking coming from inside the house grew louder. Cece stood on the front porch until Earl was safely inside. She turned and headed—not for her car—but for the barn closest to the road. She unlocked a padlock and slid open the large door.

A light flicked on inside the barn. Unfortunately, from my angle I couldn't see inside. After a few minutes the light went off, and Cece appeared with a small package tucked under her arm. She closed the door, replaced the padlock and returned to her car. When she backed up, I ducked again until she turned onto the road. The front porch light went off, and the dog stopped barking. I stared into the darkness, hoping to spot my mother.

Another pair of headlights shone in my direction and swooshed past me. I drummed my fingers on the steering wheel.

"Come on, Mom," I whispered to myself.

The passenger side door flew open, and the interior

light flicked on, causing me to squint.

"Okay, let's go," she said, brushing leaves off her arms.

"What happened?"

"I delivered zucchini to a man in need. That's what happened."

"You almost got caught. Cece could have spotted you."

"Patricia, I never thought I'd have to say this, but I think you should cut back on your coffee intake. I think it's causing you unnecessary anxiety."

I glared at the real reason for my unnecessary anxiety and started up the car.

"Did you see what Cece took from the barn?" I asked.

"It was a package wrapped in white paper. She has a chest freezer in there. My guess is meat. She must be renting the barn from him." Then she snorted. "I wonder if Earl knows he's paying an electric bill to keep Cece in steaks."

Chapter Eight

It was my hope that meeting my mother every morning at Joey's Coffee would give me a chance to pick her brain on ideas to increase business. But as I sipped on my second cup of coffee and listened to her explain in detail how next year she'd be using cover crops alongside her zucchini to increase yield, I realized these get-togethers were becoming less about running Elise's Antiques and more about her sharing her gardening acumen. My mother was a teacher at heart, and at the moment I was her only student.

"After our little adventure last night," she said enthusiastically, "I came up with a great idea."

"What's that?" I asked.

"I'm going to buy a chest freezer to store my zucchini bread."

"You've been making zucchini bread?"

"I will be after I get a place to keep a freezer. What do you prefer—with chocolate chips or without?"

"With, definitely," I said.

"I guess I could make both. I'd have to charge more

for—" She stopped mid-sentence and leaned sideways. Her eyes widened. I started to turn my head, but she reached across the table and grabbed my hand.

"Don't look," she hissed. "It's too awful."

Taking her tendency for exaggeration into consideration I looked anyway. Then wished I hadn't.

Richard hobbled toward us, bending awkwardly at the waist, walking as if the floor were made of ice and he'd forgotten his skates. I tried to turn away, but I couldn't. His attire had changed dramatically; he'd transformed himself into a professional cyclist. Above white knobby knees were neon green shorts that included suspenders that covered a neon yellow tank top. On top of his head teetered a helmet in bright orange. On top of that sat a camera, which I could only guess was filming my mother's open mouth.

"Why, Genevieve, how nice to see you," he said. "And good morning to you, Patricia."

Richard's crotch was now at table level. Did bike shorts come with extra padding, or was that all him? My cringe meter hit the red zone. I now knew more about Richard than I ever wanted to.

He grabbed onto our table with one hand to steady himself, put down his coffee cup, then reached behind him to steal an empty chair from a table next to us.

My mother's eyes darted around the room, trying to look anywhere but there.

"Boy, these shoes are hard to walk in." He pointed down to a bright pair of neon orange cycling shoes. "They have these doodads on the bottom that hook onto the pedals. Great for riding, bad for walking."

My mother and I fixated on his shoes like they were

a pair of Gucci's we'd never be able to afford. We both let out a sigh when Richard got seated. But his look was still disconcerting. His lack of sleeves showed off T-shirt tan lines and white shoulders tinged with pink. Little tuffs of black hair sprung from the neckline of his tank top. He'd used neon green gauze tape to strap his small notebook to his upper left arm.

"Well, you two have lit a fire under me." He raised his coffee cup, as if to toast us. "I've started training for Bay to Breakers."

My mother smiled weakly.

"What's your routine, Genevieve?" he asked. "Are you on a strict walking schedule? Have you changed your diet at all?"

"Um, I kind of workout as the mood suits me." She took a sip from her cup. "And the only special thing in my diet is to ingest as much caffeine as possible." She looked at me and winked. When it came to java, my mother and I were two beans in a coffee can.

"Hmm, an unusual approach, but if it works, then so much the better. I'll increase my caffeine intake."

"So what do you do for a living, Richard?" I asked, hoping to get off the subject of training.

"I'm an accountant. I do books for small businesses. How are things at Elsie's Antiques since you've taken over? Have you done inventory yet?"

"It's on my to-do list. My father's an estate attorney, so he filled me in on all that."

"Good for you. I like to see a business owner on top of things," he said, knocking on the table then pointing at me. He glanced down at his watch. "Well, I see my allotted break time is over. I just wanted to say hi. Best get back to my cycling."

He stood up and, once again, my mother and I had to look away.

"Oh, I almost forgot, Genevieve," Richard said, leaning over and lowering his voice. "The police are under the impression that you were at home the evening of Donna's accident. I'm afraid I told them that I'd seen you out." He reached up to his arm and patted his little notebook.

"It's no big deal." My mom waved a dismissal. "We didn't see anything."

"But it looks suspicious when you don't tell the truth."

"Richard, I just didn't want to bother the police with such minutia."

His lips pinched together. I could see he was struggling with his crush on my mother and his strict adherence to all things authoritative.

"I think we have an obligation to be honest with the police," he said as he jutted out his chin. He picked up his coffee cup, swiveled on his spiked cycling shoes and gingerly walked away.

I leaned across the table. "Mother, what have we learned here?" I felt a combination of irritatation and fear.

Her eyes narrowed. "That white people shouldn't wear neon?"

"No," I snapped at her, even though she did have a point. "We've learned that lying can lead to trouble. I do not want to be on the receiving end of Sergeant Romano's questions about our whereabouts when Donna got hit."

She gave another dismissive wave.

I slumped back in my chair. Ish. Parents. What ya going to do?

Rather than walking directly back to Elsie's Antiques, I told my mother that I needed to buy new deadbolts. She stared at me for a few beats, since I probably had guilt written all over my face. Mrs. B had asked me to accompany her to Steve's house. I'd be the lookout person while Mrs. B examined the car in his backyard. I felt bad, leaving my mom to work at the store while I was out sleuthing with Mrs. B, but if Mom knew what we were up to, she'd want to tag along.

I hurried to the hardware store where Mrs. Butterfield and her newest vehicle, a tow truck, waited for me in the parking lot. I jogged to the open passenger window.

"Where'd you get this?" I asked.

"Jimmy found it for me."

It was bright yellow, also known as "Caltrans yellow," since the California Department of Transportation used the same hue on the yellow lines that divide streets down the middle, as well as their work trucks. The sign on the door in pretty purple script read, "Trixie's Towing."

"Do you like the name Trixie? I do. Sounds kind of bubbly. I'm tying it out as a new persona." Mrs. B was dressed in mechanic coveralls, in the same bright yellow as the truck, and her nametag read: "Trixie" in purple script that matched the sign on the door.

"What's wrong with Betty Butterfield?" I asked, referring to the name she assumed after becoming a contract worker for the FBI. Betty had impressed the bureau after blowing the whistle on an auto dealer who was scamming insurance companies.

"Betty Butterfield is too staid. Trixie's got some sass to her."

"Is Betty Brewer sassy?" I asked, referring to her real name.

"Well, that name is the name of my youth. And, honey, everyone's sassy when they're young."

"Do you mind if I run into the hardware store? Mrs. M thinks I should replace the locks on the doors to the store."

"Smart thinking, that woman," Mrs. B said, as she slid out of the truck.

Inside, I made a beeline for the lock section and Mrs. B headed for the gardening department. After I selected a set of locks Mrs. B reappeared at my elbow.

"I just heard something interesting," she whispered.

I raised an eyebrow at her.

"I saw that Cece woman having some keys made."

"What's interesting about that?" I asked.

"She had a lot of keys on the counter, so I pretended to be engrossed in the key chain display, so I could get close to her. 'That's a lot of keys,' I said to her, and she says to me, 'I work at Green's Used Autos. We like to have extra keys for our cars.' And then she whips out a business card and starts asking me about what kind of car I drive."

"Sounds like her, never passes up a chance to sell."

"But the thing of it is, the keys she was having duplicated were house keys, not car keys. These days most car keys can't be duplicated at all because they have chips in them."

"I'm not following Mrs. B."

"Patricia, the easiest was to break into a house is to use a key."

I stared at her blankly. "My mind doesn't work the way yours does. You're going to have to explain in detail."

"I think she's going to use those keys to break in to someone's house. And not one someone, a lot of someones."

"But how would she get those keys to begin with?"

"If I was her, I'd snoop around a house looking for a hide-a-key, swipe it, have it duplicated, then put it back."

"But you'd have to be able to find the key without someone spotting you. Plus you'd need a reason to be on their property."

"Like a postal delivery person."

"So you think Donna and Cece were working together?"

She shrugged her shoulders. "It's a theory. Think about it. Every house Donna visits, she could be looking for a hide-a-key. When she finds one, she takes it and passes it to Cece to have it duplicated. Cece makes a copy, gives it back to Donna, and Donna puts it back where she found it. Then they wait until Donna gets a request to hold someone's mail, which would indicate how long the house would be empty, and Cece uses the key to break in."

"That's pretty complicated," I said.

"Yes, but if they kept their heads and didn't get greedy—maybe just lifted a piece of jewelry or some cash—the victims might not even realize they've been burgled."

We moved down a few aisles until we could see Cece

standing at the register paying for her keys.

"If you're right Mrs. B, Cece's going to carry on without Donna."

We pulled out of the hardware store's parking lot and cruised by the Phoenix building, where we easily spotted Steve on the roof engrossed in his painting. Turning onto his street, I started to feel nervous, as anyone would before doing something illegal. But Mrs. B whistled a happy tune, like she didn't have a care in the world. She parked the tow truck on the street and got out. She hoisted a toolbox out of the bed, and we walked up the driveway, past the Victorian, past Steve's rental and into his backyard. The little convertible's hood was still up.

"These old Karmann Ghias are very temperamental; plus it's hard to get parts," Mrs. B said. She leaned on the side fender and proceeded to examine the engine. "Check the inside of the car. See what you can find."

The car was unlocked. I slid into the driver's seat. A large bag of unopened M&M's was on the passenger seat along with two empty Atomic Fireball wrappers. Popping open the glove box, I pulled out the registration.

"The registration says the car belongs to Donna," I said, getting out of the car.

Mrs. B nodded. She didn't seem surprised. She held a cardboard box in one hand and a piece of paper in the other.

"This," she said, gesturing to a blue tarp laying on the ground covered in auto parts, "is a torn apart carburetor. And these," she said, shaking the box at me, "are new carburetor parts."

"Okay."

"And this," she continued, waving the paper at me, "is the packing slip for this." Again she shook the box.

"Mrs. B, we don't have time for you to put a carburetor back together, I need to get back to the store."

"I couldn't rebuild the carburetor if I wanted to, because the gaskets are missing."

I stared at her, not comprehending.

"You can't rebuild a carburetor without new gaskets, but the packing slip says there should be gaskets in this box."

"So they forgot to include them."

"No." She furrowed her brow. "The packing slip has a checkmark next to the word gaskets. The packing person must have included them. Someone's taken the gaskets."

She made it sound like someone had stolen the Hope Diamond.

"Maybe they're in the house," I said.

"Possible, but I doubt it," she said. "Patricia, you're not understanding the significance of this. Someone swiped the gaskets for the sole purpose of having this car stuck here, which means someone wanted Donna on foot the night she got hit."

Mitsy paced on the sidewalk in front of my store. It had been ten minutes since I'd returned from my outing with Mrs. B. My mother was in the back alley waxing water rings off the top of a coffee table. I sipped on my third cup of coffee and watched Mitsy's routine. She disappeared to my right, heading in the direction of Yvonne's Jeweler's, then reappeared, and walked passed me toward Lucchesi's Italian Restaurant. Occasionally she'd stop and look at my front door, then shake her head and continue on. She held Kiki close to her chest; and the little dog bounced in rhythm to her march. What could be causing Mitsy such angst?

She finally slammed opened the door and stepped inside with her head held high.

"Are you alone?" she asked.

"Yes."

She stomped over and stood directly in front of me.

"I want to hire you to follow my husband," she said.

"Oh?"

"I require your private investigative services."

"Well, Mitsy, I'm not actually a licensed private investigator." I had to be honest with her, but the possibilities intrigued me. She'd hand over her home address, and I'd have reason to go snoop around their house. Maybe I'd get into their garage and have a chance to inspect their cars.

Her eyes turned to slits as she glared at me. She reached down the front of her blouse and produced a folded up one hundred-dollar bill. Putting it on the counter, she used her one free hand to spread it out flat. Kiki leaned forward to inspect the bill, then let out a yawn, her pink tongue curling into a lazy circle.

"Are you a PI now?" she asked.

"Mitsy, just because your husband never told you that Donna went to bingo doesn't mean he was cheating on you."

"He's been lying to me." She thrust her chin forward in an attempt to hide her hurt, but the tears that threatened to smear her troweled-on eye liner revealed a deep pain. "Sometimes he disappears in the afternoons."

"Most relationships just need more communication," I said, thinking if I could fake a private investigator's license, maybe I could fake a counselor's license too. "So where did he say he'd been?"

"After sputtering like a hard-water encrusted teapot, he claimed he'd been out shopping for rare books, but you don't get sunburned by opening musty old tomes."

"There's probably a simple explanation."

"Well, if there is, I want you to find out what it is."

She reached into her blouse again, and a second folded hundred fluttered onto the counter top. Kiki whimpered, alert to the fact that I wasn't worth that much money. I took a deep breath and continued to mull over the idea. Maybe I'd find out her husband's name, and my nosey curiosity would be sated. I'd give her one last chance to back out.

"Look, it's probably just a misunderstanding. Why don't you give it a couple of days, let him tell you in his own way." For her sake, I hoped her birthday and the new dog would arrive soon.

Another bill showing Jackson's profile appeared. Geez, did she have a vault down there? Kiki pulled her lips back to fully reveal her canine fangs, showing her disapproval of Mitsy's largesse. I tapped my fingers on the counter. That was enough money to put a dent in my cable bill. Using Kiki's judgment to assess my value, I pushed two of the hundred dollar bills back across the counter and kept one. "Just so we're clear, Mitsy, I'm not a licensed private eye. But I'll do some checking and see what I can find out. If I find nothing, I'm giving you back this hundred." I raised an eyebrow waiting for her understanding and her acceptance.

She nodded.

I pulled out a small pad of paper and handed her a pen. "Why don't you give me your information: address, cell phone, and a description of what cars you own."

She wrote as she spoke: "He's supposed to be at bingo at the Mastodon's Association on Tuesday evening."

"Give me a call on Tuesday when he leaves."

I picked up one of Elsie's Antiques business cards, wrote my cell phone number on the back, and handed it to her.

She thanked me, placed the pen down on the counter, and as she walked out, a delivery man came in and held the door for her. I glanced at the paper Mitsy had handed me, it showed her address and phone number. As for cars, she'd written Mini Cooper, Toyota and Chevy, but not year or model.

The delivery guy placed a large envelope on the counter, then handed me an electronic tablet and tapped his finger in a rectangular box. "Sign here, please." At the sound of his voice, I looked up. Something seemed familiar about him. He had dark skin, close cropped, curly black hair, and a black beard that almost swallowed his mouth. Mirrored sunglasses hid his eyes, and a windbreaker gave his upper body a shapeless form. I did as he requested. After he left, I opened the envelope and pulled out a small stack of papers. At the top was the name Earl Gray. I slapped the folder down and ran to the door just in time to see the delivery guy jump into his truck and whip off his glasses. It was Beatrice Johnson, practicing her undercover skills. She gave me a thumbs up as she drove off.

I returned to the counter and flipped open Earl's file. It began with current information of address and phone number. Then it went back to his military days. He'd been drafted during the Vietnam War, but due to poor eyesight he'd been stationed as a mechanic in Hawaii. After returning to California, he'd had a variety of jobs, mostly car repair. His last known job was at a tire store.

He'd been arrested once for pot possession in the '80s. But what stood out was his horrible driving record: running red lights, driving the wrong way on one-way streets, speeding, and numerous parking tickets. I counted seven moving violations in the last five years. His car insurance must be sky high. No wonder he didn't want anyone knowing he'd hit a deer—if Andrew's story was correct. Earl could be close to losing his license, and my guess was that if he didn't have a license, he couldn't get to work.

I tapped my fingers on Earl's file and realized how helpful it would be to have this kind of information on Mitsy and Hubby or even Helena.

As I turned into the parking lot of the church, I instinctively scanned the cars. Never mind that I couldn't imagine someone committing a hit-and-run, then blazingly driving around with a dented hood or smashed windshield.

Jimmy leaned against a silver Audi. Owning a used car lot gave him access to an ever changing variety of vehicles. His dark blue suit was accessorized with a gold watch that sparkled in the sunlight.

As I opened the car door, I repeated the words: "Be nice. Be nice. Be nice." I hoped a simple mantra would overcome my distaste for the guy, and I could power through the afternoon without dumping coffee in his lap.

Earlier, I'd decided on a light gray skirt and jacket, a summer suit left over from my short lived corporate life. But that meant I had to forgo my comfortable flip-flops for gray high heeled pumps.

I stepped out of the car. Jimmy's head tilted down. His reflective sunglasses made him look like he was with the Secret Service. He peered at me over his shades, and his eyes went from my toes up to—and stopped at—my chest.

He removed the toothpick from his mouth. "Patty Cakes," he said, in a deep voice, "mourning suits you."

I slammed the door to my car and stomped past him. "Stuff it, Jimmy." What had I been thinking? Being nice was overrated.

When I reached the long, flat concrete steps that led up to the oversized doors, he grabbed my elbow.

"No touching," I said, pulling away.

He sighed. "Patricia, you take the fun out of funerals."

Standing in the back, I surveyed the church's interior. Steve sat in the front pew next to his daughter, Magnolia, and an older gentleman. Behind them were Earl and his grandson, Andrew. I also recognized a few folks from bingo: Helena and Cece, plus Mitsy's husband—Hubby, but no Mitsy.

We sat in the back on thin-cushioned pews. Jimmy immediately removed a phone from his pocket and turned on a video game. The Yarn Barn lady sat two rows in front of us. She looked over her shoulder at me and glared. I'm not sure which Merchant Association bylaw I'd broken that afternoon, since my mother was watching the store. Maybe it had to do with my gray attire instead of conventional black. She, of course, wore the funeral-appropriate color, and when she turned her head back around, I noticed that she extended this tradition all the way to the adornments on her beehive hairdo which were two shiny black knitting needles.

The air felt cool when we first entered, but the crowd forced the temperature up quickly. I slipped off my jacket, and Jimmy cast a sideways glance at the front of my shirt.

"Keep going," he whispered.

Eeww. I crossed my arms.

The organ music died down, and the minister began the service. A black speaker box hung on a large concrete pillar close to us, but apparently it wasn't working. I couldn't hear a thing. After thirty minutes of standing, sitting and fanning ourselves with the program, we adjourned to the reception hall.

While Jimmy walked ahead of me to get in the buffet line, I leaned against the wall to examine the crowd. Round tables covered with white tablecloths filled the floor space. Two waiters entered: one carried an oversized platter of cold-cuts, the other carried a steaming serving dish, which he slid onto a heating tray.

Also in line for the buffet was Hubby, flanked by two men. I made a mental note, just in case Mitsy might want to know, that at least for one afternoon, her husband was not cavorting with females. Helena was also in the food line. She wore a soft yellow wrap blouse over a bright pink skirt. She spoke to a woman next to her, then titled her head back and laughed out loud.

I edged around the outside of the room hoping to overhear some tidbit of information that might help me understand Donna better. I wasn't interested in talking with the family or other downtown merchants. I was hoping to find her co-workers. But since government-sanctioned navy blue shorts were not typically worn to funerals, postal workers blended in with everyone else.

At the table closest to me, sat a group of five women who talked of school menus; they raved about the lasagna, but complained about the hot dogs. The people at the next table were discussing football. The third crowd I sidled up to sounded a little more promising. They discussed the closing of a post office in a rural area. Luckily, a table adjacent to them had a few empty chairs, so I sat within eavesdropping distance and pulled out my phone to give the appearance I was not listening to them.

"If they close the main branch, mail will be rerouted through Oakland, and I'm not commuting all the way to Oakland."

"Oh, I doubt it will come to that," said a dark skinned man with large brown eyes. "The government's not that stupid."

A woman with dreadlocks pulled into a pony tail, leaned over to a thin-faced woman with straight brown hair and whispered into her ear. The two rose. I decided to follow, but not before glancing around to see Jimmy sitting across the room, talking with the voluptuous woman that owned Lucchesi's Italian restaurant. Thank goodness. I didn't want to be distracted by his annoying chit-chat.

The two postal workers disappeared into the

restroom, and I hesitated outside the entrance. A woman exited and I slipped inside, walking on tip-toe so my heels wouldn't alert them to my presence. Luckily, there wasn't a line, and two of the three stall doors were closed. I was alone with the women.

"Did you hear about the investigation they'd started on Donna?" one of the women asked.

"Because some of her packages went missing?"

"Uh-huh. Someone told me Donna had been talking to the police. Do you know what it was about?" the other replied.

"No, but missing packages are handled internally. So I don't know why the police would be involved."

A toilet flushed, so I moved to the entrance, opened the door, and walked heavily, clicking my heels on the floor. The woman with the straight brown hair cleared her throat as I went into the open stall. The other toilet flushed. Then I heard the sound of a faucet followed by the noise from the hand blower.

When I emerged, the two women had gone, and Maggie leaned against the tile wall, her arms folded in front of her. She wore a black wrap dress, and the same long dangly earrings she had on the day I met her on the roof. The look on her face told me she wasn't happy to see me.

"Why are you here?" she snapped.

"I came with Jimmy—"

"Leave my dad alone. He didn't have anything to do with what happened to Donna."

I sighed and turned to the sink, watching her in the mirror.

"It was an accident," she continued, her voice rising

so it echoed inside the small room. "Accidents happen."

I lowered my voice, hoping she'd do the same. "Maggie, if someone did hit Donna on purpose, wouldn't you like to find out?" Her eyes filled with tears, and she pulled at an earring, showing the Band-Aid still on her hand from the spill she took on her bike. At the moment, she seemed more scared than she did grief stricken. The image of Andrew limping when he dropped off his granddad's truck at Jake's popped in my mind. I took a wild stab in the dark. "What if that same person was the one who hit you and Andrew on your bikes?"

"How did you know?" Her eyes got big. "No, no, it can't be," she said, wiping her tears. "Just stop, okay? Just stop." She went into the stall and slammed the door.

I took a quick intake of breath. It hadn't crossed my mind that she might be in danger. I could hear her sniffling. I felt bad that I'd upset her, but finding out that she suspected that Donna was hit on purpose, and that she may also be a target was vital.

After drying my hands, I pushed open the restroom door and almost ran right into Helena. I smiled and said "Hi," not sure if she'd remember me from book club. She smiled back, but her eyes were glossy and barely focusing. She was also close enough for me to smell alcohol. The woman was lit to the gills, as Nana used to say.

I turned away from the reception area, wanting to avoid another interaction with Maggie, and headed for a side exit. Just as I was stepping outside Sergeant Romano stepped directly in front of me. He looked a tad overheated with a jacket over a dress shirt and tie.

"Ms. Schuster," he said, using the formal title like he always did when we met in situations where he suspected me of doing something illegal.

"Sergeant Romano," I said, matching his formality.

"I didn't realize you knew Donna personally," he said, making it sound like an accusation.

I narrowed my eyes and let the silence build up between us. For a moment I thought of letting our staring contest go on just to see where he'd go after that statement. But since he's Jake's dad, I did the polite thing and lied. "She delivered mail to Elsie's Antiques, plus she —you know—right in front of my mom's house. So it seemed right."

"Hmmm," he said, probably assuming I was hiding something.

"And, you?" I asked. For a second he looked surprised, he probably wasn't used to people questioning him.

"Well, we're continuing our investigation," he said.

"Hmmm," I said, assuming that he was hiding something.

I glanced around, checking for eavesdroppers, but we were alone. "Have you had any luck finding the person who hit Donna?" I asked.

He shook his head. "Hit and runs are notoriously hard to solve. Even if you find the vehicle, it's hard to know who was driving. Early days, though."

"Have you talked to Maggie?"

"About what?"

"I think she suspects someone."

"Oh?"

"A car sideswiped Maggie and Andrew while they

were riding their bikes."

Sergeant Romano's face remained a blank, I couldn't tell if he was surprised by this news or unimpressed. "Coincidences do happen," he said dismissively and took a deep breath before continuing. "I read a report the other day from a gentleman that said he saw you and your mother out walking the night that Donna got hit."

Oh, dang that Richard and his little blue notebook. "Yeah, my mom and I took a quick walk around the block, before we made s'mores."

"Wearing camouflage makeup?" he asked.

"Did you know my mother is an artist? She was practicing face painting, she's thinking of offering her services at kid's parties," I lied.

He looked at me and sighed, a heavy exasperated sigh.

I smiled as sweetly as I possibly could, said goodbye, stepped around him, and headed for my car. After pulling out of the parking lot, I drove past the side of the church and noticed two people tucked back in a secluded alcove. It was Maggie and Andrew—in a passionate embrace. I was surprised that her emotional state could change so quickly. Was she playing me? Her desire for me to stop digging seemed authentic, as did her fear. But I felt afraid for her and Andrew, really afraid. If someone purposely tried to hit them once, they could try again.

Chapter Nine

My mom clumped up the wooden steps of Donna's Queen Anne home. Tall and narrow, the house sported multiple colors: yellow, brown, and beige with decorative orange corbels. My artistic side cringed. But the house needed more than paint. A crack ran through a large plate glass window, broken siding revealed half-inch cracks in the foundation, and the small, detached garage listed to one side.

I glanced up and down the street. Plenty of neighbors were involved in their morning routine: kids being shuffled into cars, a dog walker, and a woman in a suit hurrying to get into a sedan full of others in suits. Luckily, none of them paid attention to us, even as ridiculous we looked in our pink jumpers. My mother had insisted on wearing heels, which, at least in my mind, reduced our credibility as genuine cleaners. She and Mrs. M's look went a step further with hair that was tall on top and flat against their heads on the sides. A white carnation tinged with pink was tucked behind Mrs. M's salt-and-pepper hair. I refused both the puffy hair and the high heels. Instead, I tucked my unruly curls under a baseball cap and donned sunglasses and sensible running shoes.

Mrs. B appointed herself head of marketing for our faux business. She designed a logo, so along with the words "Flock of Maids" on the backs of our jumpers, there was also a picture of a seagull holding a miniature broom in its mouth. Or a pterodactyl-sized seagull holding a regular sized broom. I preferred the latter. She made up business cards, which read: "Flock of Maids— We Swoop In and Clean for Less." She'd even had magnetic signs made and stuck them to the driver and passenger doors of my mom's SUV. Heck, at this point, maybe we really were in the cleaning business.

The painted porch looked old but felt strong and solid under our weight. Mrs. M pulled a single key from her pocket and slipped it into the front door lock. She'd cased the house the previous evening and found a hide-a-key under a rather obvious fake pile of dog poop in the backyard. Then she made a copy of the key and replaced the original in its disgusting hiding place. It was the exact scenario that Mrs. B had described on how to easily break into a house.

My mother carried a bucket of cleaning supplies, I pulled along an upright vacuum cleaner, and Mrs. M's tote held a few empty garbage bags. "Just in case there's something we need to borrow," she informed me.

The living room was decorated with a plaid sofa, overstuffed matching chairs, and mid-century end tables. Above the fireplace hung a framed print by Georgia O'Keeffe, one of her red poppies. Mrs. B came up next to me, and we stood for a moment enjoying the picture.

"She had good taste in art," Mrs. B said.

At the far end of the living room, French doors opened into a small dining area with a round oak table and matching chairs. Another set of French doors led outside to a bricked-in patio. To our left was a set of stairs, plus a sitting room with bay windows overlooking the street.

The house smelled of sweets and old dust. A large bowl of candy sat on an entry table, as if it was Halloween. My mom dug in, pushing aside the M&M's and SweeTarts to grab an Atomic Fire Ball. She tore open the crinkly wrapping and popped it in her mouth.

"I'm starting upstairs," Mrs. M said.

"I'll take the kitchen," said my mom.

I followed Mrs. M upstairs. We each took a bedroom. My search took only a few minutes. The room was sparse; it contained a daybed, a treadmill and a chest of drawers. I pulled out every drawer. The top three were empty; the bottom one held a pair of sweat pants and a sweatshirt. The closet contained a few oversized coats. I went through the pockets but found only mittens and a wool scarf. I looked out the window into the backyard. A few bushes surrounded a dead patch of lawn. An old shed sat up against the fence, and from my vantage point I could clearly see a padlock on the door.

Next I checked the bath and found only the usual toiletries. Instead of heading downstairs, I checked out Donna's bedroom. Here were more prints by O'Keeffe: a purple-and-white iris and another of white calla lilies. Mrs. M had a nightstand drawer open. She pulled out a handful of bingo cards, each covered in purple circles.

"It looked like she saved her winning cards," Mrs. M

said. "And look at that." She held up one for me to see. "She didn't cover her free space. I like to cover my free space, makes me feel like I've got a head start." She smiled and put the cards back and closed the drawer. "So all her clothes are gone, but there's still some jewelry in the box." She pointed to a jewelry box sitting on an antique highboy.

I went downstairs to a short hallway that led to a bathroom and a bedroom. The bedroom's décor was modern and cheery. Three walls were white, and the fourth was a soft blue-gray. On the wall above the bed was a picture of a simple pink heart. A small white wicker vanity was covered in tubes of nail polish. A rectangular mirror with a white wicker frame hung on the wall; colorful plastic leis draped across one corner. Tucked into the mirror's inside edge was a series of four photos, the kind that come from photo booths at fairs. I pulled one out. The pictures showed Maggie and Andrew hamming-it-up, making silly faces—stretching their mouths out of proportion with their fingers. In one, Andrew pulled Maggie's petite ears out from her head and Maggie responded with a mock look of surprise.

In the corner sat an Infinity brand surfboard leaning up against the wall, American made, top of the line. The board was white, with a thin gold stripe that ran its length, broken only by its lazy eight logo—the mathematical symbol for infinity. The longboard was perfect for learning: not fast, but easy to paddle, and easy to catch a wave.

Two bright-blue unopened condom packages lay on the nightstand. I pulled open a drawer and found an almost full box of the prophylactics. Maggie apparently wasn't hiding her sexual activity. I could only assume that Donna must have known about Maggie's love life.

The small closet held short shorts and short skirts, sparkly sequined tank tops, and high heels. Alongside the finery was a wetsuit, also an Infinity brand. When I looked closer, I realized that the tags were still attached. This collection didn't match the young woman I met on the roof, with her chunky sandals and cargo shorts. That young woman was earthy; this young woman was ready to party.

I assumed that Donna had bought these for Maggie, yet it appeared that she never wore them.

I pulled out each dresser drawer; the top two contained lacey bra and panty sets in a wide variety of colors. But when I looked closer, again I found tags still attached; they had never been worn. I checked the third drawer. It was empty.

"Found something." I heard my mom call out.

When I entered the kitchen she was leaning against the counter, holding a stack of stapled papers. She handed them to me.

The top page was a letter from a local bank addressed to Donna. I skimmed the contents; she'd been approved for a $120,000 home equity loan. The loan officer's name jumped out at me. Mitch Carter. I went to school with an Amanda Carter, who had an older brother named Mitch.

"Look at the last part," she said.

The first page said "Contractor's Bid." Divided by projects, the proposal was broken down by new foundation, new roof, house paint, and electrical upgrade. It totaled almost $165,000. The contractor's signature appeared on the last page, but Donna's signature was absent.

"So, she was going to take out a loan for home improvements," I said. "Interesting, but nothing that would get you killed."

"But her loan won't cover the whole amount. She's short $45,000."

"Meaning what?" I asked.

"Meaning, did she have a plan to come up with the extra money?"

My mother and I took the papers to the front sitting room, which contained a desk and a plaid loveseat that matched the couch and chairs in the living room. Mrs. M sat in front of Donna's computer, trying out different passwords.

"These were in the kitchen." I handed Mrs. M the papers.

She jotted down a few notes. "Better put them back exactly as you found them. We don't want to take something that might be missed."

While my mom returned the papers to the kitchen, I opened the largest desk drawer. It held hanging file folders. I read the labels out loud: "Car insurance, Medical, Passwords, PG&E, and Phone."

"Can I have the Passwords file?" Mrs. M asked.

I pulled it out, it was empty. "Sorry, there's nothing in it."

Mrs. M sighed. "Could you check the trash?"

I picked up the wire waste basket, pulled out a few crumpled receipts.

"Put those in my tote. We'll look at them later."

A dog barked in the distance, and an uncomfortable

feeling started down in my gut. "Are you almost done, Mrs. M?" I asked.

"Yes, I can't get anything. She has passwords on everything."

We returned to the car, and loaded our cleaning equipment in the back. As I opened up the passenger side door, I noticed a small piece of paper under the windshield. I pulled it out. It read: *I need a house cleaner, please call me at*—then a phone number. That confirmed it. We were in business.

On the drive home, Mrs. M reached into her tote and pulled out a small maroon book.

"Where did you find that?" I asked.

"On Donna's nightstand. It's a collection of short stories by Ray Bradbury. Hard to pass up. I told you I needed some fresh reading material." She flipped through some pages. "Oh, what's this?"

I glanced over. She held up four photos, the same kind that Maggie had in her room.

"Who is it?" I asked.

"Donna and some guy. He looks vaguely familiar."

I took the picture. "That's Earl." The two posed cheek-to-cheek. "He was at bingo the other night. Mrs. Taylor knows him. He's the one that had his car impounded for possibly hitting Donna. I got some information from Beatrice on him."

"Oh, yeah?" Mrs. M said.

"I was going to explain it all at our meeting tomorrow," I said.

"Oh?"

"I hoped it would make up for not asking Steve about his alibi."

Mrs. M could sense my guilt. She reached over and patted me on the arm. "You're doing fine, Patricia. You're too hard on yourself."

I let out a long breath. I didn't want to let these women down, yet somehow I felt I had.

Before opening up Elsie's Antiques I walked down to Chris and Adam's surf shop. The door jangled as I entered. Chris' blond hair stood out against the dark-blue walls that depicted an underwater scene of swimming sea turtles and tropical fish. He held up a wetsuit while talking with a customer. He glance my way and waved. I mulled around trying on different sunglasses while I waited, thinking I'd treat myself to a new pair.

When Chris appeared, I looked at him through dark lenses. "What do you think?" I asked.

"Anything would look good on you," he replied.

"Flatterer," I muttered.

I returned the sunglasses to their rack and looked around for the other customer, not wanting to be overheard, but he seemed immersed in wetsuit decisions.

"So what's up?" he asked.

"Do you know Maggie Olsen?"

He shook his head.

"She's the stepdaughter—or was—of our mail lady," I explained.

"Oh, Donna's daughter? Yeah, she came in with Donna, and they bought an Infinity longboard, a really nice wetsuit, plus booties and some other stuff too. Only expensive stuff, kind of unusual for a beginner."

I nodded. That's what I'd thought too. "Did you get a sense of their relationship?"

"I got the feeling that Donna was more interested in buying the best than the daughter was. What was her name again?"

"Maggie."

"Yeah, she asked me a lot of how-to questions. I told her I'd be happy to give her some lessons. But I haven't heard from her."

"How long ago was this?"

"Hmm, two or three weeks ago. What's the interest?"

Ugh. I didn't like the feeling of my personal life crossing over into this odd world with The Ladies, the FBI, and at this moment, possibly a murder. My friendship with Chris went back to my teen years, and I didn't want to damage it by lying to him.

"It's hard to explain," I started to say. The front door opened and Chris' attention shifted away from me. "You're busy, I'll see ya later."

"Okay, if I hear from her, I'll let you know."

I walked out onto the sidewalk and could see Steve standing in front of Elsie's Antiques. He held a large box. It was ten minutes after nine. I hoped the Yarn Barn Lady hadn't spotted him. I wasn't in the mood for a lecture.

"Hi, Steve," I called out, quickening my pace.

I unlocked the front door, and he placed the box on the counter.

"What ya got there?" I asked.

"Some china."

I peeked inside. "Pretty. I'll look it up. Unfortunately, you don't get as much as you'd think for a nice set like this." I had read over Nana's books and been surprised by how little she could get for a good set of china.

He shrugged. "One more thing: I was hoping we could set up a time for you to look through Donna's house."

That evening Jake and I bounced along in Jake's run down truck. He was happy to help when I asked if he could accompany me to Donna's house and be some muscle. He put in the clutch and visibly winced as the gears ground into second.

Steve stood waiting on Donna's front porch. I introduced him to Jake. We went inside, where a sweet smell lingered. We started in the sun room. The first thing I noticed was the top desk drawer was open about an inch. Mrs. M would not have been so forgetful as to have left it ajar. Steve must have been here since our visit.

I held a clipboard in one hand and jotted down each item Steve wanted me to sell. During our initial negotiations, I'd told him I'd give him one price for everything, but some items could be a detriment. My grandmother had kept a journal as to items that sold well and what items were duds. Desks were on the dud list. But when I'd been here with our pretend cleaning crew we hadn't torn the thing apart. I'd love to find a letter taped to the bottom of a drawer written in Donna's handwriting that starts, "If I die mysteriously, look to___" with the name of her killer filled in.

"Moonlight?" Steve said. "You okay?"

"Yeah," I said. "Remember I'd talked about certain items that are difficult to sell? A desk is one of them. I'll take it, but if I have to take it to Recycle Town, I'll have to charge you for it." Even though we'd gone over this, I wanted to remind him.

He nodded, and we moved to the living room. The couch, tables, and mirror were all things that would sell easily. So would a hutch full of china cups and salt-and-pepper shakers.

"How about the O'Keeffe print?" I asked.

"No, I'll hang onto that one."

He pointed down the hallway that led to Maggie's bedroom and the downstairs bath.

"That's Maggie's room," he said. "Everything stays in there for now."

We moved into the dining area. Steve wanted me to take the table and six matching chairs, as well as a small buffet. I glanced into the kitchen. The contractor's bid and bank letter were missing from the counter.

Upstairs, in Donna's bedroom, I immediately noticed the night stands where Mrs. M had found Donna's bingo cards. The drawer was open an inch, just like the desk was downstairs. I distinctly remembered Mrs. M sliding the drawer completely closed.

"I'll hang onto those O'Keeffe prints too," he said, from the doorway. "I'd forgotten all about them."

The back of my neck tightened up. That didn't sound like he'd been here recently. Could someone have broken in after we left? We'd been able to enter the house so quickly using her hide-a-key. Someone else could easily have done the same thing.

"You can take that jewelry box and what's left in it. Maggie's gone through it and taken what she wanted."

We moved to the room with the treadmill.

"Sorry, I don't sell exercise equipment," I said.

While the two guys loaded up the truck, I went out to the porch to assess two rocking chairs Steve had mentioned. But my attention was drawn to the shed. I couldn't pass up a chance to snoop, especially with the owner's permission.

I bounded across the yard. Luckily, the door was open. Unfortunately, it contained very little: a kinked garden hose, a rusty shovel against the far wall and the smell of gasoline. As I swung the door closed, I heard a female voice calling: "Leonardo, Giorgio! Where are you two?"

The voice called again. It sounded very close. I looked behind the shed. Two fence boards lay on the ground, creating a hole, substantial enough for an adult to pass through from the alley without being seen from the house. An older woman with dark hair poked her head through the hole and looked at me.

"Have you seen two young boys? I asked Donna to close up this fence. Are you a friend of hers? She and her daughter were so nice to my grandkids."

Suddenly, there were two boys right next to me. I had no idea where they'd been hiding.

"We're here, Nona."

She waved them out into the alley. "I hope they weren't bothering you."

The two looked to be brothers. I estimated their ages to be five and seven.

"Where's Maggie?" asked the older one.

"She moved back in with her dad," I said.

"Where's that?" the younger one asked.

"A few blocks from here," I said.

"I want to play in the truck," said the younger one.

The older one nudged the younger and whispered: "You're not supposed to tell."

"What truck?" I asked.

"The white one," said the younger, oblivious to their secret.

"The mail truck?" I asked.

"Yeah. She let me steer," said the younger one. He put his arms out in a circle.

The older put his hand over his face, in classic melodramatic kid form. "Ugg, stop," he said. But the little one would not be shushed.

"Who let you play in the truck? Maggie?" I asked.

He shook his head. "She let us play with the packages," he continued. "But we don't have any now."

"Donna?" I asked.

"No," the older boy said. "I don't know her name. She was Donna's friend."

"Did you ever take packages out of the yard?" I tried to keep emotion out of my voice. I just wanted it to sound like a simple question.

"It was just the one time," Grandma chimed in. "They said they found them on the ground."

"We did," the younger boy said. "But we found some there." He pointed to the ground next to the hole in the fence.

"We told my mom," said the older boy, "and she gave them back to Donna."

"It was the oddest thing," their grandmother said. "They came home with two packages and said they found them in the alley. When my daughter returned them, Donna seemed embarrassed. She said she must have left the truck open when she was home on a lunch break."

The boys lost interest in us. The older one said,

"Race ya." And they both broke into a run.

"Huh," I said, trying to make sense of it. "But who would take packages and just drop them back here?"

"I don't know. The only reason I believed the kids is I'd seen boxes sitting out here once before that. I didn't come over and look; I assumed they were recycling." She shrugged her shoulders. "People are odd."

I nodded in agreement, and as I watched her walk away, I thought about the Postal Service investigating Donna. Could it just be something as simple as kids messing around? But if the kids were telling the truth, who let them play in Donna's mail truck? And if they did find packages in the alley, who put them there? And why?

I walked back to the deck and checked out two white wicker rocking chairs. The pink cushions were faded, but it would be an easy sell to someone wanting the shabby chic look. Next to them was a set of homemade bookshelves. Even though they were too plain to sell, I might make use of them in my storage room. I heard footsteps behind me and turned to see Jake smiling.

"Need some help?" he asked, stepping closer.

I nodded as he took one more step and put his hands on my waist. I looked up. His head tilted just a bit as he leaned down and kissed me. He tasted of oranges and smelled of musk.

I heard Steve's voice coming from the side of the house. I disengaged from Jake, thinking kissing my helper didn't project a professional image as the owner of Elsie's Antiques. Plus I didn't want an audience. But it was hard to take my eyes from his face.

Steve came around the corner. "Bad news," he said, holding up the phone. "That was Maggie. She got a call from Andrew. The police found fibers from Donna's clothes on Earl's truck. He's been arrested."

Chapter Ten

Earl's predicament hadn't sat well with me; and my sleep had been restless. Watching him with his grandson that night at bingo, I'd seen genuine caring. People who have a heart don't just hit someone and drive off and leave them. At least that's what I wanted to believe. After showering, I was on the phone to Mrs. R telling her the news of Earl. She was the first on our informal phone tree. She'd call Mrs. T to tell her the news. Mrs. T and Mrs. M live together. One of them would call Mrs. B. If no one became sidetracked we'd all know about Earl within fifteen minutes.

I felt like we needed to step up our game, so to speak. Earl shouldn't be sitting in jail. Hopefully soon, The Ladies would come up with a plan.

My day would be spent itemizing the inventory from Donna's estate. It took us three trips the previous evening to move all Donna's furniture into the store. Thankfully, Jake and Steve had lifted the heaviest items and placed them up front. When I arrived, my mother was in the office, grinding coffee beans.

"You're here early," I said.

"I needed to be here to accept a delivery," she said.

"What delivery?" I asked.

She walked into the hallway and opened the storage door. Against the wall was a chest freezer, already plugged in and humming.

I opened it; it was empty.

"You planning on buying bulk meat?" I asked hopefully.

"No, but I need a place for my zucchini."

"You have plenty of room in your garage for a freezer," I said, stating what I thought would be obvious.

"But if I keep it here, you can have easy access to it. You never know when you might need zucchini, or zucchini bread."

I forced a smile and reminded myself that my mother worked here for free. She rarely asked for favors, so if she wanted to keep frozen bread in my storage room, why should I mind?

A heard a voice calling out hello from the front of the store. Maggie stood at the counter. She had on a peach tank top, beige shorts and flip-flops. A pair of sunglasses sat on top of her head, keeping her hair away from her face. She removed her backpack and placed it on the counter.

"So what can I help you with today?" I asked.

She looked down, placing a hand on her pack. Chipped black nail polish covered her short fingernails. "Can you find out stuff about people? You know, as a private eye?"

"It matters what kind of stuff you're looking for. I'd start with an internet search, just like anyone would."

Her mouth pulled down at the corners. "I tried that." She reached up and rubbed at the back of her neck. "This person has a common name."

"After that, I'd ask questions."

"I can't do that."

"Would you like to tell me what this is about?" I asked.

"Someone is blackmailing someone I know, and I want to get something on this person to make them stop."

I squinted at her. Thankfully, my morning coffee had kicked in so I could decipher her meaning. "So you want to blackmail a blackmailer?"

She nodded.

"What did this person do?" I asked. I put my elbows on the counter and rested my chin on my hands.

"It involves me, too. If I tell you something, do I get a private eye-client confidentiality agreement?"

"Did you or this person murder someone?"

"No."

"Can you go to jail for what happened?"

"Not me, but the other person could." Maggie twisted a silver ring on her index finger. "I mean, nobody got hurt. It's stupid, really."

I stood up straight. Two people do something; one can go to jail, but the other can't? This sounded like some kind of riddle.

"Patricia!" A male voice came from the back of the store. "I brought some more things. Where do you want them?"

"Oh, no. That's my dad," Maggie said. "What's he doing here?"

"He's dropping off stuff for me to sell."

"Don't tell him I was here. He has enough to deal with right now." She hauled her backpack onto her shoulder and sprinted to the door.

I ran after her, catching up with her on the sidewalk.

She looked up at me, with an exasperated expression. "Look, never mind. I shouldn't have asked," she said.

I paused for a moment, that feeling of fear for her coming over me. "Does this have anything to do with you getting hit on your bike? Is someone trying to hurt you?"

"I don't think so. I didn't see who that was." She bit her upper lip.

"Did Donna use a notebook at work?" I asked, taking a wild guess.

Maggie nodded. "I got it for her last Christmas. Why?"

"What did she use it for?"

"Keeping track of dogs," Maggie said.

"Oh?"

"She said dogs were the most difficult part of her job. So she made notes of where the aggressive dogs were and, if she could, she'd speak with the owners, and ask if she could give the dogs treats."

"Huh," I grunted, wondering if she made other notes.

She moved her sunglasses down to cover her eyes. "I've got to get to the museum," she said. "I'm going to be late."

I went back and found Steve and my mother struggling to maneuver a large cardboard box into the storage room.

"I see you've met my mother," I said.

"Yes," Steve replied, "and thank you, Genevieve."

"Are there more boxes?" I asked.

He nodded, and the three of us headed out into the alley.

"A friend loaned me his car," he said. "But I only have it for a few hours."

At the rear of an old hatchback, my mom peaked into one of Steve's boxes and did a double eyebrow lift.

Steve reached around her and pulled the box out. "One man's trash is another man's treasure," he said, grinning.

As Steve disappeared into the store, my mom said, "Have you ever noticed it's usually the person with the trash that makes that comment?"

Mitsy called late that afternoon to inform me of Hubby's itinerary for the evening. He planned to leave the house around 6:30, stop for gas, then go directly to bingo at the Mastodon Association. Bingo didn't start until 7:30. I hoped Hubby was telling the truth. But if Hubby's evening plans involved large dogs and Frisbee throwing in his quest to adopt a new pet, I'd need to come up with a lie to tell Mitsy. And on the outside chance Hubby was seeing another woman, I might need to do some real sleuthing. In that case I'd prefer not to go it alone. So I asked Mrs. Miller to accompany me in my pursuit. She owned a wonderful high-powered camera with a telephoto lens.

My Honda Civic was actually a pretty good stake out car. Small and generic, it easily blended into a residential neighborhood. Joining me, Mrs. Miller carried a black gym bag. As usual, she smelled faintly of marijuana. I gave her Mitsy's address; and she used her phone to provide directions. I filled her in on Hubby's dilemma of picking out a dog to surprise Mitsy, as well as Mitsy's belief that Hubby was chasing other women.

Mitsy and Hubby's house sat on the corner of a busy street. Next to the garage ran an alley. It dawned on me that Donna lived on the next street.

"You know we're close to Donna's house," I said.

"How close?"

"They share this alley."

"Maybe Mitsy knew her as more than just her mail carrier," she said.

"When I heard Mitsy talking about Donna, she only mentioned seeing her at the store," I said.

"I wonder if Hubby knew she lived this close," said Mrs. M. "That would be an easy way to see someone, sneak out the back, say you're going to be tinkering in the garage, run over there, run back."

"I can't see Donna fooling around with Hubby, but Mitsy thinks he's fooling around with someone."

We parked kitty-corner to view both the front of the house and the garage. Hubby and Mitsy's new Mini Cooper sat at the curb. When Hubby came out and jumped in the car, Mitsy's face appeared at the window. She made no indication that she'd seen us.

We followed Hubby to the Mastodon Association, where he promptly entered the building. I sighed, it was all very anticlimactic. The only thing I could report was that he forgot to stop for gas.

"Well," I said, picking up my phone. "I'll give Mitsy a call. Then we can go in."

Mrs. M glanced at her watch and put her hand on my arm. "We still have plenty of time before they start calling numbers. Why don't we go back to Mitsy's? You can call her from there. Let's see what she does."

"My, you're suspicious," I said.

Mrs. M smiled sweetly as she unzipped her gym bag and pulled out the case holding her camera.

We returned to Mitsy's house and parked a few doors down within easy view of her garage.

"Mitsy," I said into the phone. "It's Patricia. Your husband went directly to the Mastodon's Association."

"Dang him! He told me he was going to get gas. The games don't start for another 45 minutes." Mitsy sighed heavily into the phone. "He's probably flirting with the woman who runs the cantina." She paused. "So what's he doing now?"

I wasn't sure if Hubby really was the playboy that Mitsy portrayed him as, or if she was letting her imagination get the best of her.

"Well, we're out in the parking lot."

"Go inside, I want to see what he's up to."

I put my hand over the phone's speaker and whispered: "She wants me to go inside and see what he's doing."

Mrs. M started to giggle.

I waited a minute then told Mitsy: "He's at the cantina."

"Really? He's ordering?" she asked.

"Yes," I paused for effect. "Now he's pulling out his wallet."

"Grrrrr," Mitsy replied.

Again, I put my hand over the speaker and whispered

to Mrs. M: "She's growling."

Mrs. M continued to giggle. I turned away; I didn't want to catch her laughter.

"That little weasel," Mitsy said. "I made us a nice meat loaf and he ate only a few bites. He told me he was trying to cut back."

Ish. I'd just given Mitsy another pretend reason to be mad at him. "Do you want me to call you at break and give you an update?" I asked.

"No, just take some notes and call me tomorrow."

"Okay." I hung up. "That's odd. She doesn't want me to call her till tomorrow."

Mrs. M took the camera out of the case, attached the long zoom lens to the front, and pointed it at the house. "I've got a feeling," she said.

"Of what?" I asked.

"Of that," she replied. Mitsy's garage door slid open to reveal two vehicles. Mrs. Miller's camera clicked. "I think she has somewhere to go."

A small truck was parked next to a car that looked older than Mrs. R's Cadillac. It was large and bulky with big rounded fenders. Even from this distance, I could tell it needed a paint job.

Mrs. M snapped a few more shots. "Sure would be nice to get a look at the front end of that big car," she said. "You know a car that size could take out a person and keep going without so much as a hiccup."

The little truck backed out. I started up my car to follow. Mitsy drove cautiously, while having an animated conversation with what looked like an empty passenger seat. I'm sure it was Kiki she was speaking to. We followed Mitsy for a few blocks before she pulled into a burger joint that had been in existence since the 1950s. Mitsy held Kiki close to her chest as she walked to the sliding window to order.

I parked across the street next to Walnut Park. On this warm summer evening, it buzzed with activity. The picnic tables were filled with adults and children of all ages. One group of kids made oversized bubbles from a flat dish of soap, using a plastic ring that must have been at least eighteen inches across. A woman walked by in a skin-tight tank top and shorts. She wore an ear bud while pumping her arms. Almost everyone had a dog—on leash and off, playing, running and yipping.

While Mitsy waited for her order, Mrs. M got out and walked to the restaurant's parking lot to inconspicuously look at the front of Mitsy's truck. When she returned she said: "The front end looks fine, and dirty enough not to have been repaired recently." She scratched the palm of her hand. "Let's go play bingo. My palm itches—I'm coming into money."

While I considered whether we should head back, a full-sized truck, with dually back wheels pulled in and parked next to Mitsy's. A tall man with sandy hair— probably in his early thirties—dressed in blue jeans and a white shirt got out of the truck and put down a small dog.

"Is that another Chinese Hairless?" I asked.

Mrs. Miller lifted her camera, pointed the long lens at the dog, and looked through the view finder. "Yep." She abruptly put down the camera. "Oh, that's disgusting."

"What is?"

She handed the camera over, and I looked at the guy through the view finder. His shirt was clean and tucked in, his zipper was up, and his dog had the same combination of cute and ugly as Kiki. "I don't see anything."

"Look at the back of his truck."

I shifted the camera. "I see a bumper sticker with a paw—"

"—under the license plate," she instructed.

I adjusted the zoom lens. Hanging below the bumper were what looked like a pair of shiny silver testicles. "Eeww, are those what I think they are?" I scrunched up my face and leaned my head against the window. "You're right, that is disgusting. Okay, I'm ready to go now."

"Wait, those two know each other."

My focus returned to Mitsy. She had also placed Kiki on the ground. I looked through the camera again. The little dog sported with more bling than a pop star. Her collar sparkled as if decorated in diamonds, while her body harness and leash glistened with blue and green rhinestones. A small anklet, also in matching blue and green, encircled her delicate leg. Mitsy and the man stood talking, while Kiki and his dog did the canine dance of sniffing noses and behinds.

Mitsy, the man, and their dogs crossed the street to the park. They carried sodas and a bag of food. They plopped down across from each other at a picnic bench. Mitsy reached into her purse and pulled out a rectangular metal object and handed it to her friend.

"What is that?" Mrs. M asked.

"Looks like—" I looked through the camera again. "It's a flask."

The man poured some of the contents into his drink, then passed it back. She did the same.

"They're nipping at the rum." Mrs. M giggled. "They must know each other pretty well. Do you think they're having an affair?"

"A May-December romance?" I shook my head. "Mitsy runs a business. I doubt she'd have the time."

We continued to watch as Mitsy and her male friend munched on French fries. Eventually, the man reached into his front shirt pocket and unfolded a sheet of paper. They talked for a while. Then Mitsy wrote on the paper, handed it back, dug into her purse, and handed him some cash.

"I wonder if Mitsy's buying a stud service," I said. "Maybe she wants Kiki to be a mom."

Kiki and her new canine friend sat on the grass behind Mitsy. A brown-and-white Chihuahua mix wandered over, and the sniffing and nose rubbing started again. But this dog was a bit more amorous and ran around Kiki a few times before jumping on her back side.

"Ah, oh," Mrs. M said. "Looks like Kiki's playing the field."

Mitsy suddenly noticed the action and jumped up. "No! Bad dog! No!" she yelled. The interloper ignored Mitsy, intent on his mission. Mitsy hopped around them waving her arms, trying to separate the two dogs with her foot. But not until the little Don Juan had completed his task did he disengage from Kiki and trot off.

Mitsy pointed at her friend's dog. The guy shrugged.

"With Hubby out shopping for a new dog, and Kiki making puppies, those two bookstore owners are soon going to have more dogs than books. Let's go," I said. By this point I'd seen enough. In fact, I'd seen more than I wanted to.

***

The Mastodon building's auditorium had wood paneled walls, vinyl tiled floors, and oil paintings of mastodons that didn't look much different from modern elephants, except they had hairy bodies and smaller ears. For years the Mastodon Association had been a male-only organization, their rituals shrouded in secrecy and their purpose for existence shrouded in even more secrecy. But sometime in the 1980s they opened their doors to women and found their purpose. They raised money for local charities such as a library bookmobile, Meals on Wheels, and the local pet shelters.

I looked around the large auditorium and didn't see a memorial for Donna. Maybe the Mastodon Association wasn't as demonstrative as the Lakeville Senior Center, or maybe they had even bigger things in mind. Mrs. B, Mrs. T, and my mother had already arrived. Mrs. R had declined our invitation, saying she had other plans. Mrs. M and I paid $30 to get six bingo cards and sat down next to my mom, who'd saved us seats.

Harvey and Judy came out on stage. "Welcome everyone," Harvey said. The screech of feedback drown out the rest of his words. He stepped back from the microphone. "Is that better?"

A few voices yelled back: "Yeah."

I leaned over to Mrs. M. "So Harvey and Judy call here too," I whispered.

"Yeah, they call at most games," she said.

"Before the games begin," Harvey continued. "I'd like to remind everyone that we're two weeks away from the Chili Cook-off. There are flyers on the back table with details. And as you all know we've lost a dear friend.

Donna has passed, and we will be raising money for a memorial garden and fountain that will be built on the south corner of the building. Please see Robby if you'd like to contribute."

A smattering of applause rose and tapered off.

"Since we have so many folks here tonight, the pots have gone up as you can see." He pointed to a chalkboard next to him, as Judy erased old numbers and put up new. "Okay, let's get going."

Harold began calling out numbers, and my mind wondered. It had been exactly a week since Donna's death. Was this the same crowd that had attended that night? Were we playing bingo with a killer?

As the night wore on, my mother won a bingo. So did Mrs. M. Finally, Harold called the last game. My mother volunteered to drive The Ladies home so I could stay behind and snoop. I leaned up against a wall in the lobby and waited until most of the attendees had left. Sauntering over to the cantina I surveyed the desserts. A woman wearing a red apron over jeans and a white T-shirt scrubbed at a grill, her brown pony tail swinging in rhythm to her movements.

"Can I still buy a cookie?" I asked.

She looked over her shoulder, and then joined me at the counter. "Sure, they're three bucks each."

I judged her to be in her mid-forties, she had a friendly face with sweet brown eyes. A plastic name tag said "Roxanne."

I picked out a snickerdoodle and unwrapped it from the cellophane. "Do you mind if I ask you a question?"

"Sure."

"Anything out of the ordinary happen during last

weeks' bingo game?"

"Hmm," she said, "they spent too much time talking about the Chili Cook-off. They do one every year. You'd think they'd have the kinks worked out by now. Why do you ask?"

"I moonlight as a private investigator; I'm looking into Donna's death."

Her eyes got big. If I was going to keep this up, I might need Mrs. B to print me out some fake business cards.

"I thought Earl had been arrested. What's there to investigate?"

Thankfully, Judy, the woman who helped Harvey with the bingo numbers, appeared and went through the door into the kitchen, interrupting Roxanne's train of thought. Close up, I judged Judy to be in her late fifties. She was easily my height and had a thin nose that gave her a noble look. Thick red-framed glasses sat on top her head. "What can I help you with, Roxanne?" she asked.

"All the extra buns need to be put into those boxes. Thanks, Judy."

"Hey, you're my ride. The quicker you're done, the quicker there's pie," Judy said. "Did you see that Andrew's here tonight?" Roxanne nodded her head. "Surprising, with what's happened to Earl."

"That's devotion for ya, isn't it?" Roxanne smiled. "Showing up to do his grandpa's volunteer job." She looked to me. "No wins for you tonight?"

"No," I replied. "I just made a donation."

A few people still hung out in the lobby. I took another bite of cookie and watched Andrew sweep the floor. Devotion was one reason Andrew might have shown up tonight; the other was he might not like being at home by himself. Cece stood next to the garbage cans containing the recycling. Luckily, I had successfully avoided Cece that evening and the inevitable sales pitch she'd throw at me for some car she wanted me to buy.

"Oh, I almost forgot," Roxanne said, bringing back my attention to her. "Last week we had a fire."

"Fire? You had a fire here?" This revelation caught me by surprise. I blurted out the words loud enough for Cece to hear. She turned her head, watching me, but from her angle she couldn't see into the kitchen. She bent over the black plastic bag, gathering together the ends, then took her time fiddling with the twist tie on the top.

"Out in the dumpster," Roxanne continued. She leaned forward across the counter and spotted Cece. She lowered her voice, "Wasn't anything big. Easily contained is what the fireman said. Someone probably tossed a cigarette butt in it. But I think it was Andrew."

"Why Andrew?"

"Before bingo started, I'd gone outside for a little fresh air, and I saw him over by the dumpster. His back was to me, but his head was down, and I could see a light, like he was lighting a cigarette." She chuckled. "Or a joint." Her eyebrows went straight up.

"But it couldn't have been him," Judy said. "The fire didn't start until a couple of hours later."

"Maybe it just smoldered for a while before it took hold," Roxanne replied. "Plus, he was late for pie."

"Late for pie?" I repeated. This was the second time pie had been mentioned.

"There's a whole bunch of us that go for pie after bingo."

Judy joined us at the counter, leaned over and checked out the room. Cece and Andrew had left.

"Well, we were all late for pie, Roxanne," said Judy. "Having to wait for the firemen, then standing around talking, trying to figure out what happened."

"That's true, but Andrew was even later than we were," said Roxanne. "Andrew had dropped off Earl earlier in the evening, but he was coming back to the restaurant to have dessert and drive Earl home, but he came in after we'd ordered."

"Oh?" I interjected.

"Andrew smelled like pot when he got to the restaurant," Roxanne said, "and acted so embarrassed. When I spoke to him; he wouldn't make eye contact. That's not like him at all. I still say he started that fire, but, whatever he was upset about, it didn't affect his appetite. He had two pieces of pie and a vanilla milkshake." She shook her head. "Wish I could eat like that. I don't even eat all my pie, and it still goes straight to my hips." She held out another cookie to me. "You like oatmeal and raisin?"

I shook my head.

"Dang that bookstore guy," she continued. "What's his name? I can never remember." She tossed the cookie back with the others. "Anyway, I buy these special for him, and tonight he only bought a coffee. Said something about cutting back. Diets are bad for business."

Judy leaned on the counter and watched Cece grab another garbage bag and head back outside.

"Cece takes care of the recycling," Judy said, using air quotes around the words "care of," then rolling her eyes. "She puts the recycling into her car and cashes in the cans for money. We have a recycle bin outside here. I don't know if she feels like she has to pull her weight so she can come for pie or she just wants the recycling money. But she doesn't have to do anything. It's just pie."

I wanted to walk the same route that Donna had taken on her last night, so I headed outside and down the sidewalk. A few others were out, walking dogs and enjoying the evening air. It was garbage night, and each house had three different colored cans at the curb: grey for regular garbage, blue for recycling and green for yard waste. Two blocks from my mom's, I glanced down a short cul-de-sac with maybe six or seven houses. A white car that looked like Cece's was parked at the curb. I heard a noise and stepped behind a tree to observe.

Someone stood on a stepstool, bending over and rummaging through a blue trash bin. A head popped up. It was Cece. With gloved hands, she dropped a soda can and a liter sized plastic bottle into a garbage bag, then continued to dig. I wondered why someone who had a job would take the time to make a few bucks stealing recycling.

Movement caught my eye, and I could see another person using a flashlight to dig in another bin.

"Ow, dammit!" came a male voice.

"Shut up, Andrew," Cece hissed. "You want us to get caught out here?"

The light illuminated Andrew as he examined his hand. "I cut my finger," he said.

"You sure are clumsy. I'm surprised you've lived this long."

Why on earth would Andrew be helping Cece? Was

she paying him? That wouldn't make sense; a person wouldn't make enough on recycling to hire a helper.

At the risk of enduring Cece's sales pitch, I decided to wander over and talk to them.

"Evening," I said.

Cece's head popped up, and her eyes squinted into slits. She didn't say anything. I nodded at Andrew. His eyes grew large. He looked guilty as hell.

"Cece, did you see Donna walking home the night she was hit?" I asked.

"No." She shook her head. "Why? You think I hit her? See any dents on the front of my car?" She pointed to her hood, but since I'd already checked it out, I knew it looked fine.

"No, I just thought you may have seen her talking to someone."

Cece's overly friendly sales persona went into hiding. She gave me her version of the if-looks-could-kill stare. "We meet for pie after bingo. That's where I was, not running my friend down." She snorted.

"But I heard you were late for pie."

At that statement, Andrew returned to digging in the bin.

Cece looked at me and shrugged. "I might have stopped to pick up some recycling."

Both Andrew and Cece were late for pie that night. If Cece had hit Donna, she'd had the car repaired, but where? Could she have gone to Marin County? I sighed. Unless I was willing to contact every auto body shop within a 100 mile radius, that line of thought would lead me nowhere.

"Enjoy your evening," I said and returned to my walk.

A figure appeared around the corner with a dog. As they got closer I realized it was Richard.

"Where's your mother tonight?" he asked.

"We went to bingo. I just needed some air."

"I hear ya," he replied. Richard's little dog, Cleopatra, circled him, the leash wrapping around his legs like a tetherball rope.

"Richard, have you ever seen a woman driving a Prius and collecting recycling when you're out walking?"

"I often see people digging through the trash bins. I don't know what kind of car they drive. I assumed they were on foot."

"Did you see anyone last Tuesday?"

"No. I would have made a note of that."

"Do you walk the same route every night?" I asked.

"No, I like to mix it up a bit." He spun in a circle, untangled his dog. "Well, better keep moving, got to keep the heart rate up. Bay to Breakers is only ten months away." He gave me a thumb's up and continued down the sidewalk.

After turning down my mom's street, I examined the road in front of her house. There were no skid marks on the asphalt. Her house was the third from the corner, and for whatever reason, Donna had chosen this spot to cross the street. A car coming from either direction should have seen her and had time to break. The car came around the corner and sped up, aiming for Donna, catching her by surprise—unless it was as Steve thought: the driver was drunk and not paying attention. But it made more sense to me that the person driving the car followed her, waited for a chance, and got it when Donna crossed the street.

I felt cold at that scenario, cold and scared.

Chapter Eleven

I guessed at the breakfast menu before I opened my eyes: sticky buns, eggs of some sort, and a large pot of fresh ground coffee. The Ladies making me breakfast lifted my spirits. After a quick shower, I dressed in blue jeans, a T-shirt, and a lightweight pale-teal jacket. No pajamas covered with dancing sheep were going to greet The Ladies today.

Mrs. B put a mug of coffee in front of me and slid the organic cream across the table. This morning she had on a soft-yellow cardigan over a yellow blouse.

Our two investigation easels held new pictures of Donna.

"Where did those come from?" I asked.

"That first one is from the photo-booth picture, you've seen that one. The others I found on Donna's Facebook page," Mrs. M said, sporting a maroon dahlia in her hair that reminded me of Animal, the drummer from the Muppet Show.

The photo-booth picture of Earl and Donna had been blown up. They were both smiling. Another showed

Donna with a microphone in her hand, singing in what looked like a nightclub. The last one was of Donna and Maggie at a restaurant. Donna had her arm draped around Maggie's shoulder. Maggie smiled, but her eyes looked off to the side, not at the camera.

"Don't Donna and Earl look happy there," Mrs. T said. She didn't have a hat on this morning, I surmised that it was in the living room, probably too big to wear to the breakfast table.

Mrs. R placed a platter of homemade pull-apart cinnamon rolls right in front of me. I grabbed a hunk and took a bite. The other three followed my lead.

"Okay, who has something to report?" Mrs. R asked.

No one answered. We all had doughy sweetness in our mouths. I wanted to swoon as an expression of pure sugary-cinnamon delight. I was flanked by Mrs. B and Mrs. T, who seemed to be in their own states of edible bliss. Mrs. M purred.

Mrs. R looked at us, sat down, and popped a bite of cinnamon roll in her mouth. Her eyes narrowed as she slowly chewed. She got the picture: no one should be asked to concentrate when indulging in such decadence.

I cleared my palate with a swig of coffee and broke the silence. "So what does everyone think about Earl being arrested?"

"Earl's a sweetheart," Mrs. Taylor said. "There's no way he did this. I know he didn't. There has to be another explanation."

"What about Andrew?" I asked.

"Same thing with Andrew," Mrs. T said. "He's a nice kid."

"But if Earl or Andrew didn't hit her," Mrs. M said,

"how did threads from Donna's clothes get on the windshield wiper of Earl's truck?"

"My mom went to a yard sale at Earl's house recently," I said. "There would have been tons of people. Anyone could have snuck into his garage and planted threads on his truck."

"Not just anyone," Mrs. Russo said, "but the person who ran down Donna and now wants to pin it on Earl—or Andrew." Her mouth turned into a thin line. "You know what this means, don't you? Planting evidence isn't the act of an accidental hit-and-run. An accidental hit-and-run wouldn't even know who they hit, no less where to plant evidence to mislead the police. No, planting evidence is an act of a guilty person. And only the guilty person would have access to threads pulled from the actual vehicle that hit Donna."

"I asked Beatrice to run some information on Earl," I said. For a split second, I thought I saw approval on Mrs. R's face.

"Tell us the high points," she said.

"Earl has a terrible driving record," I explained. "And I think his bad eyesight is partly to blame. If he hit Donna, it could have been an accident."

Mrs. T nodded in agreement. "But Earl doesn't drive at night anymore," Mrs. T said. "We need to keep digging."

Mrs. R and Mrs. T exchanged glances. "Go ahead and tell them," Mrs. R said.

"Sunny and I are going to Earl's arraignment tomorrow to post bail," Mrs. T said. "Or at least we're going to try."

"You may have to put up collateral," Mrs. B said.

"Are you sure you want to do that?"

"I own my house, free and clear, so if it comes to that, yes," Mrs. T replied. "That's how strongly I feel he's innocent."

Mrs. M stared at her plate and adjusted the dahlia behind her ear. Since she lived with Mrs. Taylor, she might not be so excited to gamble her place of residence for Earl's freedom. The idea of Mrs. T losing her house made my stomach turn. We needed to find the real killer, and fast.

"Okay," said Mrs. R, "what else do we have?"

"At the funeral, I overheard two women talking about Donna being investigated by the Post Office," I said, "for mail tampering." I took a swig of coffee. "But two nights ago I talked with some neighbor kids at Donna's. There's a good-sized hole in the back of her fence that's hidden behind a shed. The kids said they found packages in the alley. And if they're telling the truth, someone was playing a mean joke on Donna— taking her packages from her truck and hiding them, making it look like she'd lost or stolen them."

"Why were you at Donna's house?" Mrs. R asked. "When you called about Earl, I never did get an explanation as to why you were with Steve."

"Steve hired me to sell some of Donna's furniture," I said.

"Oh, well, now we're getting somewhere," Mrs. B said, rubbing her hands together.

"You're doing business with a suspect?" Mrs. R asked, not pleased.

Before I had a chance to reply, Mrs. B came to my defense. "Now, there are risks, Sunny, but if it's handled right, we could get some good information."

Mrs. R's face did not reflect confidence in me "handling it right."

"Yes," I said, "I understand I'm walking a thin line here. But last night, I had the opportunity to spend time at Donna's house, and because of that I got to talk to the neighbor kids."

"But how would packages disappearing play into Donna getting run down?" asked Mrs. R.

"I don't know," I said, baffled.

Mrs. T got up and grabbed the coffee pot.

"Did Mrs. T tell you we saw Helena and Steve together?" I asked the group.

The women nodded in unison.

"That doesn't look good for Steve," Mrs. B said. "Not good at all."

"Or for Helena," I said. "She drives an ancient truck as big as a house, and according to my mother's friend Richard, there was an old truck in the area that night."

As Mrs. T refilled Mrs. R's mug, she looked at me across the table and raised an eyebrow. It took me a second to realize I'd just deflected attention away from Steve.

"I wonder how long Helena and Steve have been seeing each other," Mrs. M said.

"I doubt their feelings for each other just materialized this last week. If Steve wanted to hold on to Donna's money, either one of them—or both of them— could have run Donna down," said Mrs. T.

Mrs. Miller pursed her lips and said something in Spanish, which I didn't understand, but I got the gist. Any way you cut it, it wasn't a pretty picture.

"So what's our next step?" Mrs. B asked.

"Rita made a good point, I'd like to find out how long Steve and Helena have been seeing each other," Mrs. R said. "But more importantly, how serious it their relationship."

"I say we break into Steve's house," Mrs. B said.

"Why don't we send him something that says he's won a free house cleaning," Mrs. M suggested.

"But he'd still have to call us and make an appointment. That could take precious time," Mrs. B said. "We'll do our maid routine; we've got everything set."

"How are you going to get in?" I asked.

"If I can't find a hide-a-key, I'll pick the back door lock," said Mrs. B. "And if we get caught, we'll say we got the wrong address and the back door was unlocked. He's a man." She gave a dismissive wave. "He'll never remember if he locked the doors."

Later that morning, when I opened up Elsie's Antiques, three men stood shoulder-to-shoulder outside the front door, each holding a coffee cup. One had a newspaper tucked under his arm. They waved enthusiastically when they saw me.

The men were tall and thin, all bald, and each sported a unique dark-brown mustache. The one on the left wore a horseshoe, which was full and bushy, hanging just below his jaw line. The one in the middle had whiskers that made a straight horizontal line seeming to defy gravity, spreading at least ten inches from waxy tip to waxy tip. The man on the right had a mustache that also was horizontal, but the ends curled around to make a circle. He looked like a barbershop singer from the 1930s. Their facial features were so similar I took them to be brothers. Dressed alike in army green coveralls and purple belts, they reminded me of a clump of asparagus.

"We heard you have Donna's sofa," the one with the horseshoe mustache said.

The other two nodded eagerly.

I pulled the door open for them and pointed to the plaid couch. Donna's furniture was arranged into a space resembling a living room, complete with coffee table and lamps. Her dining table sat close by, and her desk was against the wall. They came in, moving in unison, and sat down, spaced evenly to fill the sofa from end to end. The man with the horseshoe mustache removed the newspaper from under his arm, opened it, and handed sections to the other two, kept one for himself, and tossed what remained onto the coffee table.

As I propped open the front door, Hubby crossed the street from his bookstore. He also carried a mug of coffee.

"I heard you have Donna's sofa," he said.

Again I pointed.

"Is your mom here?" he asked.

I looked down the hallway. The storeroom door was open and the light was on. I gestured that direction. "Looks like it," I said.

Hubby plodded down the hall. A few moments later my mother appeared, went straight to one of my china cabinets, pulled out a large serving platter, and disappeared back down the hallway. Hubby reappeared, carrying the platter full of sliced bread and a stack of napkins.

Was that zucchini bread?

He offered the other men a slice then placed the plate on Donna's coffee table and sat down on Donna's matching chair. It looked like I was hosting a party.

"What else was Donna's?" Hubby asked.

"Anything that has a round green sticker," I said. "This coffee table, the end tables, the loveseat, also the dining table and chairs. Plus some of these other odds and ends." As I gestured to the items, the men ogled them.

"So what can I help you with?" I asked Hubby.

"Nothing. We're fine. Thank you," he said, taking a bite of his snack. "Tell your mom she makes excellent zucchini bread."

One of the men cleared his throat, but no one made eye contact. It was obvious I was being dismissed.

I slipped behind the counter and sat on a stool. I fought the urge to confront my mother over the whole zucchini bread thing. I hadn't realized she'd actually started baking, but that would have to be dealt with later. I pulled out a pad of paper to sketch on while I waited for something to happen. After a few minutes, I glanced up at the men. They hadn't moved. I felt totally confused by what was happening.

Then another man entered. "Good morning," I called out.

He nodded in response and picked up one of Donna's dining room chairs and put it down next to Hubby. The man with the curlicue mustache handed the newcomer a section of paper.

I watched, feeling like I was on a safari and should have been snapping pictures, rather than just staring. For the next fifteen minutes, men continued to stream in the front door, until the room was full. I recognized many of the men from the previous evening at the Mastodon Association. Each one received section of newspaper, but because of their numbers, a few men read only a single page or perused an ad insert. The zucchini bread was disappearing rapidly.

I came out from behind the counter and slowly approached the group. I didn't want to scare them.

"Is there anything I can get you gentlemen?" I realized I sounded like a waitress, so I added, "Answer any questions?"

The man with the straight horizontal mustache sitting in the center of the couch glanced up looking startled. He turned his head to one brother then the other, but when they showed no interest, he then shook his head so violently that the tips of his mustache slapped against his cheeks.

I backed away slowly, returned to my post, and crouched down behind the counter. I called Mrs. T. With her education in psychology, if anyone could understand what was going on, it would be her.

"Mrs. T," I whispered into the phone. "It's me."

"Patricia dear, I can hardly hear you."

"I can't talk any louder. There's a bunch of men in my store."

"I'm assuming you're not in some kind of physical danger, or you would have called the police."

"Well, there's at least fifteen," I did a quick estimate in my head, "or twenty now, and they're all having coffee and zucchini bread." I mustered as much exasperation as I could in a whisper. "And reading the newspaper."

She hesitated before replying: "So, how can I help?"

"I want you to find out what they want. It has something to do with Donna's furniture."

"Have you tried approaching them?"

"Yes, but they won't talk to me. I'm afraid I'll spook them, and my store's too small to handle a stampede."

"Okay, I'll be right there."

I got back on my stool in time to see Hubby coming out of the hallway with a second plate of zucchini bread and more napkins. At this rate, they'd never leave.

Fifteen minutes later Mrs. T arrived, wearing a large floppy hat covered in pink silk roses. She brought her cane to play up her non-threatening persona. She glanced around the room, then slowly made her way to the counter.

"Okay," she said to me, speaking just above a whisper. "All these men are members of the Mastodon Association. And the three Bobs are fighting for control."

"The three Bob's?" I asked.

"The men on the couch, they're triplets," Mrs. T said. "Robert, Robby, and Bob. And currently," she said, "the power structure is out of balance. Robert, he's on the left, the one with the horseshoe mustache, is usually the most dominant."

"Like the alpha male?" I asked.

"Exactly. Robert has been president of the Mastodon Association for the last two years. But a few weeks ago, Bob, the one on the right with the curlicue mustache, was elected president. It was quite an upset; he won by a write-in campaign."

I winced. "Ouch."

She nodded, then glanced back to the group. "Now, Robby, the one in the center with the horizontal mustache is trying to keep the peace between them." She took a deep breath. "I'll have to go in closer to make a better assessment."

Mrs. T circled the group at a safe distance. Robby made eye contact and nodded. Mrs. T slowly moved to the coffee table and picked up a single sheet of an ad for the local hardware store. It was wrinkled after being handed around. She stared at it intensely. Hubby stood up and offered her his seat. She thanked him and sat down.

After a few moments, I saw Mrs. T holding up the advertisement to Hubby and pointing at a picture. While looking up at him, she asked a question. Hubby leaned forward and also pointed at the ad, then began whispering while Mrs. T nodded her head encouragingly. It appeared that she had successfully infiltrated the group.

My door jangled, and I looked up to see Jimmy Chang in a dark navy suit. He stared at the group as he came over and leaned on the counter. He removed his toothpick holder, opened it and tapped out a pick with a green cellophane frill at one end. He tipped the container my direction and raised an eyebrow. I shook my head.

"What's with the geezer fest?" he asked.

"Shhh, Jimmy. I don't know, but it has something to do with Donna's furniture."

"Ohhh, so you did con Steve into letting you sell her stuff," he said, nodding his approval. "Has anyone offered to buy anything?"

"No, not yet."

"So they're just sitting here, reading the paper."

"Yep, and eating zucchini bread."

"You need to take charge of this," Jimmy said. "I'd suggest an auction."

"Why?"

"Let's pit these guys against each other. They look too comfortable. Besides you owe it to Steve to get the best price."

"We're working out a flat price for the furniture."

"Well, you need to get the best price for you then."

"But I don't know how to run an auction."

Jimmy removed his toothpick and smiled. "I do."

I cringed. "What would you charge for your services? If we cleared $1,000, I'd be surprised."

"Oh, with this type of interest, that's way low. How about this," he said, pointing in the air with his toothpick. "I'll do the auction for you, and I get to keep your Monet repro."

He was referring to a painting of boats at sunrise that I'd reproduced. He'd swiped it from my house, and had promised to return it, but so far it seemed to have slipped his mind. For me, the painting was just an exercise. I didn't care if I got it back or not.

"It's your choice," Jimmy said, while chewing on his pick.

Mrs. T placed the ad on the coffee table and slowly made her way over to us. She nodded a hello at Jimmy.

In a low voice she explained, "What I gather is that Robert wants to purchase all of Donna's furniture to put in the rec room of the Mastodon Association. But Bob thinks that's not the best use of their money. Robert hasn't let go of the presidency mantle. And if he doesn't concede this issue to Bob, it could send the whole Mastodon Association into chaos, forcing the members to openly take sides. Plus Robby would have to take a side. That could be devastating for their relationship."

"This feels explosive," I said. "Do you think they'd actually fight?"

Mrs. Taylor shook her head. "I doubt it; it will probably be something subtle." She sighed. "Relationships between triplets are very complicated."

Jimmy's eyebrows rose and he removed his toothpick before speaking. "Are you saying that those three guys on the couch are triplets and all have the same name?"

"Well, variations of."

Jimmy snorted. "Wow. What kind of meds did their mom get during childbirth?"

Mrs. T's eyes narrowed as she removed her large flowery hat. For a moment, I thought she was going to whop him with it. "Childbirth pain is no laughing matter, Mr. Chang."

"Sorry," Jimmy whispered. His sneer turned into a look of contrition. Mrs. T was not one to be trifled with.

She glanced at the group, and continued. "Some of the other men want a memento. The ones that are married, like the bookstore owner, think they can have a remembrance of Donna in their home without their wives realizing it."

"Jimmy thinks we should have an auction," I said.

Mrs. T nodded. "That's perfect. That would give them a cooling down period."

Jimmy stood up straight. "Is that the sport's section sitting on the table?"

I looked over. It was the only part of the paper that

hadn't been touched.

"That's it," Jimmy said. "Whoever grabs it wins."

As soon as the words had left his lips, Robert, the soon-to-be past president, leaned forward reaching for the unopened paper.

Mrs. T took in a quick breath.

"It's now or never Patty Cakes," Jimmy said. "Peace at the Mastodon Association lies in your hands."

"Do it," I said.

Jimmy stepped into the throng and cleared his throat. He was half the age of most of the men, reminding me of a young buck challenging the old studs.

"Gentlemen," he said. "Since there is so much interest in Donna's items, Ms. Schuster has decided to have an auction."

Robert's hand retreated, and all three Bobs let out a sigh. Robert would be able to back down from his pronouncement of buying all of Donna's furniture for the Mastodon Association while still saving face.

"It will be here on Saturday." He turned to look at me. I nodded in agreement. "At 10 a.m. Come by on Friday for a complete list of items to be auctioned."

There were nods all around, and newspaper sections were returned to the coffee table. Robert was the first to stand. His two brothers followed. As he walked by he said, "See you Saturday." The rest of the herd followed, walking single file.

After the men left, I pulled out the file folder that Beatrice Johnson had made up for us on Donna, and looked over the map of her postal route. I cross-referenced it with a list of crimes in the area over the last three months. Unfortunately, there were no meth labs or burglaries or any interesting criminal activity. It was mostly people doing stupid people things: DUIs, domestic abuse, and one of discharging a firearm. Two instances of real estate fraud that involved a man and woman piqued my interest, but there weren't any details.

I called out to my mother that I was going out and I heard her mumble a reply.

Donna's business delivery route was right outside my door. I looked up and down the street wondering who would be the most receptive to gossiping about Donna. The bank seemed the logical place to start since Donna was trying to get a loan, and her loan officer was the older brother of a friend from high school. I hoped he'd remember me.

Walking into the bank I found the cool air refreshing. I spotted Mitch immediately. His desk was next to a window, and he stared intensely at a computer screen. I made myself at home in his empty visitor's chair.

"Patricia, wow, it's been awhile," he said reaching out to take my hand.

We spent a few minutes catching up. Then he turned to business.

"So what can I do for you? You need a loan? Line of credit?"

Darn, I hadn't thought this far. Then I noticed a brochure entitled: 'Own Your Own Home? Get a line of credit.'

"I inherited my grandmother's house recently, and I was thinking about getting a line of credit to help with my business," I said, hoping my lie sounded plausible.

"How much do you want?" he asked.

"How much can I get?"

He smiled. "Let's fill out an application and go from there."

He typed while I gave him my vital statistics. When he hit the print button, I figured it was a good time to get in a question.

"I heard about some real estate scam going on in my mom's neighborhood," I said, hoping I sounded nonchalant.

He leaned toward me and lowered his voice. "It happened to one of our tellers. Young guy." He looked the direction of the counters, where a short line of customers stood waiting. "He saw an ad online for a room to rent and went to the house to look at it. He met a woman who said her son was at college and they were renting out his room to help pay for tuition."

"Oh?"

"So he gave them a cash deposit and signed a lease. A few days later he shows up with all his stuff to move in, and he couldn't get into the house. Turns out the couple didn't even live there. Did you know our mail lady, Donna?" I nodded. "Well, Donna just happened to be walking by and knew the owners were on vacation. When he explained the situation to her, she called the police."

"Were the police any help?"

"He gave them a description, but the last time I talked to him, they hadn't caught the couple."

"How did they get in?

"The police think a hide-a-key."

"Oh, boy," I said, thinking about how easy it was getting into Donna's house using her hide-a-key.

"Yeah, I felt for the guy. He'd been saving for

months for the deposit. You know, it would have been his first time living away from his parents. He told me Donna was trying to help him get his money back."

I sat up straight. "Really? How?"

"I don't know."

Mitch's attention moved back to business. He went over the details and said he'd give me a call in a few days to go over some numbers. I thanked him for his time.

As I stood outside the bank, thinking about how Donna could get money back from a couple scamming folks, I heard my name being called.

"Patricia! Patricia!"

I turned to see Cece waving from Green's Used Car lot across the street. She was wearing the same outfit as when I'd met her at the Senior Center: red jacket over a white shirt and jeans.

"How are you?" she called out.

After my conversation with her the previous evening, my first instinct was to wave and move on, but then I remembered that the car lot was on Donna's route. I crossed the street and Cece ran out to the sidewalk to greet me. She grabbed my hand to shake it and didn't let go until she'd dragged me into the throng of shiny parked vehicles.

"We had a Honda Accord come in yesterday," she said, "and I immediately thought about you. It gets great gas mileage."

"That's nice of you Cece, but I really can't afford a new car right now."

"Oh, nothing to worry about in that department; we offer great financing." She looked around the lot. "Now, where did it go?" She was in full-on sales mode.

"Oh, there it is," she said, pointing with one hand and reaching out to grab me with the other. But this time I was ready and had both hands firmly clutching my purse. This momentary awkwardness did not detour her big smile. Her outstretched hand went to her forehead and she brushed her bangs to the side. I noticed she had bright pink marks on her fingers; she must be buying the cheap bingo daubers that didn't wash off easily.

"Say, would you like a cup of coffee?" she asked. "One of the guys here has family in the coffee business. He brings in beans from Honduras. They're to die for."

Coffee from Honduras. Dang these salespeople with their hard-sell tactics.

A few minutes later, I stood inside the showroom, cradling a Styrofoam cup with both hands and sipping the most majestic coffee I'd ever tasted. If I had the voice to sing out an angelic high note expressing pure joy I would have.

A hurried voice came over the loud speaker asking Cece to pick up line three. She suggested I take a seat on a saggy couch next to a fake ficus tree and disappeared into an office that lined the wall. I could see her through the plate glass window, her smile looked strained as she answered the phone. Instead of sitting, I checked out the office closest to the front door. It said "Nick Rodriguez" on the name plate. It was dark, but on his desk sat three Tootsie Rolls. His office was closest to the front door. I wondered if Donna would stop and chat with Nick when she dropped off the mail. This must be the person that Jimmy mentioned who wanted to sell his used car at Jimmy's lot instead of selling it where he worked.

A long hallway led to restrooms and a waiting lounge.

On the wall were a line of photos for each salesperson, the first one showcasing the Employee of the Month. A man named Juan Garcia looked pleased to have received the honor. Cece looked pretty in her picture, without a hair out of place. Next to her was Nick's picture. He was a handsome man with dark hair and eyes. I could imagine Donna flirting with him.

Cece called my name and, gesturing to go back outside, she said: "Why don't you sit in the car and see how it feels."

The car sat in the shade of the building. I lowered myself into the driver's seat, put my feet on the paper mat, and sniffed the coffee to hide the artificial smell of pine that came from the cardboard tree sitting in the cup holder. Cece closed the door, and I leaned my head back on the rest. In the rearview mirror, I saw her move to the rear of the car and pull out her phone. The passenger window was down a few inches, enough for me to hear her making an appointment for a manicure.

Another salesmen had been watching us. Seeing Cece momentarily disengaged from me, he sauntered over to her. He wore black slacks and a tight white polo shirt that showed off some well-developed pecs.

"You going to lunch soon?" he asked.

"Maybe, matter how this works out." In the mirror I saw her jerk her thumb my direction.

"Maybe we could go together."

She turned her head away from him. "Look, I told you, I'm not ready to date yet. Nick's only been gone a few weeks."

"Lunch isn't a date. I know you and Nick went out for lunch together most days, so I thought you might like some company."

"When I'm ready for company, I'll let you know."

Without replying, the guy turned and went back inside. I'd just sucked down the last of my coffee when Cece knocked on the window. I opened the door.

"Do you want to take it for a drive?" she asked.

"Thanks, Cece, but I've got to get back to the store."

She whipped out her business card.

I put up my hand. "I have your card from the other night."

She nodded. Her mood had shifted; her bubbly demeanor was gone. It could have been my less than enthusiastic response to the car, or it could be that she'd just been reminded of her broken heart.

I walked up the alley to come in the back door of Elsie's Antiques, but I couldn't get in because there was a line of people. Far from being excited that folks were queuing up for a peek at my merchandise, I panicked.

"Excuse me," I said to a guy in jeans and a blue hoodie. "Can I get by?"

"Hey, no cutsies," he replied.

"I work here."

"Oh, could you get me two chocolate chip loaves?" He thrust a twenty dollar bill at me.

"Ah, just a minute," I told him, and squeezed by a young woman, who held tightly onto the hand of a small boy.

"We'd like some bread, please," the boy said looking up at me with big eyes. I felt as if I'd slipped into Oliver Twist's world.

I finally made it to the storeroom, where my mother

sat next to the chest freezer. A card table held a metal cash box.

"There you go," she said, handing a tall man in a business suit a five-dollar bill. The man clutched three loaves of bread wrapped in tin foil to his chest.

"Thanks," he said, "you've made my day."

"Mother," I said sternly.

She ignored me, while pulling bread from the freezer. "With chocolate chips, or without?" She asked the next customer.

"One with, one without."

"That will be $15.00."

Her customer handed over the cash.

"Mother," I said again, loudly.

"Yes, dear," she finally replied.

"Can I see you in the hallway?"

She raised her eyebrows at me, but complied.

"Mother, I can't sell food here," I whispered. "You need a special permit."

"That's why I'm selling out the back door," she said, as if this made it all okay. "Only to a few select clientele, no one will know."

"Really. You know all these people?" I asked.

"Well, I told Margaret down at the feed store, and she said she'd spread the word."

"And who's running the store?" I asked, through gritted teeth.

"I left a note," she replied, and returned to the storeroom.

"A note," I muttered, and hurried into the store.

There was no one around, but a yellow sticky note on the counter said, "I'm in the back, if you need me."

I popped opened the till with the push of one button, and let out a sigh of relief. There looked to be the same amount as I usually started with, plus some.

Cripes, I needed more coffee.

Chapter Twelve

The morning started out rough. A laundry basket sat in the corner of my closet overflowing with dirty clothes. My only clean underwear had a hole on one side, and the only clean bra I had was of the pushup nature, fire engine red, and very lacy. It was the kind of bra meant to be worn for romantic interludes, not criminal escapades. But the worst part was that I only had enough coffee for half a cup. I need one cup to function, two would have me happily buzzing like a hummingbird, and with three I hit Wonder Woman status. Half a cup did not bode well for the day.

Into the deep thigh pockets of my pink maid jumper I stuffed my phone, plastic gloves, a few zip-lock bags, a small package of tissues, a notepad, and a pen. I should have been ready for anything, but I felt unprepared. I truly hoped we wouldn't find anything incriminating at Steve's house. He was a nice, thoughtful dad. I didn't want to think bad thoughts about a nice, thoughtful dad.

My mother pulled up in her SUV, with the magnetic Flock of Maids signs attached to the driver and passenger doors. We picked up Mrs. B, who'd accessorized her jumper with a bright yellow scarf, and then Mrs. M, who wore a pink carnation behind one ear. Mrs. R and Mrs. T were spending the day at the courthouse, hoping to post bail for Earl.

We drove downtown, past the Phoenix building, to check on Steve. He was hard at work on his mural, painting ferns around the base of a redwood tree. We turned at the next street, drove a few blocks and circled back to the Lakeville Historical Library and Museum. Arched windows flanked four pillars that held up the portico. Above the columns were the words, "Free Public Library." Long, narrow steps led from the sidewalk to the mahogany front doors. My mother pulled into an angled parking space.

"Okay, who's going to check to make sure Maggie is volunteering this morning?" I asked. Removing her picture from a file folder, I passed it around. "I can't go in; she knows me."

"But we're dressed as maids," Mrs. B said, examining Maggie's photo. "How is that going to look? No one dresses in a jumpsuit to go to a museum."

"Just ask for directions," my mom said.

Mrs. B shrugged, and took one last look at Maggie's picture before slipping out of the car.

A woman holding hands with two young children followed Mrs. B up the steps and into the museum. A shop owner across the street wheeled out a stand of wind chimes and placed them next to a table of ceramic pots. My leg jerked up and down with nervous tension. I thought about the job ahead of us. We'd repeat the routine we used at Donna's house. We should be in and out quick. Or so I hoped.

After ten long minutes Mrs. B bounced down the steps. She opened the car door and immediately started talking.

"Okay, so Maggie's working, but I'm not sure for how long."

As my mom backed out of the parking space Mrs. B began explaining in great detail the museum's highlights. "Do you know that this building has the largest free-standing lead glass dome in Northern California?" She waved her arms as she spoke. "It's one of the Carnegie Libraries."

As hard as I tried to concentrate on Mrs. B's narrative, I couldn't shake the bad feeling about our adventure. Or maybe I just needed more coffee.

Steve's neighborhood was quiet. We pulled into the driveway, drove past the front house, and parked as close as possible to Steve's rental. But our car could still be seen from the road. Mrs. B hopped out and disappeared around the back. She carried a large yellow tote, which contained her lock-picking equipment. We busied ourselves by removing the vacuum cleaner and other supplies from the car. It felt like an eternity before she opened the front door. I took a deep breath, one obstacle overcome. My mother proceeded to the kitchen; Mrs. M took the first bedroom.

Mrs. Butterfield stayed in the living room, plugged in the vacuum, and pushed it around rather unenthusiastically. We wanted to look legitimate from the outside. If a neighbor walked by, they'd see the car advertising our cleaning business and a woman vacuuming. Unfortunately for Mrs. B, she'd drawn the short straw to be the working decoy.

I followed my mother into the kitchen, she had her head in the refrigerator.

"What are you looking for?" I asked.

"Not looking, adding."

On the top shelf were three zucchini. "Did you bring those?"

"Uh-huh," she said, smiling.

"Do you think that's a good idea?"

"Of course it's a good idea. The man's in mourning. He needs squash."

I checked out the first bedroom. It held a bed pushed against the wall, weights, and a set of drums. The old double-hung windows had tab-top drapes hanging from wrought-iron rods. Mrs. M sat on the bed with an open book in her hands.

"He likes ancient world history," she said. "Roman stuff."

"No computer?" I asked.

She shook her head without looking up. "Nope."

On the way to the next bedroom, I noticed the vacuum in the living room parked, but still running. Mrs. B sat on the couch going through Steve's mail. I hoped she wouldn't leave the vacuum there for long. With a carpet this old and worn, all that sucking might cause the fibers to disappear altogether.

The second bedroom belonged to Maggie. The walls were light pink, and gossamer curtains adorned with dragonfly appliqués hung over the windows. An old CD player sat on top of her dresser. Next to that sat an empty desk with computer plugs, but without the attached computer. Sliding mirrored closet doors stood open. Maggie's wardrobe consisted of jeans, T-shirts, and shorts. The floor was scattered with flip-flops and tennis shoes. This was stark compared to her room at Donna's house. This room held vestiges of Maggie's younger years. In this room, she could still be a kid; at Donna's house she was stepping into adulthood. The transition was tricky, but Maggie was dealing with it in a creative way: carefree youth with Dad, young adult with stepmom.

I returned to Steve's room to see Mrs. M standing at a roll-top desk, tapping her fingers on a stack of papers.

"What did you find?" I asked.

"Lots of money going out that doesn't need to be," she said.

"What do you mean?"

"Late charges on credit cards, overdraft charges at the bank, late charge for the rent," Mrs. M said, shaking her head. "It looks like he has money in a savings account but doesn't move it into his checking in time."

"When I talked with him, he made it sound like he lived pretty hand to mouth, and that Donna wasn't too happy about it."

"He's flushing money down the drain; that'd make me nuts."

I started to agree with her, but I heard a noise from the front door. Mrs. M quietly pulled the lid down on the roll top desk, covering the papers she'd just been reading.

Mrs. B's voice crooned from the living room: "Oh, I wasn't expecting you. How nice to meet you, Mr. Burton."

I grabbed onto the desk to steady myself.

"You've got to hide," Mrs. M whispered, pointing to

the closet.

"No way, nuh-uh." I was not getting in a closet. I sprinted down the hallway, Mrs. M was right behind me.

"What are you doing in my house?" I heard Steve's curt voice demanding an answer from Mrs. B.

I stopped in the hallway, realizing I couldn't make it to the back door without being seen. Mrs. M pushed me into the bathroom, and pointed to what I thought was a linen closet. But when she opened its door it contained a hot water heater strapped to the wall.

"There's enough room; slide in," she said.

"Oh, no, no, no," I replied, and went to the window above the toilet. The latch was undone. I tried to open the sixty-year-old double-hung window with sixty years of enamel paint holding it closed.

"Come on; you'll fit," Mrs. M said, waving her hand as if to shoo me in.

"I'm going out the window." I put the toilet seat down and climbed up onto the lid, hoping for better leverage. "I just need a pry bar, hand me that toilet brush."

From here I could see my mother in the backyard, she must have snuck out the kitchen door. She was crouched below a window, making her way to the car.

We could hear Mrs. B talking loud and spinning her lie: "But, the back door was opened, just like you said."

My hand slipped off the window frame. I lost my balance, fell against the wall and landed with one foot on the floor, saving myself from complete collapse.

"I don't know whose house you think this is," Steve said, his voice also becoming louder. "But, the back door wasn't open."

"Well, how did we get in then?" Mrs. B sounded defensive.

Mrs. Butterfield suddenly stood in the bathroom doorway. "Well, this is embarrassing," she said. Then she mouthed the words: "He's right behind me." Or she mouthed: "We're totally screwed." It was hard to tell. She held her hand close to her chest and jerked her thumb sideways.

My limbs felt like jelly as Mrs. Miller grabbed me by the waist and shoved me into the hot water closet, slamming the door. My breath caught with the sudden darkness. I instantly felt trapped. When I was five, Jimmy Chang locked me in a linen closet. It had left me claustrophobic and a bit afraid of fluffy towels. Okay. A lot afraid of fluffy towels. The smell of fabric softener alone could send me into a sweat.

"We're at the wrong house," Mrs. B said. "This isn't the Burton residence after all."

Mrs. M said something in Spanish and Mrs. B replied, "Vámonos, this is going to put us back all day."

My chest was shoved up against a copper pipe and my nose was inches away from a layer of dust that covered the top of the heater. It wasn't hot to the touch, but it didn't matter; I started sweating like crazy. On top of that, my ears were buzzing like I was standing under a neon light.

The Ladies' voices faded, and I imagined my mom's SUV starting up and crunching on the gravel driveway. It was so dark and stifling I thought I might pass out. With my one free hand, I slowly unzipped my jumper down to my five-inch wide belt, thinking more air would keep me conscious. I heard footsteps in the bathroom. Then water tinkling on water.

Eew, eew, eew and yuck.

I tried to picture myself at the beach. The toilet flushed, I pretended the sound was a wave crashing on the shore. I heard another buzzing noise, but this time it wasn't in my head.

"Hello?" Steve said, and paused. "Yes, it's tonight. At eight, yes. Do you have the address?" Another pause. "Good, I'll see you there. Bye."

After a few more excruciating minutes, the door closed. I stumbled out and kneeled down. Unable to see clearly, I put my palms flat on the tile floor and took deep gasps of breath. Finally, the roar in my ears subsided. When my eyes focused again, I slowly stood up and poked my head into the hall. The house was silent. I slunk to the front window. Keeping close to the wall, I watched as Steve turned out of the driveway on his bike.

I went back to the bathroom and splashed water on my face. The small old-fashioned mirror was set so high I could only see myself from the neck up. The water made my mascara run, forming moons of black under my eyes. I took some toilet paper and dabbed at the smudges as best I could.

Returning to the kitchen, I opened the back door but realized I'd need a key from the outside to lock it once I was on the porch. Steve might not remember if he'd locked the door first thing this morning. But he sure as hell would remember that he locked it after finding strangers in his house. The front door was the same. I ran from room to room checking the windows. I finally found one in Maggie's room that easily opened. Now that I knew I had an exit, I called my mom.

"Hello?" she answered.

I could hear a whooshing noise in the background. And voices.

"Where are you?" I asked.

"Ah, at a stop light."

"That will be $15.95." I heard a woman say.

"Mom, where are you?"

"Where are you?" she retorted.

"I'm at Steve's. Where else would I be?"

"Okay, we'll meet you down on the corner."

"Which corner?"

"What?" she said. "You're breaking up."

The phone went dead.

Before leaving, I thought I'd take one last look around the house. Steve's closets held nothing but clothes. His shoeboxes contained only shoes. I couldn't find anything related to Helena to indicate when their relationship started, or even that she'd spent time here.

I circled back to the kitchen. Next to the back door I found a paper grocery bag from the Lakeville Market. Inside were two packages. Before picking up the first one, I put on my gloves and then gently lifted the parcel out for further inspection. It was addressed to a woman on B Street, which was on Donna's route. The tape was firmly in place. It didn't look like it had been opened or tampered with in any way, but it did have a bit of dirt on the bottom. If those kids were right, this might have been a package that was placed on the ground in the alley.

I took out the other package. It was similar on the outside and also within Donna's route. Both were postmarked two weeks ago. I wrote down the "to" and "from" addresses then thought it time to get out.

Crawling through the window, I dropped down next to a pink hydrangea, closed the window behind me, and put the screen back in place.

I leaned up against the house for a moment, breathing in the cool earth scents. Glancing around and from where I stood, I couldn't see the neighbor's windows. If I couldn't see them, they couldn't see me. Donna's convertible sat in the backyard, the hood still propped open.

I crept to the side of the house, squatted next to the garbage bins, and peaked around to view the street. A young female jogger ran past, a black Labrador trotting next to her. While I was here, I might as well take a peek in Steve's garbage.

The first bin stank of rotting chicken and something else disgusting. The blue recycle bin contained plastic water bottles, a milk container, and various cardboard boxes. I leaned in, the edge digging into my stomach, and retrieved two boxes. Both were addressed to Steve, I dropped them back in the bin.

It had been at least ten minutes now, with no sign of my rescuers. I removed my gloves and stuffed them into my pocket. Walking out to the sidewalk I turned toward downtown, hoping I was heading in the right direction. A landscape truck rolled by, pulling a trailer full of bouncing rakes and lawn mowers. The two occupants stared at me, mouths open. A woman in a van glanced at me, her eyebrows furrowed. I looked behind me; a car of teenagers crept toward me.

When they got up alongside me, I kept my head

forward but could see a young guy hanging out the window.

"Hey, baby, want a ride?" He laughed and the car sped down the street.

At the house on the corner, a woman dead-headed roses with her back to me, while a little girl danced a bare-chested Barbie on a picket fence. The doll's blond hair flopped in front of its face. The girl stared at me. "She looks just like you," she said, putting her hand over her mouth and giggling. I'd never been compared to Barbie before, but I guessed that my hair was a mess, so I giggled right back at the girl.

I saw my mom's SUV coming up the street. She slowed to a stop, and I slid into the back seat. Mrs. B sat next to me. She turned and handed me a cup of coffee.

"You went for coffee?" I asked. "You left me trapped in a hot water closet, with a potential murderer in the house, and went for coffee?"

"It has organic cream," Mrs. B replied, ignoring my rant. "If you don't want it, I'll drink it."

But I already had the lid open and was gulping it down.

"We got banana bread too. Want some?"

"No, thanks," I said.

Mrs. B stared at me and huffed. "Now you get sexy?" she said. "A few weeks ago when I wanted you to show some cleavage, you refused. Now, when we're trying to keep a low profile, you're running around showing everything you've got."

I looked down at my exposed bright red push-up bra and fumbled with one hand for the jumper zipper.

My mother spun around in her seat, her eyes wild,

staring at me, and not at the road. "Did you have sex with Steve?" she asked, slamming on the brakes. "My god, he's your father's age."

"Mom! Drive!"

"Did you?" she asked again.

A car honked its horn.

"No, of course not," I said.

She turned back around, her jaw line tense.

"You know," Mrs. M said, "I've heard of that, when parents go through a divorce, and a child is left without a father, they go looking for a replacement."

My mother nodded. "I've heard that too."

"I'm not a child, and I'm not looking for a replacement for Dad," I snapped.

"Tsk, tsk," Mrs. M said. "This could be bad. Before you know it, she'll be sleeping with every old dude in town. And you know what that means. Less guys for us."

After the morning ordeal, everything felt claustrophobic, including sitting inside Elsie's Antiques. So after having lunch, I once again left my mother in charge of the store. I knew that as soon as the front door closed behind me, she'd open the back door for her zucchini bread groupies. But I wanted time to drive Donna's residential postal route.

Two blocks from my mom's house, I came across a mail delivery truck that I assumed was Donna's replacement. I pulled over to the side of the road a few houses down. The postal woman had a satchel stuffed with mail over her shoulder as she worked her way down the street.

I got out, looked around, and saw no neighbors out,

only a cat sitting on a porch railing intently cleaning an ear. I slid up next to the mail truck and peered inside. What caught my eye was one of those pretty writing books I'd seen at the Lakeville Bookstore. The design on the front was the same as the picture over Donna's fireplace, Georgia O'Keeffe's red poppy. Could that little book belong to Donna? I wondered how easy it would be to open the door and grab a package or two. I thought about trying the handle but noticed a small red light blinking on the dash. The truck must be locked and alarmed.

I glanced toward the cross street and saw a young man riding a bike with a basketball under his arm. He zigzagged as he went, as though he was favoring one leg. There was no mistaking it was Andrew. I ran to my car and followed him. He turned into the park. I stopped and watched him shoot free-throws for a few minutes. I wondered how to approach him. Hubby was right; I needed a dog. Dogs were the perfect ice-breaker and all around reason to be in a park.

"Hey, Andrew," I said as I walked up to him.

He turned to me and continued to dribble the ball.

"I'm Patricia. We met at bingo."

He gave me an upward nod, then said, "You're Jake's friend."

Dang, I was hoping he wouldn't connect me to the day at the auto body shop when he got so mad at Jake. He shot the ball right through the hoop, without touching the edges.

"Swish," he said, grinning.

"Can I ask you a question about the night Donna got hit?"

He grabbed the ball and dribbled it, watching me.

"Okay."

"What did you see out in the Mastodon's parking lot?"

He shrugged, "Like what?"

"I heard they had a fire in the dumpster."

"I don't know anything about that," he said.

"You were seen out at the dumpster."

"So."

He took another shot and missed. The tinny rhythmic sound of the ball bouncing on the asphalt was getting on my nerves.

"What were you doing out there?" I asked.

"Using my phone."

He raised the ball over his head, bent his knees, and took a shot.

"Did you see anyone else out there?"

The ball hit the backboard and it came right back at him. He reached out with one hand stopping it mid-air.

"I saw Donna and Helena talking."

Interesting. That confirmed what Janie had said at the book club meeting.

"Did you throw anything into the dumpster?"

"No." This time his voice was petulant.

"And you didn't light up?"

"No, I didn't start a fire in the dumpster. All I did was call Maggie."

Then it hit me: the light from his phone could have been perceived as a light from a match or lighter.

"How long were you out there?"

He shrugged. "Five minutes. Then I went inside, talked to Gramps, and left."

"I heard your grandfather's been arrested. I'm having a hard time believing he hit Donna," I said.

"He didn't." Andrew spoke so quietly I could barely hear him.

"Did you hit her?" I asked.

He shook his head. "I hit a deer a few weeks ago. That's how the window got busted. I didn't want to tell Gramps because I have so many dings on my insurance that the rates are sky high, but without the insurance money I couldn't afford to fix it. I parked it in one of the garages we rarely use. But he saw the damage when we had a yard sale, so he said I'd have to figure out a way to pay for it."

"Then you got the job with Jake," I said.

"I couldn't believe my luck, I'd get a chance to fix the truck. But Jake had to turn me in." He gave me a dirty look, like we were all in it together.

"But they found fibers from Donna's clothes on the windshield."

Andrew's shoulders slumped. "I have no idea how they got there. No one's driven the truck since I hit the deer. Look, I took Gramps to bingo, in his Camry. I called Maggie from the parking lot. I drove home; she came over. Gramps called me after bingo was over, and I met him at the restaurant for pie."

"But if his alibi is so easy to explain, why didn't he explain it to the police?" I asked.

Andrew turned his face away from me.

"Your grandfather thinks you did it, doesn't he?"

Andrew nodded. "Maggie rode her bike out to the house. We were there all evening. I told Gramps that, but I guess he didn't believe me."

I left Andrew to his hoops and continued on my way. If only Andrew had been up front with his grandfather when he hit the deer, Earl wouldn't be in the predicament he was now.

Chapter Thirteen

That evening I opened my refrigerator and found a freshly roasted chicken. Since it hadn't been there this morning, I attributed it to The Ladies. I made a fruit salad to go with the poultry and sat cross legged on the couch. Watching a rerun of Star Trek, I munched until pleasantly full. Just as another episode was about to start, my phone rang. It was Mrs. Taylor.

"Good news," she said, "we got Earl out on bail."

"That is good news," I said.

Before hanging up, I told Mrs. T about the fire in the dumpster. I couldn't see how it fit in, but maybe The Ladies could connect the dots.

After feeling somewhat uplifted by conversing with Mrs. T, I called Mitsy to report that her husband hadn't flirted with anyone at bingo the previous night, hadn't won any bingo pots, and the only thing I saw him indulging in was coffee. After that, my evening was wide open. The Ladies were at the movies, and Jake was working late. I knew that Steve had a commitment at eight. Boredom fed my curiosity. But I couldn't follow

Steve on foot or in a car. I'd need a bike.

I drove across town to my mom's, and using the keypad to open the garage, I punched in her birth year. The door did not budge. I put it in a second time. Again, nothing. Did my mother, in a fit of retaliation against my cheating father, change the code? I went to the front door and put my key in the lock. It wouldn't turn. I sighed. Well, if I were in her situation, I'd probably do the same thing.

An alternative plan would be to borrow a bike from my surfing buds, Chris and Adam. I called Chris, explained my dilemma, and headed over to his house. When I arrived, Chris was in the garage waxing his surfboard. Two wetsuits hung from the edge of the open garage door.

He rolled the bike out to me as I came up the driveway.

"I pumped up the tires," Chris said, as he pushed his blond hair out of his eyes. "You want to borrow the van too? I'd hate to see you rip up the upholstery in your car."

I looked at the beat-up 1970s Chevy. On the side panel was a picture of a surfer catching a tube wave. I hoped the engine wasn't held together with duct tape and paper clips. Against my better judgment, I said, "Okay."

I would have offered him my keys in case he needed transportation that evening, but Chris' BMW also sat in the driveway. Chris had gone to Stanford, earned his law degree, passed the bar, and moved to the North Bay to surf. He and Adam had opened a surf shop downtown. If his parents were disappointed in their son's career choice, you'd never know it by the new car they leased for him every year.

"How was the water today?" I asked.

"Awesome, three-to-four feet. We're going out tomorrow if you want to come." He grinned broadly.

The invitation was unnecessary. Chris and Adam taught me to surf ten years ago. For them, surfing was a lifestyle. They'd go every morning, barring illness, and even then, it was hard to keep them out of the water.

"I wish I could," I said, thinking about how nice it would be to get in a few waves. "But, unfortunately, business calls."

After thanking Chris for the use of the bike and the van, I drove to a park a few blocks from Steve's house.

Before I'd left that evening, I'd taken some precautions with my looks. I'd tucked my hair up under a baseball cap and put on a reversible zip-up sweatshirt that I'd found in my grandmother's coat closet. It was magenta on the outside and black on the inside, with a high collar to cover my neck and jaw line.

I pedaled to Steve's and slowly cruised past his house on the opposite side of the street. Timing this was a bit of a trick. I checked my phone: it read 7:25. Hopefully, he hadn't left yet. At the end of the block, I stopped, removed the tire pump, and pretended to put some air in the front tire. After a few minutes of fiddling with the bike, I heard a squeak. I glanced over my shoulder to see Steve pedaling my direction. Keeping my back to him, I reattached the pump to the center support bar and squatted down to re-tie my shoelace. The last thing I wanted was for Steve to stop and ask if I needed help.

After he passed, I noticed that one of the baskets that hung over his rear tire contained a Lakeville Market grocery bag; the other contained a toolbox. A large square board strapped to his back worked to my advantage, since he couldn't easily see what was behind him. I took off after him, keeping a good distance between us.

I lost him on one street, but when I reached the corner, I caught sight of him as he turned down the next. He disappeared up the driveway of a two-story house. All curtains in the front windows were drawn. I cruised by slowly and stopped behind an SUV on the opposite side of the street. Steve reappeared carrying his toolbox and board. He bounded up the steps and knocked on the front door. A car drove up and parked. A woman got out and walked up to the house. She also carried a board.

From years of art instruction, I knew exactly what was happening. I rode around the neighborhood and stopped at a park to let some time pass. At about eight o'clock I went back, dying to see what was in Steve's grocery bag. I laid Chris' bike down on the front lawn and sprinted up the driveway. A small calico cat came out to greet me, its tail up. I squatted down to pet it. I could see the corner of the back porch and Steve's bike leaning against the railing. I crept forward.

The cat ran up the back steps and meowed at the door. I poked my head into the bag on Steve's bike. It contained the two parcels with local shipping labels that I'd seen at his house. Did this mean he was planning to return them?

I heard a noise behind me.

"Moonlight?" Steve said.

I snapped upright and turned to look at Steve standing in the doorway. My mouth popped open with horror. Heat ran up the back of my neck.

"You found us," he continued. "I'm so glad you came. Where did you see my flyer? I've got them all over town." He looked back inside then to me. "Did you forget your supplies?"

I nodded.

"That's okay, I've got extra."

I stood still. My feet wanted to run, but my mind chanted, "STAY CALM!" I forced myself to move, and Steve opened the door further. I followed him inside, past a staircase and down a hallway. I glanced into the kitchen. The cat that I'd seen outside was now eating from a bowl on the floor.

We stepped into a bright living room packed with people of various ages balancing drawing pads on their laps or on easels. In the center of the room, a model sat on a chair that had been placed on a plywood platform. Her back was to me. She wore a broad brimmed hat with enough flowers on it to put any Easter bonnet to shame. The room was quiet, all eyes on the model. There's nothing like a naked body to hold a group's attention.

"I'm sorry we're out of chairs. Is the floor okay?" Steve whispered. He gestured to the spot where I stood. I nodded. "Let me get you a board and some paper. Charcoal or graphite?"

"Graphite," I squeaked.

I plopped cross-legged onto the floor and looked around the room. The only person I recognized was Helena, tucked in a corner, intently studying her drawing board.

"We're just doing one minute warm-ups right now." Steve handed me a pad of paper, a piece of graphite and a kneaded eraser.

A timer beeped. The model stood up and placed one hand on the back of the chair. She was plump and full breasted—perfect for drawing. I picked up the stub of graphite and touched it to the paper. My hand trembled as I followed the contour of the woman's body. When I got to her face, I stopped suddenly. The model was Mrs. T. Why was she here? To keep an eye on Steve? Or was she working, and this was a coincidence? I must say it was ingenious, if not extremely gutsy.

I took deep breaths and kept going. Luckily, with warm ups, you can get away with a lot of scribbling. The alarm beeped again, and Mrs. T shifted slightly to place both hands on the chair back. I made another drawing next to the previous one. No use wasting paper.

"Okay," Steve said. "Let's switch to some three minute poses."

Mrs. Taylor turned in my direction, her gaze over my head. She had to have seen me by now. But if she did, she made no indication.

After about 10 minutes I relaxed, and my hand stopped shaking. I removed my sweatshirt, wrapped it into a ball, and plopped it next to me. Then I started to worry about other things: Chris" bike was laying in the front yard, and I'd left my wallet in the van, so I wouldn't have money for the class or a tip for the model. Hopefully, Steve wouldn't mind if I paid him another day.

When we stopped for a break Mrs. T put on a teal silk robe and walked by me, making eye contact. I got up and followed her down the hall. When we got to the bathroom, she gestured for me to come in.

She leaned up against the closed door. "What are you

doing here?" she asked.

I crossed my arms. "Did you hear about what happened this morning? I got locked in the hot water closet at Steve's house."

She nodded.

There were three sharp knocks, then a single tap on the door. Mrs. T opened it to a woman with dreadlocks and large gold hoop earrings who smiled broadly. She wore a soft colored blouse in yellows, oranges and greens with loose flowing sleeves. It took me a moment to realize it was Beatrice Johnson.

"Ladies," she said as a greeting.

We shifted to make room for her. I tried not to think about how small the bathroom was starting to feel.

"Ms. Johnson has some information for us," Mrs. T said. "But finish your story, Patricia." She turned to Ms. Johnson, "Patricia got locked in Steve's water heater closet this morning."

Ms. Johnson closed her eyes. She put an index finger over each ear. I couldn't recall ever seeing her wear nail polish, but tonight she had on long acrylic fingernails sporting a French manicure highlighted with white stars. Gold bracelets jingled on her wrists. She let out a deep sigh. "I don't want to hear this," she whispered, and began humming.

"Go on, Patricia," Mrs. T said.

"When I was in the closet I overheard Steve talking on the phone about something going on tonight at eight, so I followed him here. And when I was looking through some bags he had on his bike, he caught me. So I pretended to be here for the class."

"You did a good job, thinking on your feet. So, what

did you find in the bag?"

"Two unopened packages I saw at Steve's house this morning. They were addressed to folks on Donna's postal route. I'm thinking Steve might deliver them tonight."

Ms. Johnson's humming got a bit louder.

"Had they been opened?"

"It didn't look like it."

"Then, maybe the contents aren't important."

"Why take them if you're not interested in what's inside?" I asked.

"Think about it," Ms. Johnson said, her eyes popping open and her hands coming down. Obviously, she'd been listening. "What have been the consequences of those packages going missing?"

"It got Donna in trouble with the postal service," Mrs. T said.

"Exactly," Ms. Johnson replied. "And if it got back to the police, it could ruin Donna's reputation with them. Sounds to me like Donna was on to something."

"So what's your news?" Mrs. T asked Ms. Johnson.

"I'm not sure how this fits in," she said, "but Cece Bronson's boyfriend, Nick, has disappeared. His mother filed a missing person report with the police."

"I overheard Cece talking about him," I said. "She didn't say whose idea it was to break it up, but she seemed pretty upset."

"Hmm." Ms. Johnson pondered for a moment. "His mom said he wanted to break up and had plans to return to the traveling band where he and Cece met. But he suddenly stopped calling, and when the mom contacted the band, they said Nick never showed up. She's concerned he's had an accident."

"Maybe he's taking some time for himself," Mrs. T said. "He could be off enjoying nature, out of cell phone reach."

Ms. Johnson nodded, "Could be, but it just doesn't sit right with me."

I turned to Mrs. T. "So, I thought you were going to the movies."

"This gig came up last minute. A gal's got to make a living. Now you two give me some privacy," she said, shooing us out of the cramped space.

After another forty-five minutes, the class came to a close. I rolled up my drawings and returned the unused paper to Steve.

"I'm sorry, I forgot my money," I told him. "How much is the class? I can bring it by tomorrow."

"Fifteen," he replied.

I said my goodbyes and was heading for the door, when Steve called out to me.

"Moonlight, you forgot your sweatshirt."

I turned back. He was holding it by the shoulders with the back side facing me. Once again, my mouth dropped open. The words "Elsie's Antiques" were written in black script across the bright pink material.

As he held out the sweatshirt, he said in a quiet voice, "I hope your store keeps you going, Moonlight, because your sleuthing skills need some work."

Too mortified to speak, I closed my mouth, grabbed the sweatshirt and turned away. Running on pure adrenaline, I pedaled back to the van. I put the bike in the rear and dug around in Chris' cooler for something to drink. I pulled out a coconut water and gulped it down, hoping my electrolytes and my nerves would return to normal.

Partially refreshed, I read over the street addresses I'd copied down at Steve's house and made a mental map of where they were in relation to his return route. I picked out the address closest to Steve's home and drove the van there. I assumed he was going to return the stolen parcels. I wanted to believe that Steve had recently found the parcels at Donna's house and, as a good citizen, was delivering them to their rightful owner.

Across the street from one of the appointed addresses, the houses were dark. I parked under a large tree that blocked light from a street lamp, hoping the neighbors wouldn't notice me and call the police. I cracked the window and slid the seat back.

The hands from the glow-in-the-dark dashboard clock ticked by. After twenty minutes, I wondered if this was such a good idea. Then a car pulled up behind me. Rotating blue-and-white lights flashed, suddenly blinding me via the reflection in my rear view mirror. My heart leapt into third gear. A cop. I slid my seat forward and rolled down the window. Glancing in the side view mirror, I realized something even worse. It was Jake's dad.

Before he got a look at me, I poked my head out of the window and said: "Officer Romano, how nice to see you." I forced a smile.

He stepped closer, pulled out a mini flashlight and shone it in my face. "Hold on," he said, and went back to his car and shut off the flashing lights. When he came back, he stared at me for a few moments. "Ms. Schuster," he said, "why you are parked on this street, in the dark, at this time of night?"

"Well, I was riding my bike, and I got lost."

"You're in a van."

"Yes, you see my friend's bike wouldn't fit in my car, so I had to take his van."

He leaned in and took a deep whiff. Luckily Chris and Adam didn't partake in drugs due to their intense surfing schedule. But they had in high school, and they weren't exactly clean freaks. For all I knew, if I opened up the glove box, there could be a ten-year-old bong, packed with ten-year-old weed, just waiting to be used against me.

"And they don't have a GPS," I continued, hoping that my phone wouldn't ring at that particular moment. "So I was looking at a map."

He looked down at my hands, which happened to be map-free.

"What map?"

"Um, I couldn't find one," I replied.

"Ms. Schuster, where did you grow up?"

"Three blocks that way." I pointed to my right.

Sergeant Romano's left eye started to twitch. "And you got lost," he said.

"Things have changed since I lived here." I swallowed hard. Sergeant Romano and I both knew that in this neighborhood most of the homes were over seventy-five years old.

Just then I heard the familiar squeak of Steve's wheel rubbing on its rim. Officer Romano turned to look. When he turned back he shone his flashlight into the van again illuminating my face.

"Ms. Schuster, I'm going back to my patrol car. If

you're not gone in one minute I'm going to ticket you for loitering."

"Yes, sir," I mumbled.

"If you drive straight," he said, pointing up the street, "and turn right at the next corner, you'll run into Western. Will you be able to find your way from there?"

I nodded.

He opened his mouth to speak, but all that came out was a sigh.

Steve appeared and stopped his bike in front of the house that shared the address with one of his parcels. I wanted to dawdle to see what he would do, but time was ticking. I started up the van and pulled away from the curb. As I passed Steve turned, waved, and yelled out: "Good night, Moonlight!"

Chapter Fourteen

My grandmother's landline woke me. I could see light-blue sky from the bed, and I listened while the recording clicked on. Her voice asked the incoming caller to leave a message. I continued to pay for the phone just for these moments. Hearing her always made me smile.

The caller was a little muffled at first. Then I heard a familiar man's voice saying, "…from the Lakeville Police Department. I'm at Elsie's Antiques, and I'm checking on a possible break in." I scrambled out of bed and picked up the receiver before he hung up.

"I'm here. This is Patricia."

"It's Sergeant Romano, Ms. Schuster. A fellow merchant called us, saying that the back door to your store was open. Could you come down and let us know if anything's been taken?"

"I'll be there as soon as I can."

I checked my phone. An alert had come in at 4:30, I'd slept right though it.

When I arrived, a female officer stood at the back entrance and introduced herself as Sergeant Baylor. "Any chance you forgot to lockup last night?" she asked. "There's no sign of a forced entrance."

I thought for a moment. "No, I'm pretty sure I locked it before I left. So, who called it in?"

She pointed next door. "The owner of the Italian restaurant."

"I'll have to thank her."

I went into the office first. Nothing on my desk appeared to have been moved. The safe door was securely locked. I went into the store. Sergeant Romano stood in the center of the room, hands on hips, looking around as if he'd be able to tell if something had been stolen. He looked tired; I knew his shift was almost over.

"Good morning," I said.

He nodded. I went straight to the jewelry counter. Nothing looked out of place. My most valuable item, a vintage platinum wedding ring, sat in its holder, locked inside the glass case. The key for the case was in my pocket on my key chain. I took a quick tour around the room. The vases were in place; my black marble ash trays sat untouched; nothing looked disturbed.

"I don't get it," I said. "It looks like everything is here."

Sergeant Romano pointed at the security cameras. "Are those hooked up?"

"Yes," I said, and tapped on my keyboard. "Just installed. Unfortunately, I haven't paid for the alert service yet, or you would have been contacted when the break-in happened." I opened up the software. "What time should I start with?"

"After you closed."

The screen divided into four segments that

corresponded to the four cameras. I clicked on the fast-forward button, and watched the minutes fly by on the digital clock. Just before 4:30 a.m. a light flashed. Then a figure appeared. I slowed the picture to regular speed. By build and size the person appeared female. She wore dark pants, a dark long sleeved shirt, gloves, and a ski mask that covered her whole head with just her eyes showing. She used a small flashlight. We watched on one view as she came down the hallway. Her image jumped to another view as she came into the main part of the store.

She went directly to the jewelry counter and flashed the light over each piece. She then came behind the counter, where, at the current moment, Sergeant Romano and I stood. She squatted down, and after a few seconds, when she hadn't reappeared, Sergeant Romano and I looked down.

One of the cardboard boxes Steve had left me was gone. I'd been researching some china pieces and had left them on the floor. There were still a few pieces of ghost poop scattered about. We looked back at the computer to see the woman stand up, turn and look directly into the camera. Her eyes got wide. She turned. And for a split second, I could see a dark colored curl peeking out from the neckline of the ski mask. We watched as she ran, carrying the box, down the hall and out of the building.

"What was in that box?" he asked.

"Some china, not worth a lot, less than a hundred."

"Looked like a woman. I assume you don't recognize her. There's not much there to identify her by."

"Nope," I said. But something did seem familiar. "How did she get in? There's no damage to the lock or the door."

"Who else has a key?"

The Ladies had one, since they'd recently let themselves inside to sip coffee from my fine china and spy on the bookstore owner. Jimmy Chang had one. I shrugged. It wasn't any of them caught on film. "Any number of people," I replied. "I just took over running the store a few months ago. My grandmother could have given one to any of her employees."

"Okay, I'm going to leave you my card. If you notice anything else missing, just call. I'd recommend getting new locks."

I inwardly cringed. The locks I'd bought sat on the floor in my office, still wrapped in their blister packs.

He tapped on the top of my glass display case. "This glass is really easy to break. You may want to lock your valuable items in a safe at night."

"I guess I got lucky, could have been a lot worse."

"Also, could you email me that part of the video?" he asked.

"Of, course. Thanks for your help. Hopefully Steve won't be too upset about the loss of his china."

Sergeant Romano squinted at me. "Steve? Steve Olsen?" he asked.

"Yeah," I said. "I'm selling some of Donna's items for him. They'd been going through a divorce, but it wasn't final." I studied Sergeant Romano's face. He suddenly seemed very awake.

I wanted The Ladies input on the theft. I called Mrs. T, who said she'd be right over. Then I crossed the street to the bakery for pastries and coffees.

Both Mrs. T and Mrs. M showed up.

"I feel so silly," I said, "not getting those locks changed."

"You've been busy, dear," said Mrs. M. "I'll call Betty, and we'll get it taken care of this morning."

"Thanks," I said, "I really appreciate it."

Mrs. M gestured to the computer screen.

"Can we see the video footage?" Mrs. M asked.

We huddled around the computer screen and watched the scene three times. Mrs. T was the first to speak.

"What was in the box?" she asked.

"Odds and ends of some china," I said.

Mrs. T looked at the ghost poop on the floor. "Did you take out everything?"

"No."

"Maybe something was hidden in all that packing material."

"Could be," I said. "But would the person who took the box know that? The box came from Steve."

"Let me see it again." We watched it for a fourth time.

"Looks like Helena," Mrs. T said.

"Helena?" I replied. "Belly dancing, ant hating, sneaking around with Steve, Helena?"

She nodded.

"How can you tell?" Mrs. M asked.

"Her build, plus when she looks in the camera. It looks like her eyes," replied Mrs. T.

"But you can't know for sure," I said.

"She worked for your grandmother last Christmas. Ten-to-one Elsie gave her a key, and she still has it."

"But what would Helena want with a box of china?"

I asked.

"There's only one way to find out," Mrs. T said. "Let's go see her."

"You can't be serious," I said. "Shouldn't we let the police handle it?"

"Look," Mrs. T said, "whatever she was doing here may or may not be connected to Donna's death, but it's a great opportunity to ask her some questions."

"And what if you're wrong, and it's not her?" I wasn't comfortable showing up at someone's house unannounced.

"Then we'll have a nice ride out in the country."

Mrs. M asked to stay behind and browse through Donna's items up for sale. Mrs. T and I boarded my Civic and headed for the west side of town. Beyond Earl's place, the landscape opened up to pastures and rolling hills that currently were more golden then green.

Mrs. T assumed the role of navigator. "Slow down," she said. "We'll be turning left." She pointed, and I turned off the main highway.

A white rail fence ran up both sides of an asphalt road. After about a half mile, we came to a two-story, white farm house. A porch ran along the front and down one side. On the opposite side of the road were a row of three trucks. One was the old one that Helena had driven to the book club. Straight ahead, a small group of goats huddled in the shade of an oak. I parked, and a few moments after we slammed the car doors, Helena appeared from around the corner of the house. She stopped abruptly. For a second I thought she might run.

"Morning, Helena," Mrs. T called out.

"Morning," Helena replied.

"Do you have a minute?"

She stared at us, shifting her weight from foot to foot. Gone were her flowing skirts and feminine tops. She wore black jeans and a long-sleeve black shirt over a black T-shirt, exactly like our burglar. She gestured to the house. We followed her through the back door, into a mudroom that contained a utility sink. Coats hung on the wall. The kitchen smelled of cooked potatoes and coffee. As we sat down, she offered us tea. Mrs. T asked questions about the house and goats while the water boiled. I searched the table top for ants. I didn't want to witness another one of Helena's outbursts.

When Helena put the mugs down, she wouldn't meet my eyes. She sat down, dumped a hefty dose of sugar into her drink, and sipped, while peering at Mrs. T over the rim.

"So, what were you looking for at Elsie's Antiques?" Mrs. T asked.

If I was Helena I would have spewed tea over all of us, but she calmly lowered her cup and let out a deep sigh. We waited while she collected her thoughts.

"After my Mom died last year, my Dad started going to every bingo game in town and would often run into Donna. And if you knew Donna at all, you knew she liked to talk, especially to men. Unfortunately, my dad took her friendly chatter as serious flirting." Helena sighed. "When I noticed some of my mom's jewelry missing. I asked Dad about them. He told me he'd given them to Donna. They were costume pieces, nothing of much monetary value, more sentimental, for me at least. "

"Oh, dear," Mrs. Taylor said.

"So I asked Donna about it," Helena said, "and she gave the pieces back. Dad said he'd stop. But then I noticed a brooch gone. It was one of the few valuable pieces of jewelry mom had. Plus it belonged to my grandmother."

"What did it look like?" I asked.

"It's in the shape of a fan, accented with sapphires and diamonds, set in platinum," Helena said. "It was an old piece from a famous designer. Last time I had it appraised it was worth around fifteen thousand." She shook her head. "I should have put it in the safe deposit that we have at the bank. But Dad wanted it in Mom's jewelry box."

"Oh, dear," Mrs. Taylor said again.

Helena ran her finger around the rim of her mug. "So I asked Donna about it, and she said she'd return it, just like the others. The next time we saw each other was the night she died."

"At the Mastodon Association? Outside?" I asked.

She nodded.

"But she didn't give it to you?"

"No," Helena said. "She said she'd misplaced it."

"Did you ask Steve if he'd seen it?"

Helena's cheeks turned pink. "Timing's everything, as they say. Steve and I had just started spending time together a few weeks ago. And when Donna died, it just seemed tacky to bring it up."

Helena's explanation on the surface seemed legit. But there was no way to verify it.

Mrs. T rubbed her forehead. "So you risked getting arrested for burglary just to avoid an awkward conversation?"

"I'm not a confrontational type of person." She looked at me. "It never crossed my mind you'd installed cameras. Besides, Elsie had given me a key."

"Can I have it back?" I asked.

Helena pulled her key ring from her pants pocket, removed a key and slid it across the table. "Are you going to turn me in?"

"No," I said. In the big picture, no harm was done.

Mrs. T stood up. "Helena, please tell Steve about this as soon as possible."

"I will," Helena said. "I'll get your china. The brooch wasn't in the box."

I dropped Mrs. T back at the store and drove to the Phoenix Theater to pay Steve for the art class and apologize.

I slowly climbed the wobbly metal ladder leading to the roof. At the top, I watched Steve for a moment. He was hard at work on the mural. He had pushed the scaffolding aside and was painting a small flock of white chickens in one corner, a tip of the hat to Lakeville's poultry history. Closest to me, was a vineyard showing ripe red grapes covered in morning dew.

He noticed me and grinned. "Good, morning, Moonlight. Did you enjoy the class last night?"

"Yeah, it's been a while since I've been to a live drawing class. I'd forgotten how much I like them." I reached into my pocket and handed him fifteen dollars. "Steve, I'm sorry about following you last night."

His hand holding the paint brush waved a dismissal. "Forget it," he said. "Did you learn anything?"

"That you're a good art teacher, and I'm not very

good at detective work."

He shrugged. "Maybe it's like drawing. Even though it seems counterintuitive, you have to practice. With time you'll get better."

"That's awfully generous of you."

"So what do you think?" He gestured to the mural. "Are the chickens too much?"

I smiled. "They look great."

He put down his brush, picked up a rag, and wiped paint off his hands. "I had something odd happen to me the other day."

"Oh, yeah?" I said.

"I went home for a break and found women in my house, cleaning," he said.

"Why is that odd?"

"I didn't hire anyone to clean," he said. "I also found zucchinis in my refrigerator. Have you heard of anyone doing that?" He looked up from his paint rag and stared so intently at me that I was worried he was on to us.

"Well, Steve, those could have been from a friend, or a neighbor. Everyone's got zucchini this time of year." I laughed nervously.

"Nope, I asked around." He shook his head and chuckled. "For a moment, just for a moment, I wanted to believe that Donna's ghost had visited me. There was a clean spot on the carpet in the living room. I wanted to believe that she'd materialized there." He sighed and picked up his brush. "But thoughts like that are driven by guilt. I just hope she's forgiven me."

"Forgiven you for what?" I took a step backwards. Was he admitting to killing her? An infidelity? Not paying the electric bill?

He looked down. "For being sloppy."

I imagined the life of the stereotypical obsessive artist: disappearing into his work, never doing a thing around the house, staring off into space when spoken to. I tried to make light of it. "Why? Because you didn't pick up your socks?"

"Actually, this time it was a little more serious." His eyebrows furrowed for a moment, but then he smiled. "So I have a few more things for the auction. They're in boxes on Donna's back porch, could you go by and pick them up?"

His sudden change of tone inhibited me from questioning him further on the real reason his untidy ways needed forgiving. But my disappointment quickly morphed into irritation as I switched from detective mode to merchant mode.

"I'll see what I can do," I said, forcing a smile at my client, who was causing me extra last minute work.

Mrs. R was right, mixing sleuthing with business was tricky, if not downright annoying.

Chapter Fifteen

I carried the last of Steve's boxes into the storage room of Elsie's Antiques and glanced at the time. It was almost ten o'clock, too late to attend the Downtown Lakeville Merchants Association meeting. But if Jimmy came by to give me a bad time about not showing up, at least this time, I'd be awake. Unfortunately, it wasn't Jimmy that showed up to irritate me; it was someone far worse. It was the Yarn Barn Lady.

My mother sat behind the counter, eyes narrowed, a telltale sign she was on the edge of losing it. Mrs. M stood on one side of her, Mrs. T on the other. All three had their eyes glued on The Yarn Barn Lady, who stood in the center of the store. She was a small woman, but with her arms akimbo, she looked fierce. My attention was instantly drawn to her beehive hairdo. This morning her knitting needles were blood red. One stuck straight up, the other lay horizontally. So instead of the usual X shape, they created a T. She looked at me, swiveled her head to look at my mother, and then turned back to me. When her head moved, the knitting needles clacked together in an annoying way.

"Where have you been?" the Yarn Barn Lady snapped. "We're in the midst of a crime wave, and you don't even show up for the merchant's meeting. Don't you think it would have been nice to give the other shop owners a first-hand account of your burglary?"

My morning coffee intake had consisted of only one cup. That had been hours ago. On the counter, sat my mother's mug. I moved swiftly, draining what she had left. Thank goodness it was enough to help me focus.

"What on earth are you talking about?" I snapped back at her. "What crime wave?"

"We all know that Donna was stealing things from the mail and probably has them hidden away in her furniture."

"Where did you hear that?"

"At the merchant's meeting. Mitsy brought it up. Why else would your store be broken into?" She looked around, apparently not seeing anything worthy of pilfering.

I rubbed my forehead. "I don't think this break-in constitutes a crime wave," I said.

"Did you see Jake's windows?"

"No," I replied.

"Someone graffitied all over them. Just ruined. I'm surprised you didn't get tagged too."

"Did anyone else get tagged?" I asked.

"No," she said.

"So why would they hit me?"

"It had to be Earl's grandson." The Yarn Barn Lady sneered. "Who else would it be?"

"Why would you think that?"

"Those teenage boys are all the same, always looking for trouble. Didn't you have something to do with getting him hired and fired from Jake's?"

I bristled at her assumption. "I told Jake he needed a job, but he wasn't fired—"

She held her hand up, not wanting to hear the whole story. "No matter, Jake's front window is ruined. Going to cost him a mint to fix it."

She turned to glare at my mother. "And you!" She pointed her index finger accusingly. "I'm on to you, running an illegal zucchini bread distribution center out of your storeroom. I'm reporting you to the head of the Lakeville Downtown Merchants Association."

She took a deep breath and retracted her finger. "Oh, and one more thing." She smiled, which was scarier than her fierce look. "Seth, the owner of the bike store, has generously set up a memorial fund to buy a bench in Donna's memory, to be placed in the plaza. So if you'd like to contribute, talk to him." Then she looked at me, her smile gone. "But you would have known that if you'd been to the meeting!" She stomped out the door. Once again my attention was drawn to the position of her knitting needles.

"Her knitting needles are in the shape of a cross," I said.

"Do you think she's trying to ward off vampires sneaking up on her?" my mom asked.

"I doubt it," said Mrs. Miller. "What bloodsucking creature would want a sip of that?"

I jogged to the corner and saw the Meter Dude standing next to Jake. The meter maid mobile was parked at the curb. Neither of the men looked happy. When I reached them, I understood why. Across the front of Jake's large plate glass window was the word "RAT" in black paint.

"I left at 7:30 last night and got in around 6:45 this morning," Jake said, as the Meter Dude took down the information.

Jake gave me a smile. "Officer Garcia, this is Patricia Schuster. She owns Elsie's Antiques."

The officer smiled, flashing a perfect set of white teeth. "Were you downtown last night?" he asked.

I shook my head, staring at the paint. I hated to agree with the Yarn Barn Lady, but my first thought was Andrew.

Jake looked at me, and as if he read my mind, he said, "Officer Garcia is going to talk to Andrew, but I really hope it's not him."

"Since none of the other businesses were tagged," the officer said, "it's a possibility. But it could just be someone messing around, and you got unlucky. What I don't understand is that rat is kind of an old fashioned word. Plus most of the graffiti I see is as much artwork as it is vandalism."

I went into the shop's restroom, and wetted down some paper towels. Going back outside I rubbed the corner of the letter T and the paint immediately smeared and began to come off.

"It's water based, Jake. It will come right off."

"Oh, good," Jake said, looking relieved. "I'll get Reed out here to wash it down."

"Okay, I've got pictures," Officer Garcia said. "I'll write up a report." He pulled out a business card and gave it to Jake.

Blaming Andrew made me uneasy, but who else would write that? Could it be someone who wanted us to think it was Andrew? Steve had access to window paint. I wondered if he really was okay with Andrew and Maggie's relationship. She was a bright kid, and Steve wanted her to have a good education. Would he stoop to something like this to make Andrew look bad and derail his daughter's relationship?

I walked back via the alleyway and knocked on the door of Lucchesi's Italian restaurant. I'd met the owners, Francine and George, at a party at Jake's a while back, and I hoped Francine would remember me.

When she opened the door, I was greeted with a smile followed by a waft of garlic. She wore the typical white chef's shirt with a high necked collar.

"Hi, I just wanted to say thanks for calling the police this morning," I said.

"Oh, sure. Was anything taken?"

"Just a box of china." I hated the idea of withholding information from people; it felt like lying. But telling the whole story would include exposing Helena. "It looks like someone who had a key, so I've been advised to change the locks. I never thought about that when I took over the place." I shrugged. "Over the, years my grandmother had a lot of people working for her."

She smiled. "Yes, it goes with the territory."

"I'm sure the police asked you this, but did you see anyone hanging around?"

"Just the usual," she said. "There are a couple of hardcore joggers out that early. And then there's Mitsy. I usually see her out walking, well...I shouldn't say walking her dog, since she usually carries it." We both laughed.

"Could I place a lunch order with you?" I asked, thinking that giving her some business was one way I could thank her.

"Sure, come on in. We've got lobster raviolis on special today."

My mouth watered at the thought.

When I returned to the store, Mrs. B had removed the back door's deadbolt and had just opened a blister pack that contained my new lock. Mrs. Taylor sat on the steps, enjoying the morning sunshine.

Loud voices came from inside the store. I found my mother wrestling with a customer over a cushion from Donna's couch. The customer had unzipped the cushion and was pulling out the stuffing.

"What is going on here?" I asked my mother.

"Someone has spread a rumor that secret treasures are hidden in Donna's furniture," she replied, as she stuffed the couch innards back into the cushion.

Another customer was pulling out Donna's dresser drawers and flipping them over.

"What are you looking for?" I asked the woman.

"I heard Donna taped envelopes of precious stones to the bottom of her drawers. Maybe even diamonds."

I picked up one of the drawers and slid it back into its slot. I noticed a young boy crawling under Donna's dining room table, a woman stood next to him.

"What do you see?" the woman asked him.

"Nothing, Mom, just wood."

I stood up on Donna's ottoman and clapped my hands.

"Everyone, could I have your attention, please?" I

spoke loudly. The boy peeked out from under the table. "There are no hidden treasures here. All items were thoroughly inspected before they were placed on the floor."

"Darn it," the young boy's mom said. "Come on; let's go."

Shoppers muttered as the room emptied out.

Mrs. M called me over to my computer and pointed at the monitor. "Take a look at this," she said. "Just out of curiosity, I ran the video past Helena's mad exit from the store, and look who showed up."

Just before six that morning, Mitsy appeared carrying Kiki. The sun had come up, so there was enough light to see her wondering about the store picking up items, just like a customer. She stopped at Donna's candy bowl, dug around, pulled out a piece, ripped it open and took a bite.

"Ish," I said.

"There's more," Mrs. Miller said.

The video then showed Mitsy slide behind the counter to the same place Mrs. Miller and I currently stood. I could see the back of her head. She looked down, and I looked down. In the trash, was a Mini Snicker's wrapper. Next, she leaned over the jewelry counter and peered into the glass case. Kiki looked over her shoulder directly into the camera. If I didn't know better, I'd swear Kiki's eyes widened in alarm. The dog turned and pawed at Mitsy's face, but her gesture was ignored.

Mitsy picked up an inexpensive bracelet made of polished stones held together by elastic string. She slipped it on her wrist and held up her arm. After admiring the piece for a few moments, she moved on.

Kiki made eye contact again with the camera; I swore, she looked embarrassed. Mitsy strolled down the hallway and back into the alleyway still wearing my bracelet.

"So something was stolen," I said. "I'd priced that bracelet at twelve dollars, hardly worth calling Sergeant Romano over. But, geez, the nerve of that woman."

At exactly eleven forty-five, a bus boy, dressed in a white shirt and black pants, arrived at the back door with a stack of white cardboard containers. I waved him to the front of the store, where I'd covered Donna's dining room table with a vinyl tablecloth as a protective layer, then covered that with an antique appliquéd tablecloth. Mrs. R was already seated, working a crossword puzzle. The smell of garlic was heavenly. I paid the bus boy and, along with a hefty tip, gave him two loaves of zucchini bread: one for him and the kitchen staff, and one for Francine.

Having all The Ladies around me gave me a feeling of confidence, and I turned my open sign to closed. If the Yarn Barn Lady wanted to report me to the Downtown Lakeville Merchants Association for my slovenly habit of closing at lunch time, so be it. And for the hour that we ate and drank and laughed, the horrible business of Donna's death faded into the background.

The rest of the afternoon went by quickly as Mrs. M and Mrs. T helped me unpack Steve's two extra boxes I'd picked up that morning. I updated the auction list for the following day, but Jimmy would have to make an announcement before the bidding began that items had been added for those who had already picked up a list.

A few minutes before closing, the front door jangled.

Mrs. M sidled up next to me behind the counter. "Well, look who's here," she said, speaking softly, "returning to the scene of the crime."

I looked over the top of my computer screen to see Mitsy, the bracelet thief.

"Hi, Patricia," Mitsy called out, as she strolled over to Donna's hutch where she looked over an assortment of salt-and-pepper shakers. She held Kiki in her arms.

"Can I answer any questions, Mitsy?" I asked, wondering if I should bring up the bracelet incident.

"No, just wanted to check out what's going to be in the auction tomorrow," she replied. I could hear her humming. "I saw a lot of people in here earlier—looks like there's lots of interest in Donna's things, especially after Jimmy hinted that Donna had sticky fingers." She turned to me, grinning. "But, I'm not really surprised, with all those packages she lost." The woman looked absolutely smug.

I leaned over to Mrs. M and whispered: "Didn't The Yarn Barn Lady say that Mitsy had spread the rumor of Donna pilfering packages and stashing treasures in the furniture?"

"Yes, and that makes a lot more sense," she whispered back. "Since I can't imagine Jimmy ever saying anything bad about Donna."

"Do you think Mitsy took those packages?" I asked, keeping my voice low. "It would be easy for her to leave the bookstore at lunch time, go home, and sneak down the alley into Donna's backyard through the big hole in the fence."

"And while Donna was inside having lunch," Mrs. M said, "Mitsy could open up the mail truck, take out some packages and drop them in the alley, ruining Donna's reputation with the postal service and the police."

I came around from the back of the counter, pulling Mrs. M with me. I needed a bit of courage. Both Mitsy and Kiki looked a bit surprised.

"It was you," I said. "You're the one who took those packages from Donna's truck."

"Oh, don't be silly," Mitsy replied.

Kiki glanced in my direction, she looked so guilty I felt I had to be on the right track.

"You live just a few houses from Donna's. You went in through the back fence and stole packages from her truck during her lunch hour. Then you dropped them in the alley. Plus you started the rumor that treasures were hidden away in her furniture."

"That's ridiculous. You give me too much credit."

"You think we should trust the word of a thief?" Mrs. M said, pointing up at the cameras. "There's a recording of you taking a bracelet early this morning."

She looked up at the camera, and her eyes narrowed.

"So, what?" she snapped back. "So, I swiped a bracelet." She dug around in her purse, pulled out the bracelet and tossed it to me.

Mrs. M shook her head, audibly tsking.

"I can prove you took those packages," I said, hoping I could come up with a plausible lie. "I know where two of those packages ended up." I listed the two street names that I had written down from the packages at Steve's house. "And the police can take fingerprints from those packages."

"You think you're going to get fingerprints off of cardboard?" she snapped.

I took in a sharp breath. I had no idea if it was possible to lift fingerprints off a rough surface.

"Not the cardboard," Mrs. M said, "the plastic tape." I gave Mrs. M a sideways glance, glad for her presence. "Did Donna figure out what you were up to, and so you ran her down?"

"I did not. What an absurd idea."

Kiki whined, and pawed at Mitsy's face. Mitsy looked down at the dog and hugged her close. "Fine," she said, sighing. "One day when Donna was delivering the mail, she didn't see Kiki and accidentally kicked her. Kiki bit her on the ankle—not bad—it didn't break the skin. Any animal would have reacted that way. But then every time Donna came in the store, Kiki would growl at her. Donna threatened to ticket me for having an aggressive dog. I couldn't take the chance of Kiki getting a mark on her record. She'd be barred from the Ugly Dog Competition for life. For life!" Kiki blinked frantically at Mitsy's pronouncement. "Donna had no right to take that from me, so I wanted to ruin her reputation. Making it appear that she was losing packages was a way to do it. But I didn't hit Donna." She caressed Kiki's ear. "Besides, there was no real harm done, those packages got to the right people; it just took a couple extra days."

"No harm done? Donna could have been fired from her job," I said.

"But she wasn't, was she?"

I looked at Mrs. M and sighed. Even if we took this story to the police, by this time, the packages with the packing tape had probably been picked up by the garbage company. And since Donna was no longer with us, I doubt that the police would see it as a priority.

"You need to tell Steve and Maggie what you did," I said. "They need to know that Donna had nothing to do with packages going missing." I held up the bracelet. "Or Sergeant Romano hears about this."

Mitsy glanced up at the camera. "Fine."

Chapter Sixteen

On auction day, I opened Elsie's Antiques at eight o'clock. My mom sat behind the counter registering buyers and assigning them a bidding number. Mrs. B was working with Andrew organizing the presentation of each item on the sales list. I'd created as much room as I could, pushing furniture to the walls and bringing in folding chairs. I was excited for the day. Not only would I be making some money, but this would also provide some much needed advertising for the store. When we were ready to start, Jimmy stood up in front of the crowd.

"Listen up folks," Jimmy spoke into a small microphone. "This is not a fancy auction. You bid by holding up your number. There will be no thumbing your nose to bid, no pulling on an earlobe to raise a bid, and no twisting of a mustache to indicate your highest bid." His eyes landed on the three Bobs. "You want to bid, hold up your number. Does everyone understand? And please remember there's tax and a 15 percent buyer's premium."

As I scanned the crowd, I saw mostly older men. The three Bobs had arrived early and situated themselves on Donna's couch. Beatrice Johnson stood along the side wall, and when we made eye contact she winked. One of The Ladies must have contacted her and told her about the auction. She wore a tight yellow-and-black top, held a motorcycle helmet under her arm, and when she reached up to pat her, hair I could see she had on gloves. She spoke to a tall man standing next to her with short curly hair and a close cropped beard. He also held a helmet under his arm.

I walked through the crowd, introducing myself to those I didn't know. When I got to Beatrice, I put out my hand to introduce myself to her companion. "I'm Patricia Schuster. Thanks for coming."

"She knows I'm with the Bureau," Beatrice said, leaning into him.

He smiled as he shook my hand, and said: "This is a major happening, mon." His accent was thick Jamaican.

Beatrice elbowed him in the ribs.

"Glad to meet you, ma'am." This time the accent was deep Southern, and he raised his hand above his head pretending to take off a hat.

I couldn't help but grin while Beatrice once again elbowed him in the ribs. "Ow," the man said while laughing.

"This is Hank," Beatrice finally said.

"Bee doesn't like it when I go undercover," he replied. This time I couldn't discern any accent accept for simple Californian.

"You do voice-over work; you don't need to go undercover," Beatrice said.

"Did either of you want to bid?" I asked. "You'll need a number."

Beatrice shook her head.

"I do," Hank said, and disappeared into the crowd.

"We came up to go wine tasting," Beatrice said. "I wanted to visit the vineyards sitting in the back of a limousine, but Hank had other ideas." She tapped on the helmet. "So any news?" she said quietly.

"The day after Donna was hit, her daughter Maggie and Maggie's boyfriend were sideswiped while riding their bikes."

"Either seriously injured?" she asked.

"No, but Maggie's scared. And if she's scared, I'm scared."

Beatrice pursed her lips, then let out a sigh.

"Poking my nose into other people's lives leaves me feeling spent," I said. "I'm finding out personal things that are none of my business, and even worse, that lead nowhere," I said, thinking about Maggie's nightstand full of condoms and Cece's boyfriend leaving her.

"You're doing fine, Patricia," she said. "Hit-and-runs are really hard to solve."

"So I hear."

Jimmy slammed his gavel down. Andrew stood at the front of the room next to Jimmy, holding one of Donna's candy bowls. It was made of blue glass and held at least a pound of Snickers Fun Size bars.

"First up is a blue candy dish," said Jimmy.

Andrew held the bowl up, so folks in the back could see, then walked from one side of the room to the other.

"We'll open at twenty." Jimmy had set up a mic and amplifier. His voice boomed over the crowd. "Who'll give me a twenty for this tasty bowl of sweets?"

Cards with numbers flew up into the air. I was surprised that Jimmy started with such a desirable piece, but he knew what he was doing: it instantly got everyone involved.

"Twenty." Jimmy pointed to the first number. "Twenty-five, thirty, thirty-five." At this point, Bob—the newly elected president of the Mastodon Association—put up his number. Robert—the past president—scowled at Bob and put up his number. But Bob's arm didn't flinch. When Jimmy hit forty-five dollars, all hands went down, except for Hubby, who seemed pleased with his purchase.

Jimmy continued focusing on Donna's "smalls": her salt-and-pepper collection from her hutch, the china set Helena had tried to steal, and various other kitchen and household items that slowed the auction to a crawl, but the bidders seemed to love.

After the small items had sold, we took a lunch break, and I started checking out bidders who were ready to leave. The Ladies stepped in to help match buyers with their newly purchased items.

When Jimmy returned to his post, he started in on the furniture. Bidders continued to surprise me by what they were willing to pay. Then we got to the finale: the matching couch and chair set.

Jimmy opened the bidding at two hundred dollars, and numbers went up all over the room. Both Bob and Robert had their cards up. They gave each other the evil eye as Jimmy pointed to cards, trying to follow whose hands came up first. When Jimmy hit seven hundred, three bidders remained. Bob and Robert, who were still seated, and Earl, who stood near the front door. When the two remaining Bobs realized they were bidding against someone, they turned their respective mustaches toward Earl, as did the rest of the crowd. Earl's arm remained firmly in place. The two Bobs dirty looks did not persuade Earl to drop out. When the bidding reached eight hundred, Robert, leaned over to Bob and whispered in his ear. Both of their arms came down at the same time, and Earl won the couch and chair. The crowd politely clapped.

The rest of the afternoon was chaos as the bidders paid for and gathered up their treasures in my small store. One issue I hadn't thought of was that a few people had no way to transport their furniture home. Luckily, Jake volunteered his muscle and his truck. I charged these folks a delivery fee, the money to be paid directly to Jake. At least it would cover the cost of gas, if not his time.

Overall, I was pleased with the results. The crowd seemed to enjoy themselves, and some folks hung around and shopped for things not included in the auction. One woman took photos and posted them online, swearing she'd come back to shop for Christmas presents. It was just the type of advertising I was looking for.

When my stomach started growling I decided to order pizza from Lucchesi's. The Ladies and my mom continued puttering around in the store, straightening up and trying to rearrange the remaining furniture to fill in the gaps where Donna's items had been. Jake's last delivery was Donna's dining table to a house in Healdsburg. By the time he got back, it was past closing time, The Ladies, Jimmy and Andrew had all gone home and the leftover pizza was cold.

Jake came in through the back door, and I met him in the hallway.

"How did the deliveries go?" I asked.

"Fine. I'm famished. Is there anything left to eat?"

"Cold pizza and, of course, zucchini bread."

He smiled at me, but stayed put.

"Looks like you and Andrew made nice today," I said.

He nodded. "He starts back on Monday."

"I appreciate all your help. I couldn't have done it without you."

I leaned back against the wall, a half-smile on my face. Jake moved forward slowly and put both hands on either side of me. He leaned in to kiss me, his body barely touching mine. Just as my heart fluttered, I heard my name being called.

"Patricia! Patricia!" The voice came from the front of the store. "Patricia!"

I opened my eyes and Jake pulled away. "Ish," I muttered. "I forgot to lock the front door."

A smile twitched at the corners of his lips. "Sounds like someone wants you as much as I do." He leaned forward and kissed my neck.

"Patricia!" The voice called again.

"That's Steve's daughter." I pushed him away.

Jake's mouth was a full-on grin. I stared at him for a long moment, soaking in how handsome he looked when he smiled.

"We better go see," I said.

When Jake and I came out of the hallway, Maggie stood where Donna's dining room table had been.

Mascara was smudged under her eyes. She looked as if she'd been crying.

"You've got to come," she said, grabbing my hand and pulling me to the door. "My dad's on the roof of the Phoenix building. I think he's going to jump!"

"Jake, call the police," I said over my shoulder.

"No!" Maggie said, "No police, just Patricia."

I gave Jake one last look before following Maggie out the door and down the sidewalk. We made it to the corner, past a group of teens, and down the alleyway. A vintage Schwinn bike leaned against the wall. I assumed it was Steve's.

"I'll go first," I told Maggie, and headed up the ladder.

I stepped onto the roof. No Steve. Maggie appeared and ran past me to another ladder at the far end of the mural. She pointed. I went up first. A four-foot parapet edged the upper roof. I swung my leg over and stepped onto dried tar. Odd shaped vents and machinery scattered the rooftop. I finally spotted a pair of feet, behind what looked like an air conditioning unit, toes pointed up.

"Steve!" I called out, running to the prone legs.

Steve lay on a blanket, his eyes open, and a bottle of beer in one hand. A six-pack sat next to him. Two full bottles were left, with the empties placed back in their compartments. A tripod holding a telescope stood close to his head.

"I wish we could see more stars from here," he said, pointing at the sky.

I put my hand on my chest willing my heart to slow down.

Maggie stood a few feet away, her arms crossed, tears streamed down her face. She gestured to him then covered her mouth with her hand. I knelt down and got a strong smell of beer.

Steve looked at me then up to the heavens once again.

"You know, Moonlight, Donna and I used to come up here when we first started dating. That's when I got the idea to paint a mural. Took me years to get the city and the theater and all the other powers that be," he swung his beer in an arching motion as if encompassing the whole sky, "to get it okayed and paid for. And now she's not even here to see it." He rolled over onto his side. "Moonlight, do you think she's forgiven me?"

Maggie still stood just a few feet away. I really hoped he hadn't run Donna down and that Maggie wasn't going to witness a confession. "Forgiven you for what, Steve?" I asked.

"Not fixing her car."

"What do you mean?"

"The exhaust was kicking out black smoke, so I told her it was probably the carburetor. But I lost the gasket. It was in the box. I don't know what happened to it. She always said how sloppy I was." He sighed heavily, flipping back over to again stare up at the stars. "If I'd fixed it, she would have been driving it the night she got hit." He put an arm over his eyes and his mouth turned into a line, the corners quivering.

I glanced at Maggie. She was biting her upper lip. I felt for her, thinking your dad might have killed someone is a heavy load to carry.

"Steve, the only person responsible for Donna's

death is the person that was driving the car that hit her," I said.

"It doesn't feel that way," his said softly. His arm suddenly popped off his face. "And you know what else is just perverse?"

I shook my head.

"I'm going to make out like a bandit." He looked over at Maggie. "You know how you were going to work while in school?" Maggie nodded. "Now you don't have to." He looked back to me. "Maggie got scholarships to college, but you know how expensive school is. She was still going to have to work. Now she won't have too."

Tears again streamed down Maggie's face. I got up, put my arm around her, and took her out of earshot of Steve.

"Oh, God," she said, wiping away tears. "I actually thought he might have done it. He was acting so guilty, and it was all over that stupid car."

"This has been a really hard time for you, hasn't it?" I said. She looked down at the ground and wiped her face. "How about we get some help to get your dad home?" I pulled out my phone.

"Okay."

"Do you know Earl's phone number?"

She shook her head. "I tried calling Andrew a few times, but he's not answering."

I called Mrs. T, told her the situation, and asked if she could contact Earl. I thought a third person would at least be able to help get him off the roof. I then called Jake and asked him to lockup the store.

For the next fifteen minutes, Maggie and I listened to Steve rattle on about his and Donna's relationship and lament about how light pollution separated us from connecting with the stars, and hence our true selves.

Earl's voice broke through our conversation. "Steve, you up here?"

"Over here," Steve called out.

Earl appeared along with Andrew.

"Where were you?" Maggie stood up and yelled at Andrew. "I texted you three times! And called twice!"

"My battery went dead." He shrugged. "It's not holding a charge. I think I need a new one."

I turned away from the teenage angst and watched Earl kneel down next to Steve. He helped him to his feet, and Steve put his arm around Earl's shoulder. Earl maneuvered Steve to the ladder. Steve could walk better than I expected, and I guessed that the alcohol affected him more emotionally than physically.

"I'm sorry they arrested you," Steve said. "They really shouldn't have done that."

"I know, I know, it's okay," he replied before turning to me. "Now, let me go first," he said. "Then help Steve get on the ladder. If he slips—" He looked over the edge, then patted Steve on the shoulder. "Steve don't slip."

Steve chuckled, "Okay."

Earl got on the ladder, and I hung onto Steve's arm as he swung his leg down. Maggie and Andrew were right behind me.

We had one more ladder to go, Earl swung his leg down onto the first rung. He didn't speak, but his eyebrows pulled together. He moved down a few more rungs. Steve followed and I kept a firm hold on the ladder as it scraped against the ledge.

Maggie went ahead of me and had just started her decent when Earl called out. "Hey, hey! Where's my car?"

From the roof, I looked up the alley to the main boulevard. A few cars went whizzing by; a street light lit up the exit. The other direction was dark, flanked by buildings. The alley emptied out onto a small side street whose businesses had closed up for the night.

Andrew went down. I followed. We stood stunned, realizing that in the few minutes we were on the roof, someone had stolen Earl's car.

Steve still leaned on Earl, mumbling about the stars.

"Andrew, call 911," Earl said.

"Granddad, you just parked it down here," he said. He pointed into the dark and started jogging.

"Wait, Andrew," I called out. Something didn't feel right.

Two glaring headlights appeared out of the dark and moved toward us. Andrew jolted to a stop. The driver floored it, aiming for him. He darted sideways, but not quickly enough. The car caught him and spun him 180 degrees. He fell backward and landed with a sickening thud. As Earl's car sped past us, I strained to see the driver, but the face was covered in a ski mask. The car turn onto the boulevard and disappeared.

Maggie screamed. Earl ran by me to get to his grandson. Andrew's stillness made my heart stop. I pulled out my phone and dialed 911.

The operator asked, "What's your emergency?"

Chapter Seventeen

Andrew opened his eyes and spoke to the paramedics as they put one brace around his neck and another around his leg. They gingerly placed him on the gurney, and Earl followed him into the ambulance. Sargent Romano was in one of two police cars that arrived. He approached me. I told him everything I remembered. He immediately radioed in the stolen car. He briefly talked to Steve and Maggie, but there was nothing else they could tell him. I offered to drive Steve and Maggie to the hospital, so we hoofed it to my car.

I counted the vinyl squares on the floor as I paced back and forth in the hospital's emergency waiting room. A TV hanging from the ceiling in the corner played a knife infomercial. It kept the attention of a young woman but didn't interest her two small children.

Maggie had stopped crying and sat leaning against her dad, her feet pulled up underneath her. Her eyes were puffy. She stared at the floor.

Earl appeared from around the corner, looking like he'd aged ten years in the last hour. Maggie jumped up and ran to him.

"They've got him stabilized," Earl said, "but they're taking him in for surgery on his leg. He got a concussion, too, when he hit the ground." He slumped into a chair. Steve placed his arm around his shoulder. "I thought I was going to lose him." Earl's voice quivered with emotion. "For a second there I thought he was gone." He wiped at his eyes. "He's going to be okay though." He looked at Steve then gave me a quick smile. "He's going to be okay."

Maggie eased into the chair next to Earl. He looked at her, as if suddenly realizing she was there. He put his arm around her shoulder and pulled her in for a hug.

I moved away from the little group and found an oversized upholstered chair in the corner. After slumping into it, I called Jake. I explained what had happened. He offered to come to the hospital, which I thought was very kind of him. But I said no. After I hung up, I realized that just hearing his voice had made me feel better. I called Mrs. T and went through the story again. She said she'd relay my message to The Ladies. I laid my head back on the chair and closed my eyes. Then I felt a hand on my arm.

"Ms. Schuster," said Sergeant Romano.

I opened my eyes and squinted. I felt completely disorientated.

"What time is it?" I asked.

"Six-thirty," he replied.

"Six-thirty in the morning?" I couldn't believe I'd slept through the night.

He nodded. "Sorry to wake you. I have some information you might want to hear."

I got up, stretched, and followed him over to Steve.

Maggie was asleep leaning against Steve's shoulder. I didn't see Earl. There was another uniformed officer talking with a nurse at the check-in counter.

Steve smiled at us through sleepy eyes. "Andrew came through the surgery just fine," he whispered, and looked sideways at Maggie. "I doubt he'll be awake for a while, Earl's back there with him now."

"Good to hear," Sergeant Romano said. "We found Earl's car, it was parked around the corner. Because of the circumstances we're going to place an officer outside Andrew's room. We believe that Donna was hit on purpose, and I'm not sure how this ties in, but I want to cover all our bases."

Steve's eyebrows came together. "What about Maggie?"

"Keep her close to home if possible, and don't let her travel on her bike."

Maggie woke up and stretched. For a moment she looked like a child. Then her memory kicked in. Steve reassured her of Andrew's condition.

"How about I buy you two some breakfast?" I offered.

"Go on, Maggie, I'll catch up with you in a few minutes," Steve said. "I'd like to ask Sergeant Romano a few questions."

After shuffling through the cafeteria line we found an empty table. I wolfed down my breakfast of scrambled eggs, toast and coffee.

Maggie picked at a bagel. Her eyes looked dark and sunken.

"I'm glad to hear Andrew's going to be okay," I said.

She didn't reply. She opened her backpack and pulled out a small red book with Georgia O'Keeffe's red poppy on the cover. "Did you want to see this?" She held it out to me. "I found it in Donna's mailbox. Her replacement must have dropped it off yesterday."

I snapped it up and started leafing through it. There were extensive notes on dogs and vacation times. Dogs were mentioned by house number, type or size, and whether they were barkers, or lungers. I also saw scattered notes about mail not being picked up and assumed these people had been gone for short periods of time, probably not long enough to request a mail hold. I turned to the last entry. Donna had written two words: Where's Nick?

Humph, I thought. Get in line Donna. Everyone wants to know where Nick is. I felt disappointed. I'd hoped for something more.

I glanced at Maggie, feeling that she might know of a missing link to Donna's death. Pushing her at a time like this would be unfortunate, but I was scared for her. "Andrew's had quite a few mishaps recently," I said.

Maggie bit her upper lip, but said nothing.

"Did Andrew paint those letters on Jake's Auto Shop window?" I asked.

She stared at her bagel, and nodded. "He was so angry. He felt like he finally had a chance to do something besides grunt work, and just like that, it was taken away."

"Jake did what he thought was right about having Earl's truck checked out. And Jake never said Andrew couldn't work for him. It was Andrew's choice to leave."

"Andrew thought he needed to stick up for his grandfather," Maggie said.

"I understand. But, Jake and Andrew made up yesterday, Andrew's going to start working for Jake on Monday."

She shook her head. "It won't last, not when Jake finds out."

"It was water-based paint; it came right off the windows. It's old news at this point."

"Not that," Maggie said.

"I don't understand."

Her eyes filling with tears. "Andrew's being blackmailed."

"For what?"

Maggie dug into her purse, and placed a folded five dollar bill on the table. "Like I tried before—I'd like to hire you."

I didn't touch the money. "But I'm not—"

"Andrew and I have been sleeping together," she said.

"And this person threatened to tell your father?"

She shook her head. "The police."

I finally understood her riddle of one person doing something illegal and the other person not. "Because you're under age and he's not."

"He turned 18 a few months ago." Her gaze shifted to the ceiling, and a tear ran down her cheek. "He could go to jail. He'll have to register as a sex offender. They can ruin his whole future."

"Wouldn't they have to prove it?"

Her mouth turned into a thin line, as tears flooded her eyes.

"Oh no. You didn't tape it, did you?" I asked. "Please tell me that you and Andrew aren't on the internet?"

Maggie let out a snort of a laugh as she used a napkin sop up her tears. "We're not that stupid."

Whew. "Then how?"

"My bra."

"Your bra?"

"This person has my bra."

"So?"

"Well, there's DNA on it, isn't there?"

"Maggie, no one's going to pay for DNA testing for a couple of young people having sex. Plus it wouldn't prove anything anyway. Did you check on the details?" I asked.

She shook her head.

"It might not be as bad as you think."

As I pulled out my phone to call my lawyer, Maria Sanchez, Maggie rummaged through her purse. She pulled out a mini pack of tissues and placed them on the table. There was a little clunking sound. She picked up the tissues, and there, lying on the table, was Helena's brooch: fan shaped with sapphires and diamonds set in platinum.

"Oh, crap, I meant to give that back to Donna. She'd been asking about it," Maggie said.

Maria Sanchez's paralegal answered before I could respond to Maggie. I placed the phone on speaker so we could both listen. I asked how California's statutory rape laws would apply in this type of case, without mentioning Maggie's name. The paralegal explained that because the guy was so close in age to the gal, he could be charged with a misdemeanor. He might pay a fine, but there would be no jail time, and he would not have to register as a sex offender. But even a misdemeanor charge was rare, as it was considered a waste of courtroom time. I thanked her and disconnected.

A corner of Maggie's mouth twitched downward. "She said legally it was rape. She said it would follow him forever. That for sure he'd spend time in jail. Why did we believe her?" Her eyes rimmed with tears again. My heart ached for her. Right in front of me, I was watching innocence being lost. This had nothing to do with sex, and everything to do with trust.

"We are so stupid," she said.

I leaned back. "You're not stupid. As a kid you have to believe what adults tell you or you'd go psychotic. So, who's blackmailing Andrew?"

She sighed. "Cece."

"Cece!" I still had my phone in my hand and immediately wanted to hit redial to talk with Maria's office again. "Wait, is that why Andrew's been working for her?"

She nodded.

"Oh, man, that's low." It crossed my mind that instead of calling Maria, maybe I should call Jimmy Chang and let his thuggy friends go after her. "Okay, you're going to need to tell me how she got your bra."

"Well, this is kind of embarrassing."

"Sex often is," I said.

"Andrew likes to do it in cars."

I tried to keep my face neutral unsure if that was the embarrassing part.

"It's kind of a game," she continued, "so whenever we can get away with it." One eyebrow went up along with a shoulder.

"Okay."

"So Cece rents the garage on Earl's property. She keeps a padlock on the big door, but there's a door on the back that Earl has a key to. Andrew found the key." She paused. "Cece has a car in the garage. So we were in the car, and, you know." Her shoulder came up again. "She showed up."

The hairs on my arms stood up. "Cece showed up in her car, but she has another car parked in the garage?" I asked.

Maggie nodded.

"And what night was this?" I could barely wait for her answer.

Maggie looked down, and whispered: "The night Donna got hit."

"What kind of car was in the garage? Was it a Prius?"

She stared at me. "I don't know."

"What do you remember?" I could feel my heart rate going up. "What color was it?"

"White, I think. It has a cover over it, which we pulled up to get the door open, but we didn't take it all the way off. It was really small inside."

I remember Earl finding a bra in Cece's car the night she was so rude about the Cadillac. "And you left your bra in it? A purple bra?"

She nodded. "How did you know?"

I jumped up. "That's how she did it!"

"Did what?" Maggie looked horrified.

"Cece killed Donna, and I know how to prove it."

I thought about Donna's last entry. Where's Nick? Maybe that was the link. I picked up the book. "Can I take this?"

"Okay."

"I've got to find Sergeant Romano."

"Oh, no, you can't tell him."

"You might need to tell him that you two were in the garage. Hopefully, we won't have to go any further." I looked down at the brooch. "And, hold onto that brooch, I know who it belongs to."

I ran down the corridor toward the emergency room lobby. I met Steve halfway there.

"Is Sergeant Romano still here?" I asked.

"No," Steve replied. "He got a call about a fire out at Earl's house. He took Earl with him."

My stomach sank. This wasn't good.

When I pulled up to Earl's property, the fire department was there, shooting streams of water high onto what was left of the barn. I got out and blinked against the smoke.

"You-hoo," a woman's voice called out. "Patricia, over here."

I turned to see Mrs. Butterfield, Mrs. Taylor, Jimmy Chang and Earl across the road. I jogged over to the group. Earl stood apart from them looking concerned. The other three looked a bit too happy for the situation.

"I can't believe it's gone," I said, gesturing to the barn. "The car that hit Donna was in there." I felt like crying.

"We know, dear. But don't speak too soon," Mrs. B said, pointing behind me.

I turned and watched the fire hose lowering and smoke coming from what was left of the building. When the air started to clear I could see that only a section of the 100-year-old structure had burnt. The firemen had arrived in time. A small car, partially hidden by a dripping wet cover, sat inside.

Sergeant Romano crossed the street to us. He looked a bit disheveled and definitely grim.

"What are you doing here?" he asked the group, hands on hips.

"We'd like to look at that car," Mrs. B said, and pointed to the barn.

"Why?" Sergeant Romano asked.

"We think it's the car that ran down Donna Olsen."

Sergeant Romano crossed his arms and raised an eyebrow. "Explain," he said.

"Yes, explain." Earl stepped forward. "Those two have been friends for years. I can't imagine Cece doing such a thing."

"Well," said Mrs. B, "Jimmy and I were talking business recently, and Jimmy mentioned that he had signed paperwork authorizing him to sell Nick Rodriguez's Prius, but Nick had gone missing."

Jimmy unfolded some papers and held them up as if we could read them from where we stood.

"Nick Rodriguez? He's been missing for a few weeks," Romano said.

"We suspect that the license plate on that car will match my contract," Jimmy said, tapping on his paper and looking pleased with himself. "But the VIN numbers will not."

"And why would that be?" asked Romano.

"Because Cece Bronson, who also owns a Prius, switched the cars and license plates after hitting and killing Donna Olsen" Mrs. B explained. "The car that's in that barn is Cece's car, with Nick's license plate. And the car that Cece is currently driving is Nick's car with Cece's license plates."

We all turned and stared at the barn.

"The cars are identical?" asked Sergeant Romano.

"Yep," replied Mrs. B.

"Let's take a look," Sergeant Romano said.

Our little crowd trudged across the street. We stood a ways back from the barn while Sergeant Romano spoke to a firemen. The two men looked in our direction and the fireman shook his head. They spoke for another minute before Sergeant Romano returned to us.

"We can't go in until they know the structure's safe. Plus they suspect arson, so they'll being doing their own investigation," he said. "But he's willing to take a look."

We watched the fireman approach the car and pull off the wet car cover. The front of the car looked remarkably good for just having been in a fire—if you didn't take into account the broken windshield and the huge dent on the hood.

"Well, look at that," said Sergeant Romano.

"What's the last three numbers of the vin?" the fireman called out.

"Four-eight-five," Jimmy called back.

The fireman looked at the door's edge and shook his head. "They don't match," he said.

"Anything in the back seat?" Mrs. Butterfield yelled out.

The fireman peered through the window, then came back to us. "There's a black garbage bag, a purple bra, and what looks like a gasket of some sort."

"I knew it," Mrs. Butterfield said. "If that is a gasket

for a carburetor that goes in a '67 Karmann Ghia, it proves that Cece Bronson hit Donna on purpose. It was no accident."

"Again, you're going to have to explain yourself," Sergeant Romano said.

"Cece, Donna and Nick all knew each other, right? Cece and Nick were seeing each other, Donna and Cece were old friends from the band, and Donna delivered mail to Green's Auto where Nick and Cece both worked. Now, in case you don't know, Sergeant Romano, Donna liked to chat, especially with men. So it's not hard to believe that when Donna dropped off the mail, she flirted with Nick. Jimmy, tell us what Nick said when you met him."

"Nick came in to sell his car. He said he was having a midlife crisis and wanted to quit his job and get away from his crazy girlfriend. But, at that time, he hadn't told either of his plans."

"Okay," said Sergeant Romano.

"I think Nick told Donna that he and Cece were involved in the real estate scams, and he wanted out. So when Donna is out delivering mail, she comes across a young man who can't get into a house he's supposedly rented. Since Donna knew about the scam, she thinks she can get Cece to give back this young man's deposit money. When Donna brings it up with Cece, Cece realizes that Nick had been blabbing."

At that moment Hubby came walking toward us. He had a German Shepard on a leash.

Sergeant Romano stepped forward. "I'm Sergeant Romano, and you are?"

"He's with me," Mrs. T interrupted. "He brought his

sniffer dog."

The sergeant looked down at the dog. "To sniff for what?" he asked.

"For Nick," Mrs. T replied.

Sergeant Romano's head snapped up. "What?"

"I suspect that Nick is buried here," Mrs. T said, pointing up the hill, "and I think this dog can find him."

My legs felt heavy. I started to feel sick. "Where's Nick?" I whispered to myself, repeating Donna's words from her notebook.

Hubby walked past the old garages to the edge of the field. He gave a command, and the dog immediately pulled at her leash.

"How did you come to this conclusion?" Sergeant Romano asked.

"I saw Cece making copies of house keys," said Mrs. B, "but Cece lied and said they were car keys. It was then I started to connect the dots."

"I think Cece believed that Nick might turn her in," said Mrs. T. "All this happened when Earl and Andrew were in Alaska and Cece was here housesitting and taking care of Earl's dogs. Nick comes here and tells Cece he's leaving her. She snaps and kills him. Then buries his body up there." Mrs. T pointed at the hill, which was partially covered in blackberries.

"I'd check the tools in those garages," said Mrs. B, pointing at the other outbuildings.

Earl grunted. "When we got back from Alaska, I noticed that backhoe had been moved." He shook his head, looking grim.

"When Nick disappeared," Mrs. B said, "Donna must have asked Cece too many questions. And that's where the gasket comes in. Donna mentions to Cece that Steve was going to rebuild her carburetor. So Cece sees an opportunity. She goes to Steve's house, steals the gasket from the carburetor to keep Donna carless, so Donna is on foot the night of the Mastodon's bingo game. Cece follows Donna in her silent Prius and hits her. Then Cece comes here, switches her car with Nick's, and changes out the license plates."

"But there was a problem," I said. "Andrew and Maggie saw her."

Sergeant Romano raised an eyebrow. "What do you mean?"

I realized at this point, that being explicit about Andrew and Maggie's reason for being in the garage was not needed. "Andrew and Maggie were at Earl's place the night Donna was hit and saw Cece swap out the cars."

"So Cece's been after Andrew and Maggie ever since," said Sergeant Romano.

"Cece was the one that hit Andrew?" Earl asked, looking pale.

Sergeant Romano stepped forward. "I'm sorry Mr. Grey, but it appears so."

Earl turned away and headed to the house, his shoulders sagged.

Less than twenty minutes later, Mrs. T was proved right. Hubby's sniffer dog found Nick's body shallowly buried under a blackberry bush, covered in a red and white table cloth with his phone lying underneath him.

Sergeant Romano put out an APB for Cece, wanted for questioning in connection with the deaths of Nick Rodriguez and Donna Olsen, attempted murder, and arson.

Epilogue

The back of my mother's SUV was stuffed with baskets. Brown weave, pastel weave, wire, and rattan. Each one carried zucchini. My mother and I were on the prowl again, looking for targets of my mother's excessive gardening.

"This time, we'll stick to the senior center," my mom said. "Those folks nod off by eight o'clock. We'll get there by nine, home by eleven. Easy peasy."

"Don't you remember that Nana had insomnia?" I countered. "Plus those folks have lots of little dogs, and little dogs have to tinkle at night." I sat shotgun, wishing that this time I had worn camouflage makeup. "Don't you need a code to get into the building?"

My mother waved a dismissal. "We'll figure it out."

Next to the senior center was the Lakeville Senior Complex. A three-story building with balconies and elevators. Sixty-five units—two bedrooms, one bedrooms, and studios. Now we didn't have enough to give away to all sixty-five, but we had a lot. We'd start on the second floor, since the first floor contained the manager's offices, the dining hall and the recreation room. If we were questioned, my mother knew four residents that we could claim as "relatives."

With four baskets on each arm, we stood in the bushes like bashful burglars, waiting for someone to emerge from the stairwell. Finally, a group of three ladies exited, each with a small dog under her arm. I nudged my mother with my elbow; she shrugged in reply. Before the heavy metal door closed, I made a run for it, sticking my foot in the opening. My mother went in first, going up the stairs to make sure the second floor door was unlocked. Once she had it opened, I let the door slip closed and followed her up the stairs.

We came out on one end of a long corridor next to some potted plants and what used to be a cubby for a pay phone.

"Oh, no," my mom said.

"What?" I whispered, peering down the hallway. "Is there someone there?"

"No, but there has been. Look." She pointed.

In front of most of the doors sat a bundle of zucchini wrapped in twine. I assumed the occupants of apartments with nothing in front had already discovered their squash. "Oh, fudge" I said. "Who would have done that?"

"I'll be right back." She unloaded her baskets onto the floor, sprinted to grab a bundle, and ran back. In her hands she held three evenly sized zucchini. These were store bought, not home grown organic. The plain brown tag read: "In loving memory of Donna. The Zucchini Fairy."

I sighed. "Mom, you've been bested."

***

I sat on my mother's couch, eating popcorn and watching the late news. She paced back and forth, periodically blocking my view of the TV. The weather was on, showing a five-day forecast of fog in the morning and sunny afternoons, a typical Northern California summer.

"This isn't good," she complained. "I'm done. Through. The end of the line."

"Done with what?" I asked.

"Zucchini runs. I can't go out again. Don't you see what this means?" She stopped in front of me.

I shook my head, "I don't see anything, not even the TV."

She resumed her pacing. "If I go out again, I'll be labeled a copycat. Not the real Zucchini Fairy." She grabbed a handful of popcorn and continued. "I know, we'll just have to drive further. We'll go to Bodega Bay. Start fresh. No one knows anything about the Zucchini Fairy one way or another out at the coast."

Ish, there goes my potential for a good night's sleep. "Mom, why do you care?"

"I thought I didn't, but I guess I do. It would have been a nice addition to my résumé."

The anchor woman with perfect hair and perfect makeup smiled broadly at the camera. "West county supermarkets were cleaned out of zucchini today. Apparently, it all ended up at the Lakeville Senior Complex in Lakeville." They cut to a reporter standing in front of the complex, showing a clip from earlier in the day. She held a bundle of zucchini tied in twine.

My mom sucked in a breath. "Is this a San Francisco station?"

I nodded.

She sighed and plopped down next to me. "Oh, Patricia, my time has passed," she said. "I'm washed up, a has-been, driven out by an inferior mass-marketed product. Just like Beta tapes and TIVO."

The reporter continued: "A generous donor delivered zucchini to all members of the senior complex, wiping out the zucchini supply on the county's west side. Each bundle held a card saying: In Loving Memory of Donna, which refers to Donna Olsen, believed to be the Zucchini Fairy of Lakeville."

"Oh!" My mother popped out of her seat. "I've got it! We'll take my zucchini by the grocery stores and drop them at the back entrance. That way people will have access to the delicious squash by morning. People shouldn't be without squash."

"Mom, no store is going to sell vegetables when they don't know where they came from."

She sat back down again. "Okay, how's this? We sneak the zucchini into stores that are open 24 hours. And put them in the vegetable department."

"And what are we going to sneak them in with? A gym bag? This late at night, they'll think we've showed up to steal stuff, not deliver stuff."

She cradled her head on her chin.

I sighed. I hated seeing her so deflated. "Didn't Nana have a friend that worked at the food bank?"

"Yeah, Shirley," she replied.

"Call her tomorrow, and see if we can bring them over. Since she knows you, I'm sure she'll take them."

"That's a good idea."

Relief flooded every cell of my body. Now, was that so hard?

The doorbell rang, and I looked through the peep hole. Sergeant Romano stood on the steps. I opened the door to greet him.

"Ms. Schuster," he said.

"Sergeant Romano," I said, returning his formal greeting.

My mom came up behind me.

"I thought you'd like to know," he said, " that Cece confessed to running Donna down with her Prius. She claims it was an accident. But because we found the carburetor gasket in the back seat of her Prius, the DA thinks they can prove it was premeditated. Under the advice of her lawyer, she's not talking about Nick's death."

I sighed. "Two people dead, such a waste."

"The bank teller who got scammed has identified Cece as the woman who took his money under the pretense of renting him a room. If Donna would have come to us, instead of trying to get Cece to give his money back, this might have been avoided." He looked at me. "I wanted to thank you and your friends for your tenacity. Without it, we might never have known what happened." He turned to go then stopped. "So what were you and your mother really doing out the night that Donna got hit?"

My mouth dropped open.

He looked past me to my mother. "It wouldn't have anything to do with zucchini would it?"

Meet the real mural artist of the Phoenix Theater building in Petaluma:

Ricky Watts

Ricky's colorful murals and intricate paintings can be found throughout the United States. His client list includes artwork for Louis Vuitton, Google and YouTube. Ricky Watts currently works out of his Sebastopol, California studio and spends his "free time" raising energetic twins.

Visit his website to buy prints and other great merchandise. https://watts.art/

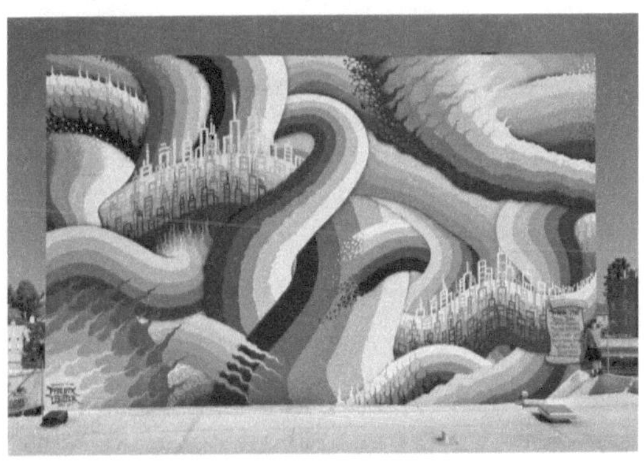

For those of you that don't know, the city of Lakeville, is a fictionalized version of Petaluma, California. During the time I lived in Petaluma I often thought that the Phoenix Theater would be a great place for a mural. When I started writing Zucchini Fairy I wanted an interesting physical structure for some of the scenes, and the theater was perfect. My character Steve and the story line was well underway when I realized that an actual mural was going up, so nothing in my story is based on Ricky. What struck me as a fun coincidence was all the times I thought that the Phoenix building really needed a mural, Ricky was probably thinking the same thing. ~ Ann Philipp

Happy Reading!